SUMMER IN TINTAGEL

SUMMER IN TINTAGEL

AMANDA JAMES

URBANE
Publications

First published in Great Britain in 2016 by Urbane Publications Ltd
Suite 3, Brown Europe House, 33/34 Gleamingwood Drive, Chatham, Kent
ME5 8RZ

A CIP catalogue record for this book is available from the British Library.

ISBN 978-1-911129-78-3
EPUB 978-1-911129-79-0
MOBI 978-1-911129-80-6

Design and Typeset by The Invisible Man
Cover by Chandler Design

Printed and bound by CPI Group (UK) Ltd, Croydon, CR0 4YY

urbanepublications.com

The publisher supports the Forest Stewardship Council® (FSC®), the
leadinginternational forest-certification organisation This book is made
from acid-free paper from an FSC®-certified provider. FSC is the only forest-
certification scheme supported by the leading environmental organisations,
including Greenpeace.

For Tanya

Acknowledgements

I would like to thank all my friends and family, but especially these lovely people who lent an ear, an eye, or a heart along the way.

Celia Anderson, Kelly Florentia, Elaine Hardy, Margaret James, Angie Marsons, Chris Stovell, Sue Watson and Anne Williams.

A big thanks to John Lewis of Lewis's Bed & Breakfast for allowing me to put his wonderful establishment in my book - and him too! Lewis's is a real place, not a figment of my imagination, and if you're ever in Tintagel, Lewis's is the place to stay.

CHAPTER 1

*R*osa kneels on the lawn. It is summer, but the grass is damp under her bare legs and she wishes that she had taken the picnic rug that Mummy had tried to give her just now. Mummy said she was wilful, would have to learn by her own mistakes. Rosa wonders what wilful means as she pours water from the plastic teapot into a tiny cup and places it in front of Barney, her oldest teddy bear. Wilful is perhaps the same as stubborn. Daddy often says she is stubborn.

'Would you like tea too, Miss Jemima Puddle-Duck?'

A stuffed green and brown duck looks at her from its one glassy eye, but says nothing. Rosa nods. 'Yes, of course you would. You can have a biscuit too.'

Rosa puts cups in front of her remaining toys and looks back across the long expanse of grass towards her house. The sun hides itself behind a cloud, but that isn't the reason she has goosebumps forming along her arms. She feels her heartbeat quicken and she tightens her grip on a biscuit. It crumbles and leaves a sticky smear of chocolate on her fingers. Rosa licks the chocolate, but her stomach rolls and she tries to blot out a voice in her head. Daddy will be angry, very angry.

A scream pierces the silent afternoon. It comes from the house and it sounds like her mother. Rosa leans her back against a tree and draws her knees up under her chin. She looks at a grass stain on her white sock and her whole body begins to shake. A siren wails up the valley and she knows

1

that something bad has happened. Very bad.

She has been under the tree for what feels like a long time, but then she sees Daddy burst from the house as if he has been fired like a bullet from a gun. His hair is messy and he runs his hands through it with wild, jerky movements. Daddy's tie is pulled to the side and he doesn't look at all neat. Being neat is something he is very proud of. Rosa tries to make herself small, but he has seen her and runs towards her ... fast.

Daddy kneels beside her and puts his big hands on her shoulders. He shakes her roughly.

'This is all your fault! Dabbling in evil always ends in disaster, do you hear me?'

'I ... I ... haven't done anything ...'

'Don't lie! All this mumbo jumbo about ghostly old ladies appearing in my house and warning you to ...' Daddy's face looks like a Halloween mask and his mouth twists down at the corners. 'Never mind. You are going to your room and you will stay there for the rest of the day!'

Rosa's arm hurts where Daddy is squeezing it as he drags her back to the house. Her eyes fill, but she won't let him see her tears. She is glad she is going to her room, because she doesn't want to know exactly what has happened; the bad thing that has made Daddy so angry. Rosa has a good idea already and this makes her so sad that she can hardly breathe ...

Rosa's eyes snapped open. Terror gripped her heart - the walls were too close and she didn't know where she was. Then she remembered and struggled to take a few calming breaths. She had jolted awake in Gran's rocking chair from some weird dream, and thought the walls were closing in on her. The dream had begun to fade now, leaving just whisperings in the corners of her mind ... herself as a little girl on a lawn ... a toy's picnic ... something bad had happened … and her father was angry. Rosa had never been claustrophobic, but in the dream she'd felt like she couldn't breathe; and now as her chest tightened, she knew that if she didn't get the window open, she'd have to run outside.

Suspended in a shaft of sunlight dust motes, shimmered like flecks of gold, twirled and resettled. Rosa caught her breath, mesmerised by their simple beauty. A layer of dust had been dispersed from the frame of an ancient sash window during her struggle to release the rusty catches. These labours had involved much cursing and a grazed knuckle, but still the catches remained stuck fast.

Why didn't she just give in and open the door? No. It was a battle now. The stubborn window mocked Rosa's youth and inexperience with its age and craftsmanship. Surreal as the thought may be, she was determined the window wouldn't win; she set her jaw and gripped the wooden frame again. A rattled protest, then at last the sash squealed open a few inches, grudgingly allowing the scent of rain-soaked grass and lavender into the moribund sitting room.

Rosa drew sweet air into her lungs and slowly exhaled. Silence reclaimed the sitting room. Moribund was not a word that she would have associated with her gran's house years ago. Nor silence.

As children, Rosa and her brothers had filled this house with excited laughter and the thud of running feet, their joy and enthusiasm alive in the fabric of its interior and the strength of its foundations. Rosa's memories of those days were sometimes winter-warm with open fires, Christmas candles and the scent of pine. Other recollections were summer-fresh with the zing of cut lemons and cloudy lemonade, a blue gingham picnic cloth on a green lawn, a rope swing and the sting of antiseptic on grazed knees.

Moribund was as far away from those times as the most distant planet in the firmament. Today, it was a perfect description of the house. Dull. Decaying. Waiting to die. Upstairs, Rosa's grandmother waited too, in a drug induced slumber.

It was inconceivable to Rosa that such a vibrant robust woman could have succumbed so quickly. But on her seventy-third birthday, Jocelyn Nelson had been given the unwelcome present of a terminal diagnosis. The consultant had said around nine months. Three had passed already.

Rosa absently trailed her fingers through the dust on the windowsill and across the weather-stained pane. Gran would be ashamed to see it. She had always been fastidious and reluctant to accept help around the house. Latterly, Polly, Rosa's mother, had organised a cleaner once a week to do a 'quick whizz round', as Polly put it. Perhaps the cleaner couldn't see the point in wasting precious whizzing time on an old sash window, given that the occupant of the house was unlikely to look out of it ever again. Or to even leave her room again. Not with her … disease.

Rosa crossed her arms over her chest and watched the lavender bordering the overgrown lawn shivering in the strengthening breeze. A shiver ran through her too. The thought of what the disease was doing to her gran made her feel like the lavender looked – fragile, vulnerable, weak.

The disease.

Its name refused to sit well on most tongues. Instead it was reduced to whispers or euphemisms, because if uttered, the word *cancer* would somehow manifest, its physical reality eating into the organs of those uttering it. That's how it seemed to Rosa anyway. 'Big C' was comfortable - reliable even - like some universally accepted logic impossible to live without.

Never one to dwell on the meaning of life and the sadness of human mortality, Rosa had surprised herself when she volunteered to stay with Jocelyn for a few days while Polly 'popped' back to France for some essentials. Polly tended to pop, whizz or nip. Rosa had noticed that her mother's choice of verbs since her own mother had got cancer were clipped, speedy little words, as if she thought that employing longer words might use up the time that Jocelyn had left.

* * *

Four little sugar lumps sat in a metal dish next to a ceramic milk jug and two china cups and saucers on a wooden tray. Rosa couldn't remember when she'd last seen cups like these; old-fashioned, floral, gold-rimmed. Holding the cups up to the light, Rosa marvelled at their weightlessness and near transparency, and then for one heart stopping second almost allowed them to slip from her fingers as an imitation of a train-whistle shattered her contemplation.

Who used shrieking kettles nowadays? Rosa had forgotten how loud the old thing was. Blowing away the steam, she thumbed the lid from the spout and poured boiling water into the teapot. In fact, who used sugar lumps, china cups, milk jugs and teapots nowadays? Jocelyn did and Rosa was glad. It reaffirmed her gran was special.

Established, some might say pernickety, ways of doing things were part of who she was. That didn't mean that Gran was a stick in the mud or a killjoy, quite the contrary. Large in Rosa's childhood memories was the sound of Jocelyn's laughter. Laughter that provided a soundtrack to vigorous demonstrations of hopscotch, flailing on the rope swing with her skirt tucked into her knickers, or rolling down the hill wrapped in an old rug.

A shadow fell across Rosa's heart as a futile longing to hear Jocelyn laugh like that again, see her on the swing again, crept through her. A look outside at the old silver birch tree confirmed the rope was still there. Tattered, weather-beaten, grey with age, but still there ... and so was Jocelyn. For now.

The door creaked open accompanied by the ceramic rattle of assorted crockery on the tray. Rosa held her breath. It looked like Gran was asleep despite having asked for tea, though the poor woman *had* been waiting a while due to her granddaughter's unscheduled nap in the rocking chair. And now to cap it all the less than silent entrance might have disturbed her. Retreat seemed the way forward, but as she backtracked, Jocelyn struggled to a sitting position.

'I'm not asleep, love, come and sit by me.'

Rosa placed the heavy tray on the side table, drew back the curtains a little and sat down on the bed. Before she could stop herself she asked, 'How are you feeling, Gran?'

What a fatuous question. Jocelyn looked out at her from pale green eyes dulled with morphine and pain. Her skin was almost translucent, stretched thinly across protruding cheekbones; her once plump lips now a slash in the white landscape of her face.

'I have been better, Rosa.' Jocelyn managed a smile and tried to tidy her faded chestnut curls with shaking fingers.

Rosa swallowed, again cursing at her thoughtless enquiry after her gran's health. Of course she'd been better, but what were you supposed to say to a dying loved one? Rosa inclined her head towards the bottle of morphine on the bedside cabinet.

'Would you like another dose of Oramorph?'

'Not yet. I'll see how I go.'

'So what about a cuppa?'

'Of course, I'd love one. And then I have got something to tell you. A secret that I have never told a living soul.' Jocelyn's determined jaw and serious tone conveyed both pent up emotion and excitement.

A feeling of trepidation welled in Rosa's belly and then trickled down again, dragging away her confidence like waves sucking at the pebbles on a beach. She was not at all sure that her shoulders were broad enough to carry the weight of a deathbed confessional. Besides, it should be her mother or even her older brothers, Simon and Ben, who had this dubious honour.

Innate within her consciousness was a little kitten of contentment meowing, 'I'm not good with serious or sad things. Please don't feed them to me'. The kitten must have been asleep when Rosa had packed her weekend bag and headed back up here to Skipton from her London home.

And for the first time since she had arrived, Jocelyn looked more like her old self, eager, excited, alive. At twenty-eight Rosa should be mature enough to hear a secret, shouldn't she? She forced the struggling kitten out and said, 'That sounds a bit ominous, Gran. What on earth is it?' Then the kitten slipped back through the cat flap and wrapped its little body around her vocal cords. 'But don't you think you should tell Mum ... or someone else instead?'

Jocelyn's hands shook even more and tea slopped into the saucer. 'Your mum is in her second home in France, not because she has to get 'essentials', but because she can't cope with my situation.' She took a tentative sip of tea. 'Besides, I decided long ago never to tell her, and who else would I tell? You are the perfect person to confide in, little one.'

Little one. That term of endearment, a blast from the rope swing days, sent prickly nettles behind Rosa's eyes. Perfect? She hadn't even visited this house for nearly three years, seeing Jocelyn only at family get-togethers and the occasional visit to her mother's house. Rosa blinked a few times and took a sip of her own tea. In her defence, her job as a travel journalist had taken her far away, but in hindsight she should have tried harder to see the woman who had meant the world to her years ago – still did.

'So are your ears pinned back?'

Rosa pretended to pin them and nodded.

'Okay. You remember your grandad was a bit of an old grump?' Rosa nodded again. She had been fond of him, but her grandparents' relationship had been more chalk and cheese than yin and yang. 'By the time you knew him he'd mellowed.' Jocelyn nodded at Rosa's raised eyebrows. 'He was a right old bastard when your mum was little.'

This time it was Rosa who slopped her tea. Never in her life had her grandmother used a word like that and the venom with which Jocelyn had spat it out twisted her stomach.

'But ...Why? What did he do?'

Jocelyn rested her cup down on the quilt, leaned back against her pillow and stared at a point somewhere behind Rosa's head. A sigh. 'Oh, many things. He drank too much, stayed out all hours, thought he was still a lad with no responsibilities.' Jocelyn gave a short bark. 'Always said I'd got pregnant to catch him, snare him

Snare him? If he'd been a rabbit caught in a snare, I'd have broken his sodding neck … often wish I had.'

Rosa's stomach twisted again. She didn't like where this was headed and neither did the kitten. An adequate response eluded her, so she just said, 'I always thought you seemed happy and Mum never said—'

'Your mum never knew. I made sure of that. It was one thing me being miserable, but I wouldn't allow *her* to be. If he came home in a mood or drunk, I would take her out for a walk or round to my mother's, anything so she didn't realise what a monster she had for a dad.'

Jocelyn closed her eyes, her chest rising and falling as she tried to regulate her ragged breathing. Anyone could see that this revelation was taking its toll. Rosa wanted it to stop.

'I honestly don't know what to say, Gran. Perhaps you should rest now, all this is tiring you out.'

'I'll be at rest soon enough and for long enough.' Jocelyn smiled wryly. 'No. I'll have a dose of that morphine jollop and carry on with my tale.' She opened her eyes and looked at Rosa. 'If you are willing to hear it?'

Rosa administered the Oramorph and sat back down again. If her ears were needed, then she had to listen. It was suddenly important to know how it had been for Polly as a girl. Rosa had had a very happy childhood created by parents who loved each other. They'd been comfortably off; Dad was a science teacher and deputy head, and Mum had her own bridal wear business. She and her brothers had grown like little seeds in the warmth of a perfumed garden - seedlings nurtured by love into fragrant blooms. She took a breath. 'Was he nice to Mum?'

'Nice? Yes, most of the time, especially when he'd had a drink. The only person that really mattered to him in the end though was himself. As long as Malcolm could do exactly as he pleased, then things were okay. As you know he worked on building sites and he made good money, though much more than a run-of-the-mill builder does. I think he did a bit of dodgy trading too, but I never

asked outright. I learned not to ask questions because his answer would come on the end of a fist.'

Rosa gasped. 'What? He hit you!'

Jocelyn patted Rosa's hand and took another swallow of tea 'Yes, in the early days … until I "knew my place".'

Rosa's heart lurched, turning indignant anger into words. 'The bastard! That's outrageous. Why didn't you leave him?'

Jocelyn gave a ghost of a smile. 'I came close … so very close … but in those days it was easier said than done. I had your mum and nowhere to go. My own mother was ill with 'her nerves'. It would be called depression nowadays. Dad had died before Polly was born, and though I didn't ask, I knew my mother couldn't cope with us living in her tiny house. My sister Helen had three children of her own She'd offered to take us in but it wouldn't be fair. She and her husband were struggling as it was.'

The unbearable pain in her gran's eyes made looking into them impossible. Rosa switched her gaze to the window and the tops of the fir trees waving in the late afternoon sun, and wondered how many more poor women had lived such desperately unhappy lives fifty years ago. She guessed a fair number, and she'd bet that kind of desperation wasn't confined to those days either. Absently stroking her bare ring finger, Rosa also guessed there was much to be said for being single. Still staring through the window she whispered, 'I can't bear to think of you being so unhappy … all those wasted years.'

'Not all wasted, nor unhappy; I had Polly and my friends.' Jocelyn traced a finger down her granddaughter's cheek. 'You look so much like your mum when she was younger, cute as a kitten with your auburn curls and jade eyes.' Jocelyn sighed and rolled her eyes up to the left as if trying to remember what she'd been saying. 'Yes, so not wasted. And as I said, he wasn't so bad later.'

The 'he wasn't so bad' was hardly an accolade and didn't do much to lift Rosa's spirits. Bewildered at this awful account of a past she'd never been privy to, and would never suspect, she rubbed her eyes and tried to make some sense from her tangled thoughts.

Eventually a thread of clarity unpicked itself. 'You know when you said you came very close to leaving him?'

A ghost of a smile returned to Jocelyn's lips, a spark alive in her eyes. She handed her empty cup to Rosa 'Yes, love.'

'Where would you have gone, Gran?'

Jocelyn lifted her head from the pillow, her eyes danced and a radiant ear-to-ear grin exorcised the ghost of a smile. 'Oh, I had somewhere … and someone … a very special someone. And that, Rosa my little one, is the secret I want you to hear.'

CHAPTER 2

$\mathcal{A}$cting had never been one of Rosa's strengths. A fear of pretending to be someone else purely to elicit a favourable audience reaction had always left her nauseous. In drama class at school, the donning of heavy layered Elizabethan silks, or wigs, masks and black gowns, in order to hubble and bubble, ironically left her feeling naked under the spotlights. Rosa hadn't really known who she was at fifteen, so how could she pretend to be someone else?

Thirteen years later as she prepared for an audience of just one, she felt the same trepidation and gut-rolling anxiety. If she was honest, she still didn't know who she was. You could say that she didn't feel particularly comfortable 'in her own skin'. This often-used phrase always struck her as accurate but odd. It was useful in that it succinctly covered a plethora of feelings about one's shortcomings or anxieties, but 'her own skin'? She sure as hell wouldn't feel like borrowing someone else's to compare.

The opening speech of her soon-to-be-performed act scrolled through her mind as she shook her umbrella and ran up the granite steps to her London office. Even to her own ears it sounded like a boring monologue. A memory of her drama teacher, Mrs Postlethwaite, muscled in to add criticism. 'It needs to be more of a flighty, summery little piece, tip-tapping from your mouth Rosa; not a monotonous dirge.'

What she said had to be believable, not just a thinly disguised excuse to carry out Jocelyn's request – a legacy of the secret she'd bestowed upon Rosa last week.

11

Rosa's boss, Shelley Harrison, editor of *Travel the Turning World*, wasn't easy to convince at the best of times. Years ago she'd worked as a Fleet Street journalist presiding over many a cut-and-thrust exclusive scandal and political naming-and-shaming story. Even now that she'd left gossip and scandal behind to become the boss of a travel guide, she could still see through schmooze. Her sharp dark eyes pierced the schmoozer's fakery like powerful headlights through thick autumn fog.

Before today Rosa had no cause to worry about Shelley's penetrating gaze. In fact, she'd never got on the wrong side of her. Rosa's assignments since she'd become a travel journalist were often far-flung, always exciting, and extremely fulfilling. One of her journo friends on a local paper back home in Yorkshire once said that she'd kill for a job like Rosa's. Rosa had replied that she could see why, as it was the best job in the world, the turning world, *hardy-har*. But today it was yarn-spinning time. If Shelley was less than convinced by her performance, it could place their hitherto comfortable relationship in jeopardy. Though, after careful consideration, Rosa had decided Jocelyn's quest was worth it.

Rich aromatic coffee percolating in the tiny kitchen next to Rosa's office created a comforting ambience, and her lungs expanded to take full advantage of the welcome. On the drainer a large mug had her name on it - literally. She picked up the pot, sloshing coffee to the brim. Then the first few sips of the day, hot and bitter. As the caffeine raced through her system she was reminded that she had a body, not just an overloaded brain. An Arabica path spread down her gullet, warming her stomach and lifting her spirits.

Through the window, watery rays shone a spotlight on the rain-soaked pigeons. Wings slick and tucked in tight, they strutted along a balustrade like hopeful extras in a production of *Grease*. Spring rain always made everything so fresh, even here in the middle of the city where patches of green were rarer than hen's teeth. Why hens? Why not ducks or ... Rosa sipped her coffee and cleared her mind of irrelevant thoughts. She wondered how Jocelyn was feeling today.

Jocelyn's secret had been divulged to Rosa over a period of an hour or so as the older woman had slipped in and out of consciousness. The telling of the story had left Rosa's emotions balanced on a tightrope between happiness and despair, her whole being concentrating on the happy ending, willing it with all her heart to be the tale's final destination – yet she knew it wasn't, of course. How could it be? Jocelyn was here, on her deathbed, remembering the best time in her life. A time that was achingly beautiful, yet all too fleeting.

* * *

Last week, as the sunset lengthened tangerine fingers across the May sky outside Jocelyn's bedroom window, she'd made herself comfortable and began to talk.

'It was the August of 1968. The month began rainy and stormy and your granddad had a temper to match. We were supposed to have gone to the seaside for a few days, but because of the weather he didn't want to bother. He spent the holiday money on booze.'

Rosa shook her head sadly. 'Poor you … poor Mum.'

'That's nothing. No, he'd excelled himself this time.' Jocelyn rubbed her eyes and smoothed the sheets firmly, as if trying to erase the past. 'He started an affair with Gloria, a barmaid at the Rose and Crown. Silly cow. I didn't blame her really, she'd lost her husband and mine was readily available. She must have been desperate to have fallen for Malcolm though. Oh, don't get me wrong, he was a handsome man back then, but his beauty was very much skin-deep.'

'So how did you find out?' Rosa cupped her chin in her hand and stared at a threadbare teddy on a stool in the corner. She wanted to scoop it up, give it a cuddle, galvanise her feelings against the grim truths of Jocelyn's past. But she left it where it was; concentrating on Jocelyn's feelings was more important.

'Oh, he told me. He revelled in it … came home in the early

hours one night stinking of booze and perfume.' Jocelyn cleared her throat. 'I asked him where he'd been until then and he just laughed and said 'Fucking someone else, and by heck, she's so much better in bed than you."

Rosa's head snapped up at the shock of gran's words and the matter of fact way in which she recalled what must have been a hideously painful moment. 'But that's … awful.' Rosa felt empty, hollow. And then increasing fury at her grandfather's actions whipped through her like wildfire.

'Yes. But then as I told you, he *was* awful, I just grew to live with it. I was very hurt at the time, of course, devastated in fact. Something inside that was holding it all together, tethering me to his side, something that was already frayed, just snapped after that night. The next morning I grabbed my "rainy day" money from under a loose floorboard, dropped your mum at my sister's and bought a ticket to Cornwall.'

'Eh?' Rosa wondered if her gran would ever stop surprising her that evening. 'What rainy day money? And why Cornwall?'

'It was money that I'd squirreled away from the bit I earned in my part-time cleaning job. Some also from going through Malcolm's trousers when he'd had a win on the horses and was too hung over the next day to remember how much. No idea why Cornwall really. It was pretty far away, which was good. I'd have gone to the moon if I could. Anyhow, I just looked at the schedule and went to Bodmin.' Jocelyn's snowdrop-white face flooded with colour. 'And I am so glad I did or I wouldn't have met the love of my life. My Jory. Such a lovely name. It's the Cornish version of George.'

So that answered Rosa's earlier question about surprises. 'You met the love of your life in Bodmin?'

'Yes and no. We met in Bodmin, but fell in love in Tintagel.'

'Tintagel? Isn't that the place where King Arthur was supposed to have lived?'

'There are lots of stories. Truths and legends all intertwined like a tangled vine, my love. Nobody really knows. But one thing I know for sure, it is a place of magic and mystery all right.'

Jocelyn looked like she was about to drop to sleep all of sudden, so Rosa tapped her hand. There was no way she was missing this now. 'Okay. So you went to Bodmin. How did you first meet him?'

'Hmm? Oh, he was the taxi driver. I bought a little tourist map of the area and the first interesting place I saw was Tintagel Castle. Now I'd heard of it, of course, but couldn't for the life of me remember much about it. The blurb under the picture said an exciting place of legends and mystery, so I just plumped for that. I could have done with a bit of bloody excitement I can tell you.'

'So you went by taxi to Tintagel Castle?'

'Yes. Well, not the castle of course because that's just a ruin, but the village. And by the time I got there it was pretty late; the train journey had taken forever and I had no plan of what to do at the end of it. I hadn't booked a room anywhere either. Jory and I chatted on the way and by the time we arrived in Tintagel, I think I was already a little bit in love with him.'

Jocelyn looked more awake now and her eyes had regained the old twinkle.

'I was watching him through the rear-view mirror all the way. He was tanned and had dark curly hair and the most infectious laugh, rich and deep and joyful. Oh, but his eyes, Rosa. He had these eyes as deep as the ocean, blue as an August sky and yet green too, you know? Like sea-green depths of swell under an anchored boat.'

Picturing such long-ago summer eyes in the gloomy and darkening room was a bit of a tall order, but Rosa tried her best. 'I think I know, yes.'

A nod. 'And because I was in the back of the taxi I could only see the top half of his face. In the mirror his mouth was missing from the picture. Of course I saw his mouth later on. It was wide and full and quick to smile, and even quicker to kiss, but at the time I didn't know that, as I couldn't see it. But that made him sexier and more mysterious – the fact that I couldn't see all his face somehow? You know, like a man at a masked ball?'

Rosa wasn't altogether sure she felt comfortable talking about sexy smiles and kisses with her gran. It felt a bit weird. Masked balls weren't on her agenda and she was surprised her gran had ever been to one either. Still, she just shrugged and nodded. 'And did you stay with him that night?'

Jocelyn's eyes grew round. 'Eh? What do you take me for? I wouldn't have slept with a man the first time I met him. And I was a married woman, don't forget!'

Rosa held up her hands. 'Okay! No need to have a heart attack.'

'You youngsters have a lot to learn about these one night stands. Don't you think about HIV anymore?'

That rankled. 'Hey, hang on a minute. I've never had a one night stand in all my life as it goes.'

Jocelyn's face softened. 'Really? Oh I *am* glad.' Then her eyes narrowed but she made her voice casual. 'I haven't really heard much from Polly about your … er … friends.'

'Really, Gran?' Rosa said, trying not to smirk. How obvious was she? In the long silence Rosa could almost hear the cogs ticking over in her gran's head.

Jocelyn cleared her throat and fixed her stare on the tops of the trees outside. 'No. I was actually wondering if you liked girls instead, but didn't know how to tell your mum. No shame in it you know. Even though I draw the line at one night stands, I'm open-minded about sexuality.' Her questioning eyes slid back up and across her granddaughter's face.

In spite of the direct question, Rosa had to laugh. 'You don't beat about the bush, do you?'

'I haven't time for shilly-shallying, and I would like to see you happy.' She folded her arms and stuck out her chin. Then into the awkward silence she snapped, 'So is there someone?'

'For Christ's sake. Having a partner is the route to all happiness, is it? I wouldn't have said that was always true looking at *your* marriage.' Rosa hadn't meant to be so harsh but Jocelyn's blunt manner had hit a nerve. The truth of it was that Rosa was beginning to wonder if she had a 'keep off' sign tattooed on her head. The longest relationship she'd had lasted six months and that was two years ago. Since then, there had been a few dates, but that was all.

In the past she'd not worried too much. Her job had taken her all over the world, sometimes at the drop of a hat, so making firm plans was never possible. But recently she had noticed that many of her friends had married or formed long-term relationships.

Jocelyn looked away. 'No. I guess I asked for that. Sorry if I upset you, I—'

Rosa heaved a sigh and shook her head. 'No, please don't apologise. That was out of order; I guess I was beginning to wonder why at the grand old age of twenty-eight I had nobody significant in my life. Romantically, I mean. You're pretty significant, Gran.'

'Oh, my little one. Don't worry, one day you will find Mr Right … or Miss.' Jocelyn smiled and reached for Rosa's hand.

'If such a person exists … perhaps I will. I'm not overly worried, I have a fabulous job and that's keeping me busy, there's plenty of time. And for the record it's Mr.'

'Mr?'

'Right.'

'Oh, I see,' Jocelyn chuckled.

A glance outside told Rosa that the last brush strokes of sunset had tailed off into the velvet navy of evening, and a pale moon slowly grew brighter in the sky. She put her hand out to switch on the bedside lamp but Jocelyn shook her head.

'No, love. Leave the room like this. I love watching the moon rise through my window. I feel like I'm sailing across the sky on it.'

'That'll be the medication, Gran.'

'No, that jollop barely touches this damned thing nowadays. I might have to get one of those syringe-driver contraptions soon. It's connected by a needle into your arm and it releases morphine as and when. They said I might need one nearer the time. The nurse comes round and fills it up, makes sure that everything is working okay.' Jocelyn's voice was ironed flat. The sparkle faded, became subsumed by defeat.

Once again the hateful disease had muscled its way back into the room, filling every nook and cranny, suffocating any spark of hope under its immeasurable weight. Though, if Rosa was honest, it never really left, just hung about at the periphery of their consciousness waiting for a chance to grab the attention again. She wanted to scream, shout, ride a charger into its lair; shoot burning arrows into its belly and yell, 'Leave my gran alone, you bastard!' But of course she couldn't. Those fantasies belonged in childhood fairy tales. She was no longer a child and there was no magic sword or bullet to protect gran from death.

Jocelyn's hand felt cool and paper-light in Rosa's. 'You look exhausted, Gran. Try and have a nap and I'll go cook you a little something.'

'No. I'm not hungry, and I need to tell you the rest. Give me a drink of juice and let me finish my tale.'

'I think the tale can wait until tomorrow—'

'Please, it won't take long.' She sipped her juice and settled back against the pillows. 'Anyway, when we get to Tintagel I tell Jory I hadn't booked anywhere to stay and did he know of anywhere. Unbelievably, his sister Meredith ran a B&B nearby, at the top of the road that leads to the castle. And she had a room free. He introduced me to her and then I went to say goodbye. It was then that he explained he'd a week off starting the next day and wondered if he could show me around the place.'

'He was from there?'

'Yes. He worked in Bodmin and around the more populated areas, but he lived right there in the village.'

'Bit forward for those times wasn't he? Didn't he ask about your personal life? You'd have thought he would've seen your wedding ring.'

'Oh, he did. Asked me all about my life in the taxi on the way. I told him that my husband had abandoned me and our daughter and I wanted a bit of time to recover.'

'Gran! That was such a big fib!' Rosa remembered that Jocelyn always made a point of the importance of telling the truth when they'd been growing up.

'In a way it was true. He was having an affair with Gloria so he had abandoned us really. And when he was home with us, he wasn't really "with us". He'd be on the sauce or looking at the racing pages.'

Rosa nodded. 'Was Jory single?'

'Widowed at twenty-six, three years before – so sad. His wife had only been twenty-five, some kind of leukaemia I think. They had an eight-year-old daughter, Daisy, who was looked after by Meredith when he was at work. Lovely little girl, I met her once.'

'Right. And did he come round the next day?'

Jocelyn's eyes lit up and crinkled at the corners. A smile curled her lips. 'Yes, and the next day, and the one after that. We spent almost a whole week together, walking amongst the ruins. He told me there was ancient power in those stones; spirits of the past still walked there and so forth. And do you know, I felt it too? That place is very special. We went around and about as well, visiting all the local beauty spots, kissing under the stars. I thought I'd died and gone to heaven. I have never been so happy before or since.'

The joy of those memories was almost palpable in the room and Rosa felt her heart plummet as she asked the inevitable question. 'Such a shame that it had to come to an end. What happened?'

Jocelyn swallowed hard and Rosa was saddened to see tears standing in her eyes. 'We'd gone for a moonlight walk along the cliff path, past an old church that is on the other side from the castle, and we made love for the first time under the stars right there on the headland. After, he'd put his arm around me and we looked out to sea. I rested my head on his shoulder, inhaling the warm, male smell of him, the salt air on his skin. It was one of the most perfect moments of my life … I adored him and never wanted it to end.

'The thing was, I had been there six days and I needed to see your mum. My sister had said everything was fine and Polly was having a whale of a time, but Malcolm kept coming round, demanding to know where I was. She hadn't told him of course, and he'd got right nasty at one point.' Jocelyn took another sip of orange juice.

'God, you must have been in a state,' Rosa said, blinking

moisture from her eyes.

'That's putting it mildly. Anyway, on that moonlit night, Jory turned to me and told me he loved me, wanted me to stay there with him, marry me in the old church behind us.' Jocelyn's voice cracked. 'We'd send for Polly, of course.'

'But that was fantastic ... you already told me you adored him, so why didn't you stay?'

'Because Malcolm hadn't abandoned us, as you rightly pointed out a few minutes ago.' Jocelyn pinched the bridge of her nose and sighed. 'I came clean and told him everything. Jory was furious on my behalf and said that there was nothing stopping me making a new life here and that Malcolm would never find us. He practically begged me to stay, told me that he never thought he'd love anyone again until he met me. I told him I loved him too and I'd sleep on it. But the next day I got up early, took the first bus out of there and went back to Malcolm.'

'What? Why?' Rosa had to force herself to keep seated. She wanted to jump up, rage around the room, vent her frustration.

'Because I knew Malcolm. Even though he didn't want me, he would never have let anyone else have me either. He'd have tracked us down, snatched Polly, God knows what else. I paid for it in bruises even though I went back to him. I couldn't allow him to hurt Jory, tarnish the beautiful thing we had. Once he'd set foot in Tintagel the whole place would have been sullied.'

'Jesus, Gran. Didn't you let Jory know why you left? Ring him or something?'

Jocelyn's face crumbled and a sob escaped her. 'God forgive me, no. But I did ring his sister a while after and found out he'd been devastated by my leaving. I'll be with him again though soon. He told me that the other night.'

Rosa thought she'd misheard. 'What do you mean the other night? Has he been here to see you?'

'In a manner of speaking, yes ... he came to me as I slept, told me we would be reunited and that I needed to tell you to visit the castle.'

So this was the morphine again. 'He wants me to visit the castle?'

'That's what he said. Jory couldn't stress enough how important it was. It had to be you … especially as you had um… since you were little. Never mind, I'm saying too much.'

Rosa hoped a change of tack would clarify. 'Do you mean he died, and you dreamt about him? And I had what since I was little?'

'So, will you visit, little one?'

Jocelyn was obviously not open to clarification. Rosa shook her head. 'I don't think I could get the time—'

'Please.' Jocelyn clutched at her granddaughter's shoulder and heaved herself into an upright position, her breath coming in short huffs. 'I know you probably think it's the jollop talking, but I know it's the truth.'

The colour that had returned to her gran's face earlier drained, and she swayed slowly from side to side as if the effort of sitting up had interfered with her balance. 'Gran, lie down; you don't look right.'

A short burst of humourless laughter was followed by, 'That's because I'm not. Please, Rosa. Please say you'll visit … and soon … I want to be alive to hear all about it.'

'But I have my work, how—'

'Please, I beg of you. I failed him once … terribly. I couldn't bear to fail him again.'

* * *

The squeal of the hot water tap turning brought Rosa's mind back to the small office kitchen. Rinsing her coffee cup, she girded her loins for the meeting with Shelley. Could she pull off the casual, carefully rehearsed, 'I have to go on holiday in the next few weeks, but I can combine work with pleasure' routine? And work the, 'Yes, I know I was due to go to Canada to ride husky-drawn sleighs, but this place is *really* special and I have a particular angle I'd like to explore' earnest enthusiasm?

If the answer was no, she only had one other option. Rosa would have to resign, because the look of joy on Jocelyn's face when she'd agreed to go to Tintagel was worth more than any job in the world.

CHAPTER 3

$\mathcal{T}$he audience of one failed. After the first carefully rehearsed line, the act crumbled. Under the immobilising sweep of Shelley Harrison's oncoming headlights, Rosa had done a brilliant pastiche of a rabbit in the middle of a road. A subsequent combination of fear and a shot of adrenaline had given her the courage to just come clean about the whole thing.

Shelley, black-suited and white-shirted, had listened in silence, her dark eyes giving nothing away. She then left her desk and walked to the window, turning her expensively tailored back to Rosa The vista over Camden was much wider and grander than the one from Rosa's office. No pigeons strutted here, just a sweep across the canal, rooftops and blue sky. Blue sky? It had been drizzling ten minutes before, but then perhaps Shelley could order favourable weather as well as order people around.

'I once had a grandma I loved her so much; she brought me up after my mother dumped me,' Shelly said, her voice distant yet heavy with emotion Though unrehearsed, her lines were far more convincing than Rosa's.

'Oh, I didn't realise … I guess that was … tough' Rosa stumbled into silence and looked at her feet, heat spreading through her face and neck. She'd never been allowed into the closed box that was Shelley's personal life, and now the lid had been lifted a little, she felt uncomfortable about trying to prise it off.

'Why should you realise? I never make a song and dance. But

yes it was tough' Shelley turned around to face Rosa, tucked her blonde bob behind her ears, and then touched her mouth briefly as if wondering whether to let any more personal words out. She sighed and sat back at her desk before speaking again

'My mother was a cocaine addict. I never knew my father, and my grandmother, a widow, worked her fingers to the proverbial to make sure I valued education and never wanted for anything. She had a heart attack and died when I was in my last year at university.' Shelley picked up a pen and looked at it. 'It was very quick. I hated the fact that I wasn't with her and would have done anything to be there.'

The crack in Shelley's armour was made larger by the one in her voice.

Rosa cleared her throat. 'Oh, Shelley, I'm so sorry …'

'Yes. But I don't want you to be in a similar boat in the future. You have been given a last request. Perhaps the ex-lover thing is all to do with the morphine, but in the end it doesn't really matter. Take two weeks. Go tomorrow.'

'But what about Canada?'

'Someone else will do it. You haven't had time off for …' Shelley frowned, 'I don't remember to be honest. Anyway, go.'

'If you're sure. And as I said, I'll do a report too for work.' Rosa heaved a sigh of relief, feeling the knots constricting her stomach loosen She couldn't believe how easy it had all been

'Whatever you like. Now, I have work and I'm sure you need to get your desk in order before you go.' Shelley opened up her laptop and began to type, the crack in the armour now welded neatly and expertly shut.

Rosa nodded, said thank you and left.

* * *

'If you told me sooner I could have come with you,' Willa muttered. The scowl on Rosa's flatmate's face resembled the particularly evil looking gargoyles seen on medieval buildings, and Rosa had to turn away to smile. 'You know how much I love Cornwall.'

'No. You love surfing,' Rosa said, folding a pair of jeans and placing them in her case. 'Where there's a Willa there's a wave, don't you always say?'

Willa's scowl deepened and she ran her hand over her closely cropped blonde hair. 'Yeah, well I look at the scenery too, *obviously*. And Tintagel's right by all the best beaches down that north coast … can't believe you didn't mention it.' She sat down cross-legged in the middle of her bed, her long angular limbs tucked and folded like some easy-bend pipe cleaner model.

Rosa had shared a flat with Willa for two years and normally found her unruly 'teenager' strops amusing, but the woman was actually twenty-six and just lately the strops seemed more like spoiled brat syndrome. Willa worked in a homeless shelter and wore her 'caring for others' role like a badge of honour, a kind of moral one-upmanship.

Newly introduced to Willa, lesser mortals whose jobs didn't involve rescuing teenagers from the streets, drug rehabilitation and the like, would receive the 'raised eyebrow of superiority'.

Though Willa looked the part - tattooed ankle, shoulder and inner wrist, with the recent addition of a pierced lip - on occasion, and to her eternal shame, her cultured accent escaped - unwelcome as a fart in a lift. Willa would then do a damage limitation job, dropping aitches all over the place and wiping her nose on the back of her hand in a parody of how she imagined a working class person to behave. She was far from working class however.

'So if I had told you earlier,' Rosa stopped packing and looked at Willa, 'which would have been impossible because I didn't know for sure until today, you could have taken time away from your vitally important job at a drop of a hat then, could you?' Rosa noted the extension of Willa's bottom lip and her avoidance of eye contact. *That'll be a no, then*. She turned back to her packing.

'I might have. I've not had a holiday for months.' Willa stretched out her legs and flopped back against the pillows.

This act was wearing thin now. Even if Willa could get the time off there was no way she'd want her tagging along. 'Just go somewhere on your own then … why you want to come with me is a mystery. I mean, it's not as if you need to share costs or a room is it, not with your income.'

Willa's hazel eyes shot a 'that was way below the belt' glare and she turned to face the wall. 'That's not the point,' she mumbled. 'Just thought it might be nice to travel together, that's all … forget it.'

Rosa's cheeks flushed. Damn it. Why had she been so bitchy? She picked up socks and rammed them into the case. The stress of her gran's imminent death must be taking its toll. Still, the break apart would do them good. Perhaps the poor little rich girl might seem more palatable when she'd done Jocelyn's bidding.

About a year ago, Willa had spilled her twenty-four carat gold beans when she'd had too much to drink one evening. Of course, Rosa had already been a little suspicious of her flatmate's seemingly endless supply of cash, not commensurate with such a low paid position - and of course because of the slips in accent from time to time. And, as Willa had drained her fourth glass of cheap red, she'd opened up.

Her full name was Wilhelmina Farquharson. Her parents had a country seat up north and, unfortunately for them, their daughter's 'coming-out' was the antithesis of a traditional debutante ball. Willa had one day calmly explained why she wouldn't be dating the eligible and well-to-do bachelors champing at the bit outside the stately walls. She had 'come out' all right and then been quickly 'sent out'. A lesbian daughter was not in the grand plan and she'd been ordered from the ancestral home, not in so many words, but it was clear how the land lay. Willa had fled from the garden parties, the hunt balls, the pitying looks and village tittle-tattle of Little Snobbery-upon-Bigot. Mummy and Daddy had sent her substantial monthly cheques, of course, a tacit arrangement that actually shouted 'stay away and there'll be more where this came from'.

The truth was that with that kind of income Willa needn't have worked at all. She could have bought her own flat (certainly didn't have to share with Rosa) and had a comfortable life. Willa was bright, well-educated and could have turned her hand to anything, but she was a kind hearted soul - odd really, given her background. Immediately upon arriving in London she'd secured the flat-share and had thrown herself into helping those less fortunate than herself. She'd told Rosa that she wanted to be thought of as ordinary, just another person making her way in the world.

After a while, Rosa had wondered why Willa tended to spend her evenings with her male friends or in the flat. When she was sure they were friends she'd asked. Although she was at ease with her sexuality, Willa apparently hadn't the desire to seek out a girlfriend. 'I'm happy doing my job and hanging out with my mates. If it happens, it happens,' she'd said waving a hand dismissively.

Rosa had wondered if Willa had a thing for her, but the more than obvious match-making attempt Willa made between Rosa and her mate Greg from work had put paid to those thoughts.

Zipping her case closed, Rosa turned back to Willa. She still faced the wall, her whole posture rigid and unforgiving. She looked so vulnerable sometimes. What her parents had done must have hurt, still must be hurting. She saw them a few times a year but they always came to London.

Rosa felt guilty for her impatience at Willa's behaviour earlier and juxtaposed her flatmate's lifetime of rejection, nannies, boarding school, university and then booted out because she didn't fit the mould, against her own warm cocoon of childhood and careful nurturing through the teenage years. No wonder the poor woman was acting like a kid. She'd never really had the chance to be one, to be loved even.

She took a step forward intending to give Willa a hug and then stopped when she remembered that on her last visit, Rosa's mother had hinted that such shows of affection might give her friend the wrong impression. Realisation dawned. *That's* where Gran had got the idea that Rosa was gay. Damn Polly. While her mother was not

27

quite a bigot, unlike Rosa she was hardly the most liberal thinker in the world. Rosa would be having words next time they spoke.

Kneeling lightly on the bed, Rosa placed her hand in the small of Willa's back. 'Hey, I'm sorry. I guess I'm just stressed because of my gran's situation, and this whole trip is unorthodox to say the least. Fuck knows what I'm actually supposed to do when I actually get to Tintagel.' A shrug from Willa was all she received. 'Look, do you fancy a quick pint in The Dog? I'm all packed and I could do with relaxing a bit before bed.'

Willa turned over, her eyes already crinkling at the corners. 'Last one there buys the first round!' She jumped from the bed and ran out of the door.

Rosa laughed and ran after her. It really was like living with a big kid sometimes. Perhaps she should work harder at making Willa smile more often when she got back from Cornwall.

* * *

The three-hour and forty-two-minute train journey from Paddington felt like six. Though the train rattled through the lush greenery of spring in her finest clothes, all Rosa saw was grey. As she travelled further from London a dull ache started in the pit of her stomach and grew more raw with every passing minute. It felt as if she had a barb hooked deep in her guts, the other end tied firmly to Camden.

Plans and organisation were bread and butter to Rosa, the mainstay of her job. Without a meticulously plotted course she felt at sea, anchorless. All she knew about the immediate future was that she'd be due into Bodmin station at 15.48. Beyond that ... *Here there be dragons.*

With another forty minutes to go Rosa tried to read to take her mind off what was ahead, but found her eyes gliding over the same few words again and again. At one stage she'd convinced herself that it would be for the best to just ring Jocelyn and ask her what exactly she wanted her granddaughter to achieve. Was it some desperate attempt to live the best time of her life again vicariously through Rosa? If that was the case, she'd be happy to take a few photos of the area and the damned castle. The problem was that Rosa knew her gran wanted more. What the more was however remained locked inside Jocelyn's head as she lay watching the shadows of the past slip across the face of the moon.

The train slowed into a station and an announcement revealed that they had arrived at Bodmin Parkway. This was it then. Better make the most of it. Gathering her belongings and a buoyant mood from deep within her resource bank, Rosa decided she should just let herself float anchorless and see where she washed up.

A practical voice, probably her mother's, heckled, *let's face it, you haven't an awful lot of choice*.

* * *

A step off the train was a step back in time. The station, if it could be called such, was a tiny little building at the side of the track. In fact, it resembled more of a glorified bus stop. A man and a woman sat on the bench inside, unmoving, unsmiling – a Madame Tussauds' exhibit had more life. The only other structure was a footbridge over the track resplendent in black and white and so much grander than the station. The only neighbours to left and right were tall trees marching alongside. Rosa took a photo. Jocelyn would be pleased to see that little had changed.

Rosa stood alone, the only passenger to alight here. The train moved off again on the way to Penzance, and its slipstream pushed the smell of diesel and country freshness into her lungs. The forced buoyant mood applied in the train began to feel more natural as she took in the quiet beauty of the area. And as she walked towards the exit, mid-May delicately introduced herself via the purple Campion, yellow buttercups and bluebells along the hedgerow.

From the back pocket of her jeans she pulled a folded bit of paper with a local taxi company and the name of the B&B she'd booked written upon it. A few people walked past and one went into the station, but apart from these few souls, the length of the country road was deserted. Her fingers keyed the first numbers into her mobile phone and then stopped as she noticed a no signal sign flash across the screen. Oh buggeration. She'd forgotten that Cornwall was beyond the back of bloody beyond, and then beyond that a bit further. Now what?

Her deep frown was soon smoothed by the sight of a red Honda coming to a halt a few feet away. *Terry's Truro Taxis* graced each door and a balding man in his thirties, presumably Terry, jumped out and began pulling suitcases from the boot. A middle-aged round woman huffed out of the back seat and jammed a hand into the side compartment of her shoulder bag.

'Did you say twenty or thirty?' She waved a twenty and ten pound note at Terry.

'I said forty.' Terry put the last bag down and narrowed his eyes at the woman.

The woman grunted and rummaged in her bag again. 'Well, I only have thirty, take it or leave it.'

'I quoted forty in Truro and even then I was selling myself short. You said okay.' Terry's voice was calm and even, though Rosa could tell he was only just keeping a lid on his temper.

'Ah, well, I thought you said thirty. Anyhow, I have to go as my train's due in a mo— Oi, what you doin' with me bag?' The woman hurried forward as Terry took the small bag and put it back in the boot.

'I have to take this to cover my petrol. I'll sell it on eBay, should get twenty quid or so.' Terry slammed the lid down, folded his arms and leaned against the taxi.

'You can't do that, it's bloody stealing!' the woman shrieked, flecks of white spittle peppering her chin.

'So's the way you duped me into coming all this way for peanuts. That's daylight robbery in anyone's book, my dear.' Terry smiled and winked over at Rosa.

Rosa covered her mouth to stifle a grin. The woman pointed at Rosa 'Hey, did you see him take me bag? He's a bloody thief, he is.' Rosa shrugged and looked away. Though she wasn't always an excellent judge of character, she was sure that Terry was the wronged party here.

'Right, I haven't got time to stand round here being insulted. I have fares to pick up.' Terry walked round the car and made as if to get in the driver's door.

'But I need that bag! It's got all me toiletries in it.'

'And I need that tenner. Pay up and I'll give it back.'

The woman stamped her small feet and muttered an expletive worthy of a hardened soldier in a war zone. 'Bleedin' cheeky swine, you are. I'm only paying up 'cos I got to get me train.' She jammed her hand into her bag pulled out a roll of notes, peeled off a rubber band and slapped ten pounds on the bonnet. Terry pocketed it and then almost threw the bag at the woman. She stuck two fingers up at him and scuttled off into the station.

Terry looked at Rosa and shook his head. 'Well, I've seen some mean buggers in my time, but she is currently top of the list for this year so far.'

Rosa nodded. 'I couldn't believe the size of the wad she pulled out.'

'I could, because I saw it when I was putting the bags in the car in Truro. She was counting it in the back seat and thought I couldn't see, cheeky mare.'

'That's awful!'

'Yeah, but it goes with the territory sometimes.' Terry pointed at her bags. 'You got a lift?'

'No. I have a cab firm, but no signal on the damned phone. I want to get to Tintagel.'

'Hop in. I've got no one booked. But it's about twenty-three miles so it will be thirty pounds, that okay? Should be more, but I like your face.'

Rosa chuckled. 'Would you like to see the money before we go?'

Terry just pulled a face and started the engine.

* * *

The delicate introduction made by mid-May grew into an onslaught of colour, smell and taste as the rich tapestry of the Cornish countryside in full bloom hurtled past Rosa's partially open window. The breeze tugged at her curls and she leaned her head against the glass to inhale the pungent wild garlic, meadow flowers and now and then, the earthy smell of cows.

Turning from the window she said to Terry, 'This area is stunningly beautiful.' A glance at his eyes through the rear-view mirror reminded her of the life-changing taxi ride her gran took all those years ago. The corner of Terry's eyes crinkled in a smile but they were brown, unremarkable, certainly not 'deep as the ocean, blue as the August sky and yet green too, like sea-green depths of a swell under an anchored boat'.

'It sure is. We're taking the scenic route, so just wait until we go through the little village of Treknow, that's lovely in itself but you can see the sea too.'

'I love the sea. It's been a while since I saw it, in this country at least.' Rosa pulled a book about the history of Tintagel out of her bag. She flicked through it as Terry asked about her job, her 'holiday', chatted about this and that and the time passed as quickly as the train journey had dragged. Terry told her that he'd visited the castle a few years ago and 'didn't reckon much to it'. He couldn't see the fascination of an old ruin up some of the steepest steps he'd ever been forced to climb by his much more adventurous wife.

Not far from their destination, the road became little more than a track, certainly no wider than eight feet. At one stage Rosa was worried that the taxi would take the door off the car next to them as they inched past each other, sandwiched as they were between the huge Cornish hedges on either side.

Treknow was indeed 'picture postcard' material, and to her left, the Atlantic Ocean twinkled invitingly under the yellow sun, while green rolling fields stretched down to the blue waters. Rosa had seen some fantastic sights on her travels abroad, but this view ranked up there with the best of them. The taxi turned into the village of Tintagel a few minutes later and Terry parked up next to Lewis's B&B, a delightful ivy-covered building that Rosa had booked before leaving London. It was in the middle of the village and within walking distance of the castle.

She thanked and paid Terry, and standing on the pavement, Rosa turned in a circle, linked her fingers and stretched her arms above her head. After few lungfuls of fresh air and one more stretch, she felt the travel weariness roll away as a sudden rush of excitement tingled through her. The palms of her hands felt clammy and a light sensation settled in her head. It was the kind of feeling she'd had as a kid before a birthday, Christmas, or on the eve of a holiday somewhere new … the spirit of adventure?

As Rosa took a quick glance at the array of shops and ancient buildings up and down the street, the weight of history supporting their walls, another tingle ran through her. She began to feel for the first time that she was no longer chasing after Jocelyn's wild goose, but was here for an important reason. That reason was as yet unknown, but Rosa had the unshakeable notion that it wouldn't be too long before she discovered what it was.

CHAPTER 4

$\mathcal{A}$s the taxi disappeared down the street, a little bit of Rosa's excitement drained away and ran after it. The sensible, organised and level-headed part of her, which was usually dominant in her persona, wanted to yell for Terry to come back and take her to the station to catch the train home and back to normality. But as she turned to an arched iron gate set in the old stone wall, her eyes were drawn up the path to the B&B and the runaway excitement was back at her side.

From the website, Rosa remembered that the building was sixteenth century. The old heavy bricks offset by long multi-panelled white framed windows and round turret wall covered with large green ivy leaves, certainly gave it the gravity of age. Yet it was stunningly pretty too and Rosa decided as she ran her hands along the spirals in the iron gate, very 'secret garden-ish'.

Across the road, a not so aged building watched from stained glass eyes, and next to it, white writing on a blue sign informed the reader that they were looking at Tintagel Methodist Church. To her right, the street inclined towards the main shopping area and Rosa couldn't wait to explore. But first she had to check in, freshen up and unpack. Organisation demanded it, and then the village was her oyster.

A jovial grey-haired man opened the door and welcomed her inside. He introduced himself as John Lewis and Rosa smiled. Firstly, she'd imagined that the owner's first name would be Lewis, not John; and secondly she couldn't get a certain large department store out of her head as he led her upstairs to her room.

Of the four beautifully furnished ensuite rooms, The Rose Room had seemed the best choice when she'd booked, as it had a balcony and views of the ocean. Once she stepped inside, her smile grew into a wide grin, my goodness had she picked the right one. It was so perfect, right from the huge brass bed, antique furniture and fresh flowers in a decorative vase by the window, to the light flooding in thorough the balcony door. 'Oh, thank you, Mr Lewis, it is such a gorgeous room!'

'Glad you like it,' he said, placing her bags on the settee. 'And please call me John, everyone does.' Then he explained about breakfast times and where it was served and left her to unwind.

The view from the balcony was stunning. The greenery of the garden against the blue of the ocean took her breath away, and if she narrowed her eyes she could almost believe she was on a ship at sea. Rosa wrapped her arms around herself and laughed out loud. It had been too long since she allowed herself to just relax and let her imagination off the leash for a good run. Willa had said recently that she was acting like an old woman. Well, right now Rosa felt about twelve, and couldn't wait to get out and explore properly.

A change of top - blue to green - a slick of lip-gloss and a quick comb of her long curls and she was ready. Rosa smoothed a crease from her black crop-trousers, looked at her reflection in the mirror and noted that there was more colour in her cheeks and sparkle in her eyes than she'd seen for some time. Adventures were good for her it seemed. Tintagel felt good for her too, even though she'd only arrived an hour ago.

As she turned from the mirror she noticed that Jocelyn's familiar half-smile kissed her own and a pang of sadness turned her mouth into a hard line. Rosa knew how much her gran would have loved to be here. But sadly this was one adventure she'd have to enjoy alone. Rosa however had promised to ring Jocelyn regularly, so in a way she'd be alongside her, if not in body, then in spirit.

* * *

Now past six in the evening, Rosa was glad to discover that the evening air was still pleasant. A salt breeze lifted her curls and carried upon it a delicious aroma of food wafting from The Tintagel Arms Hotel, just as she passed the door. Her appetite had been whetted by the unusually named Granny Wobbly's Fudge Pantry two doors down, and next door to that, Granny Wobbly's Ice Cream Parlour. The shop had drawn her from across the road with its bold pink exterior, and once at the window the delicious array of 'handmade crumbly fudge made daily', cakes, pastries and ice-cream had made her stomach rumble. Rosa knew that sampling such delights would be on her list tomorrow, but she needed a proper meal after having only a synthetic cheese sandwich on the train. She nearly ducked into the pub to sate the need, but wanted to spend just a little more time exploring before she did.

With that in mind, she hurried back across the road to a shop that demanded attention. A blue and gold circle sat in the centre just above the shop window depicting a tree and two moons. The words Willow Moon, formed from the roots of the tree, arched underneath them. A witch held a sign to the left of the window. Upon it Rosa read: *Willowmoon - Tarot readings, Reiki healings, Unique gifts crafted by local artists, come in for a spell.* She chuckled at the pun. This was the kind of place that would be great to explore.

Though the shop was closed for the day, she could smell the incense and essential oils seeping through the wooden door frame. The tarot stuff she dismissed as a bit of fun, designed to lure tourists hungry for mysticism and magic. But Rosa added Willow Moon to her list as she'd love to see what gifts she could find for family and friends.

Sadly too late in the day to explore properly, Rosa thought she'd have a brisk walk down to the end of the main street and back to get more of a feel of the place, then she'd seek out some food. Each step took her past more pubs, shops, and across the road an ancient

Post Office run by the National Trust. That was another place for her mental list, there seemed so much to do and see in a place so small and she'd not even clapped eyes on the castle yet – her main reason for coming.

As if her thoughts had been spoken out loud, a little way ahead was a wooden signpost directing her to Tintagel Castle. Rosa realised that at this time in the evening the place would be closed, but it was tempting to nip down and have a look.

The 'nipping down' proved to be more of a trek. In her mind's eye the guide book had showed her pictures of people walking down a paved path and then huge cliffs and ruins next to a beach and crashing ocean There was a paved path, but it was a lot steeper and longer than she'd imagined and her stomach was sending her rumbling reminders about food, or the lack of it.

The path turned into a small road a bit further on, and at last the ocean came into view and a cluster of white buildings nested together as the road ended. Puffing towards her up the incline, four ruddy faced, middle-aged folk in stout walking shoes stopped and took photos of a fast flowing river to her left. As she grew closer, Rosa surmised they were two couples, and one of the men took several photos of an information sign about the castle.

'What you taking pictures of that for, Don? We *do* have a leaflet all about it.' One of the women said, making a rude sign behind his back to the other woman

The other woman giggled. 'Yeah, should have done that on the way down We have *been* in the damned place after all.'

'Because I think that the more information one has, the more one knows,' Don said pushing his glasses up the bridge of his nose.

'Ooh, does *one*, indeed?' The first woman said in a fake upper class accent and then cackled like a witch Rosa thought that she would get on her nerves pretty quickly if she had to spend more than a nanosecond in her company.

'Oi, leave him alone you misery. Let's get up to the pub; I'm gagging for a pint.' The other man turned in Rosa's direction

'So what's new?' the second woman said. Then as Rosa passed

them she called, 'Excuse me, there's no point going down there, love, it's shut. The folk who run it were just packing stuff into a Land Rover as we left.'

Rosa considered just walking past, but 'being polite' was instilled - a hard thing to ignore - so she said, 'Yep. Just going for a look.'

'But you haven't the right footwear. If you slip down the rocks in them flimsy sandals you'll do yourself an injury won't she, Rachel?'

'You're not wrong, Gill.' Rachel pointed to her feet. 'You want strong boots like these. And you don't want to be on your own There's all sorts of strange ghosts around and Merlin might get you!' She cackled again and Gill joined in

Rosa waved her hand dismissively and hurried past. She'd had enough of this double act. 'I'll be fine thanks. I don't believe in ghosts.'

'Shh, don't let them hear you!' Gill hooted after her. Rosa didn't look back and quickened her pace.

* * *

Just as she thought she was free of interfering 'do-gooders' - or 'do-badders' in the case of Gill and Rachel - a Land Rover came up the hill. One pulled to a halt and an attractive young woman wound the window down. 'We're shut now, and so's the cafe,' she said, trying to tuck her long dark hair behind an ear as the wind lifted a few strands across her eyes.

Rosa could see an older woman in the passenger seat and in the back seat, the top of a guy's head as he looked for something in a bag. 'Yes, those people up there told me.' She flung a hand in the direction of the 'do-badders'. 'I just wanted a quick look, but I'll come back tomorrow for a proper visit.' She was beginning to feel a bit of an idiot to be honest. Everyone must think she was.

The woman pulled a face. 'God they can talk for England! We were waiting to lock up and it took us ages to get them out of the visitor centre.' She looked at the sky, down at Rosa's sandals and re-tucked her hair again 'The wind is getting up, sure to be followed by rain You're likely to get drenched. Wanna lift? There's room in the back next to Talan'

Talan raised a hand but not his head and carried on rootling, and the other woman leaned over, looked Rosa up and down and said, 'Hmm Not the best gear for wandering about down here.'

Rosa noted her smile while ostensibly sympathetic, held a trace of insincerity and more than a little derision That did it. Though the offer of a lift was tempting, her pride wouldn't let her admit defeat. 'No, honestly I'll be fine. I'll just stay ten minutes and then walk straight back up to the village. But thanks for the offer.'

Rosa waved in farewell and hurried past towards the buildings at the edge of the bay. The woman was right, the wind was strengthening, but she was glad of it to cool her burning cheeks. How could she not have realised that these strappy red sandals were about as much use as a snow in harvest time for clambering about the Cornish coast? But then, she hadn't meant to come all this way in the first place had she?

She wrapped her arms around herself and hurried past the two buildings which turned out to be a visitor centre on the left and a cafe on the right, just as a fat raindrop spattered on her forehead. Damn it. Damn it to hell! She wouldn't have time to see anything at all now.

At the edge of the land, the Atlantic Ocean pitched itself against a little beach, and on her right, a steep cliff and grassy incline, the lower reaches of which headed out into the water and curved up and around a headland. On the left, even in the drizzle and in the gathering gloom, was one of the most spectacular sights she'd ever witnessed.

A huge mass of rock and cliff jutted out into the incoming tide joined to the mainland by only a precarious bridge and sheer steps. Along the high edges, old stones formed arches, walls and ramparts. Rosa wiped her forearm across her damp face, and despite the weather and her stupid footwear she felt a tremor of excitement. At last she was looking at the ruins of Tintagel Castle, the place that

Jocelyn had adored, and according to legend, the stronghold of King Arthur.

Tucked away under the gigantic rock face was an entrance to a cave. Because the tide was coming in, Rosa couldn't see much, but she remembered from the guide book that at low tide 'access to the deep and mysterious dwelling of Merlin was readily available' as was 'the feeling of wonder as the traveller walks in Merlin's sandy footsteps'.

Feelings of wonder were already beginning to unfurl. Even just looking at the place made Rosa want to throw caution to the wind and race along the path and up the steep steps. But then the fat raindrop which had spattered a few moments ago brought reinforcements in the shape of a huge black cloud directly overhead. The wind threw caution back at her and hurled a few stinging raindrops into her upturned face. Great. Together, the elements seemed hell-bent on single-mindedly blowing Rosa off her feet and drenching her through.

The only bit of cover she could see was in the doorway of the visitor centre and she made a run for it - there was no way she would get back up into the village before the deluge came. Rosa tucked herself as far as she could into the doorway and watched the scene from behind a grey curtain of rain. The curtain sometimes flapped around her ankles thanks to the gusting wind, and when it parted, she noticed that the ocean had morphed from warm blue to cool mercury.

Rosa rubbed her arms to try to get rid of prickly goosebumps and swore. Why hadn't she just gone to the pub? Her grumbling thoughts echoed in her stomach as she remembered the lovely smells that had wafted out into the street. And given the fact she'd not gone to the pub, why hadn't she taken notice of the 'do badders' and the woman in the Land Rover? If she'd accepted the lift she *would* be in the pub right now tucking into something delicious … or something not delicious - anything at all would do, she was starving.

The curtains parted again and a man sauntered along the path by the ocean where she'd stood a little while ago. Rosa's heart turned over. She was all alone here ... but something worried her more than that, something felt wrong about the man. Rosa shoved her hand through her damp hair and peered round the doorway to try and see where he was going. His back to her now, he walked up towards the castle and as he did, the rain eased, affording her a better view. It was then that she realised what was wrong. He wore dark jeans and a grey sweater, his dark curls bouncing in time with his long easy stride.

But he wasn't wet.

Not even damp.

Rosa's pulse rate galloped up the scale and goosebumps came back again prickling along her arms and down the back of her neck. That was impossible. The guy looked like he was out for a Sunday stroll in August ... oblivious to the weather and he had ... Rosa swallowed hard ... and the man had ... The words jumbled around in her head refusing to assemble in the required order, and then they did...

The man had sunlight on his hair.

That was enough for her. She was getting out of there.

* * *

In the pub at last, Rosa went straight through to the ladies and ran hot water into the basin. A few seconds after she'd fled the shelter of the doorway the deluge had turned to light rain, and by the time she'd scrambled up the path and hurried through the village, that rain had become a feeble drizzle. Nevertheless, she was still cold, damp and dishevelled. Rosa placed her hands flat on the bottom of the basin and allowed the heat from the water to rise through her fingers and up her wrists. Despite the speed at which Rosa had galloped up the hill, her extremities felt as if she'd been in a deep freeze.

Eyes that still struggled with what they had seen down by the castle stared out at her in the mirror, the jade orbs darkening to emerald as they re-ran the shocking experience. Rosa dabbed a wet tissue at her smudged mascara and she reapplied eye liner and lip gloss, watching her hands complete these tasks as if they were someone else's going through the motions. They should be trembling, refusing to move, just as her legs had a split-second before she'd forced them into flight mode at the castle. But no ... her hands were still, calm.

The sensation of standing apart from her body swept over her. She continued to watch her hands. A wide toothed comb was found at the very bottom of her bag and dragged through her rain-fresh curls, a purse was placed on the sink and coins and notes were checked and counted. *Yes, enough for dinner*.

A corner table was selected and a menu studied. How could she possibly be considering dinner now? Now that she'd seen...

A shutter wound down, presumably courtesy of a coping mechanism, and she flashed a dazzling smile at the waiter. 'What would you recommend? I will warn you that I'm starving.'

'Well that's good, because tonight our special is the sirloin steak and homemade Stilton sauce, served with seasonal vegetables and either chips, new, or jacket potatoes.'

'Sounds delicious. I'll have that medium-rare and chips please.'

'And would you like the wine list?' The waiter tapped his pencil against his lips and gave her a lopsided grin. And did he just wink?

'No thanks. I'll get something from the bar.' Rosa stopped smiling and watched the waiter walk away. The last thing she wanted at the moment was unwelcome advances. Though she had to acknowledge that with his short blonde hair, cool blue eyes and easy manner he was distractingly attractive. Perhaps that's what she did need actually, a distraction - something to block out the image of a man walking through the sheeting rain with sunlight on his hair. And he was dry. Dry. As. A. Bone.

Leaning on the bar, Rosa eyed the optics as the lone barmaid flitted between one customer and the other like a slightly frazzled butterfly. A few stiff drinks might do the trick, quick, cheering and much less messy than a fling. And Rosa reminded herself that she didn't do flings anyway. Though a gin and tonic would hardly compliment the steak, she ordered a double, downed it pretty much in one and then asked for another. The frazzled butterfly blinked a few times but noticing Rosa's 'yes, and?' stare, chose to keep quiet and placed another on the bar.

Half a slice of lemon rocked against the ice in her glass as she walked back to her table. Rosa's bloodstream reacted to the swift injection of alcohol on an empty stomach, sending a wobble to her legs and a heat rush to her face, the colour of which, Rosa imagined, rivalled the red tablecloth. She needed to slow down or she'd be under the damned table in a few minutes. A giggle surfaced at that mental image and she coughed to cover it. Folk would think she was nuts sitting alone giggling at nothing. Ah, good, Mr Distraction was walking towards her with a huge plate of food.

'Wow, this looks delicious,' she said, practically drooling as the combined aromas of Stilton sauce, hand-cut chips and freshly grilled steak wafted into her nostrils.

'And it is!' The waiter winked again as he placed cutlery beside the plate. 'Anything else I can get for you?'

Rosa could tell exactly what he meant by that and was tempted to give a smart reply but said, 'Just some water, thanks.'

The plate of food disappeared nearly as quickly as the first gin and tonic and the initial alcohol-related giddy feeling along with it. A few glasses of water also helped to focus her mind, but the thoughts filling it couldn't be magicked away quite so easily. The silly 'do-badders' warning of Merlin and ghosts kept sounding in her ears, as did her own voice replying that she didn't believe in ghosts. And nor had she, until she saw the man … the man in the rain.

She pushed the last bit of steak around her plate to catch the remaining sauce and savoured it slowly while she thought about the man again. Rosa tried to convince herself that she'd imagined the sun on his hair. He'd just been a crazy guy who liked wandering about in the rain. Her dad, ever the science teacher, had always said there was a rational explanation for every seemingly strange phenomenon. Maybe even a stray sunburst had strong-armed through the deluge for a second or two. That would be feasible, wouldn't it?

The waiter's voice broke in. 'Did you enjoy your meal, madam?' Considering she was still swallowing the last bit he was a bit quick off the mark, but she had and told him so. 'Lovely. And can I interest you in a pudding? I can recommend the homemade clotted cream ice-cream and locally grown strawberries, a melt in your mouth treat!' He grinned and licked his lips.

'Sounds delicious but I am stuffed.' Heat built in her cheeks and settled at a low simmer as she saw the flirty look in his eyes.

'Coffee, then?'

Rosa eyed the still half-full gin glass and thought it might be wise. 'Thanks, black no sugar.'

The waiter picked up her empty plate. 'Are you here on holiday?'

'Yes, just for a week or so. Not decided yet.' It was easier than explaining the real reason.

'Great. There is a lot to do here. Been to the castle yet?' His eyes swept over her face and settled on the V of her T-shirt.

Rosa wondered how to disguise the furnace rising up her neck again, so her mouth just spewed out everything that had been running around her head. 'I hadn't intended to, but my feet kind of took me there, you know?' She flapped her hands in imitation of feet walking and giggled. *God what was she doing?* The waiter nodded and looked back at her face. 'A woman I met on the way warned me of Merlin and ghosts. I mean how stupid? I told her there's no such thing. People come here with all sorts of twaddle in their heads don't they?' Her face was still tamale-hot so she took a big swallow of water … except it was gin. Great.

The waiter put his head on one side and pursed his lips. 'Merlin, perhaps. But ghosts … some might say it's not twaddle. This place is well known for mystery and magic.'

Rosa looked at him. He seemed serious. 'But isn't that just for tourists? Fool the gullible city folk?'

'Some say yes, some say no. My mother would say no and so would lots of folk around here.'

Rosa looked at her hands. Please don't let him pull a bit of hay out of his pocket, shove it in the corner of his mouth and say, *'You'm not from round these parts, are ee?'* She glanced up. His eyes had lost their mischief and there was an air about him of what Rosa could only describe as disgruntlement. She had the distinct impression that her scoffing had offended him.

'Right. Have you seen anything … you know, spirits?' she said with what she hoped was an encouraging smile.

A curt nod. 'Not sure I want to discuss it. I'll get that coffee.'

Watching his ramrod-straight retreating back, Rosa guessed her smile wasn't encouraging enough. The guy obviously believed in ghosts, and so did quite a few others it seemed. Rosa looked into her glass and swirled the remnants of gin and tonic. The ice cracked as it melted, and into the whirl the man in the rain appeared in her mind's eye again. Perhaps what she'd seen couldn't be explained away by rational explanation this time - it sure as hell seemed as real as the gin and the smudge of Stilton sauce on the red tablecloth.

An invisible cloak of fatigue floated over her eyes and draped itself heavily across her shoulders. It had been a long day and the last thing she wanted now was coffee. Before the waiter came back she hurried to the bar, paid her bill, and told the frazzled butterfly that there was a free coffee with her name on it if she wanted it.

* * *

At last under the sheets in the Rose Room's big brass bed, she flicked off the switch on the lamp and forced *Rain Man*, as she now called the 'ghost' by the castle, out of her mind. Tomorrow she'd wake refreshed and explore properly with a logical mind and a good pair of walking boots. Everything would look better in the daylight. It always did.

CHAPTER 5

$\mathcal{D}$aylight looked more than better. It looked fresh and new and quite wonderful as Rosa gazed out to sea from her balcony. The breeze gently twirled her shower-damp hair, bringing with it the scent of salt and pine, while glorious birdsong provided the soundtrack to her morning. After a few feeble attempts at resurfacing, *Rain Man* was now firmly squashed in a strong box, the lid nailed shut by a refusal to accept such nonsense. Unless proof arrived with a claw hammer and set him free of course.

Immediate plans involved a full English and at least two cups of coffee, then on with the walking boots and off to the castle. A phone call to Jocelyn was earmarked for late afternoon when Rosa guessed she would have more to tell than the crazy happenings of yesterday. She hadn't the first clue how she would explain it and still sound sane.

* * *

Preparation is key her dad always said, and he was right as usual. Sturdy walking boots, jeans, and T-shirt - not forgetting a waterproof tucked into a rucksack on her back along with snacks, sun cream and water - made Rosa feel more than ready to face the day. Though all the places on her list from yesterday beckoned enticingly as she passed, she kept on walking. There would be plenty of time for shopping later. Her main mission was to go to the castle. Her gran's wish would then be fulfilled and she could spend a few days relaxing and go home.

Of course the feeling that she'd had yesterday that she was here for an important reason, and it was a place of mystery and magic, had all just been part of the emotion of coming to the place where her dying loved one had been the happiest in her life. Today was about the castle and paying homage to Jocelyn's happy memories. Any more was fantasy. *Rain Man* rattled around his box a bit and then became quiet.

Even though it was just past ten, Rosa had plenty of company when once more she walked down the steep path as it wound to the sparkling blue ocean. Still a little way off, the white buildings of the ticket office/shop and cafe reflected the glare of the sun that brightened the late spring day, and Rosa, feeling smug, pulled a pair of sunglasses out of her rucksack. There. Prepared for every eventuality, there was no way the Land Rover woman from the ticket office could look her snootily up and down now.

The cool of the shop matched the expression on the woman's face behind the desk. Great it *would* have to be her. Where was the other woman, or the guy? Rosa decided to ignore her and browse around first before she bought a ticket. Perhaps she'd watch the video about the history of the place that was advertised on the English Heritage notice board too. There was a good range of books, ornaments, maps and local honey and jams and the obligatory tackier gifts of King Arthur mugs and miscellany. The video was only twelve- minutes long and quite informative, though Rosa would need a book on its history if she was to really find out about the place properly.

On her way back to the desk, a sign on the wall caught her eye. It informed her that there were sometimes guided tours/events round the castle at certain times and to ask at the desk.

'Hello, I was wondering if I could book to go on the guided tour,' Rosa said to the woman, and dug her purse out of the rucksack.

'Hello. Weren't you the one we saw last night in those red sandals?' The woman twirled a dyed blonde curl around her finger and pouted her pink lips. 'Gosh, hope you didn't get a soaking.'

The twinkle of humour in her eye told Rosa she hoped quite the opposite. 'We said after we left you that you'd probably look like a drowned rat by the time you got back up to the village …'

'No actually. I sheltered in the doorway here.' Rosa glared at the woman. She was tempted to say if I'm a drowned rat, you're a dead ringer for Miss Piggy. 'So about the tour?'

The woman folded her arms, stopped 'smiling', and cleared her throat. 'You'll have a wait. Next one is August,' she said in a flat monotone. 'We only have one or two events at certain times of the year.'

Rosa shrugged and smiled. There was no way she would share her disappointment, and perhaps she could ask the other lady from last night more about the place. 'I see. Okay. I'll just pay for a ticket then. All on your own here today?'

The woman raised a quizzical eyebrow.

'Just wondering about the lady with the long dark hair who spoke to me last night?'

The woman took her money and issued Rosa with a ticket. 'No. It's Kate's day off and Talan's on a break.'

Rosa heart sank. She didn't feel comfortable about asking 'misery personified' anything. She didn't allow her face to show it though and said, 'Oh Talan, the guy that was in the back of the Land Rover yesterday?'

'Yes. So if there's nothing else?' The woman turned and began to re-arrange models of knights in a display.

Rosa walked out of the shop. Just what was that woman's problem? Perhaps she'd always wanted a pair of strappy red sandals but had a wooden leg. A smirk lifted the corners of her mouth and she set off up the steps towards the castle … the very steps that *Rain Man* had taken. Rosa tapped a merry little tune on the handrail and hummed as she walked to drown out his attempts at a noisy escape. And by the time the steps had given way to a windy path next to the crashing ocean, he was quiet and forgotten. This place really lifted her spirits.

Ignoring protesting thigh muscles, she hastened her ascent up the hundred or so almost vertical stone steps and then at the top, her breath caught in her throat from the sheer beauty of the ancient archway and wooden door set into it. Rosa stepped through the door and entered the ruin of Tintagel Castle, her heart thumping with the strain of the climb, but mostly with the exhilaration of seeing such a beautiful and ancient setting.

She looked back the way she had come. The doorway framed the crashing ocean as the sun angled in, illuminating the stones and the wings of a seagull gliding past. Turning again, on her right, the ocean stretched around the rocky headland, and in front of her, more arched ruins and squat slate remains of thirteenth century rooms awaited. It was all she could do not to laugh out loud and set off at a run to explore it all as if she was a little child.

Information from the video she'd watched connected with the notification on various stones and plaques dotted around, and she learned that there had been a settlement of sorts here during the fifth century. Then some bloke called Geoffrey in the twelfth century had started a legend about Tintagel being the place where King Arthur had been conceived. A hundred years later or so, a Cornish lord had built the castle, by all accounts simply to show off. But in the end it didn't matter what the truth was, who had lived here and why, this place was pretty special - anyone with a soul could feel that.

The sun was high in the sky, but when Rosa touched the ancient slate walls in the Island Courtyard, leaned her head against an archway and looked out to sea, she felt that the stones were more than sun-warmed. An inner-peace and spiritual belonging that she'd just glimpsed the muted edges of the other evening, grew and spread through her like vibrant green shoots.

The little paths and more steps led her ever upward past ruined gardens, chapels, halls and lookout points, until she was at the very tip of the island. Nothing stood between herself and the windswept ocean apart from a few steps of tussocked grassland. If there weren't little groups of people here and there, she would have given into the urge to throw her arms wide and tilt back her head, allowing the wind to tangle her hair into auburn streamers and whoop for joy. It was one of those rare moments of unadulterated happiness. A moment when she felt the power of nature running through her veins, felt at one with the elements, powerful and wild like the landscape surrounding her.

Spongy grass underfoot and the sun on her back added to the feeling of wellbeing as Rosa set off back down the paths. Even though she was still none the wiser about the reason for her mission, she was more than happy to stay for a few days and see more of the village and the surrounding area. From the path leading down to the castle she had also seen a lovely little church nestled on a green hill, and she'd spotted it again just now from across the water. That would be worth a visit too.

The immediate future either held a cream tea or a crab sandwich at the Beach Cafe opposite the shop. Both had been advertised on a board as she'd passed, but she just couldn't decide which she fancied the most. In the near distance a man rose from a sitting position on the grass and walked up the path towards her. There was something familiar about him, his long easy stride, his dark curls bouncing in time with his gait and sunlight on …

Fear clamped a hand over Rosa's mouth, immobilising her steps and chilling her bones. She found she could do nothing but stand rooted on the path and wait for him to pass.

As he got close he nodded and said, 'Lovely day for it?'

Rosa couldn't reply, but felt her hand come up to shield her eyes as she looked at his face and felt the hairs on her arm rise and crackle with static. Then he'd passed and she heard his footsteps growing distant, but she couldn't physically turn her head. Rosa was aware that she couldn't hear the sea, the seagulls, the wind – nothing. It was if she was trapped in a vacuum, and then whoosh, her ability to move and hear was returned in one splendid cacophony of noise.

Rosa spun round but there was no sign of the man, just the path and an ancient stone arch at the bend in the path. Half of her wanted to run after him, the other didn't. What was she thinking? This guy was no spirit; he'd not disappeared in a puff of smoke, just turned a corner and walked on.

But his eyes, Rosa, his eyes had been ... Jocelyn's voice whispered in her memory. *As deep as the ocean ... blue as the August sky and yet green too ... like the sea-green depths under an anchored boat.*

Aware of a pain in her left palm, Rosa saw that she had unconsciously been digging the nails of her right hand into it - probably in her attempt to hang on to reality. Damn it, she was really *not* listening to this fantasy again. No way. Fuelled by adrenaline, she set off at a jog down the path, giving herself a good talking to all the while.

Eyes the colour of blah blah? But were they, were they really? You only saw them for a second or two. She reached the steps leading back to the entrance and cafe. *And he spoke to you, just normal, right? How many spirits have you heard of that pass the time of day?*

Nearly slipping a few times in her haste to get down, Rosa grabbed the handrail, calmed her breathing, and forced her feet to walk steadily past the little beach and on to the cafe. Before she entered the cafe, a random thought made her trip up the step.

The thing is, he didn't actually speak out loud, did he? You just heard him in your head.

* * *

Almost on autopilot, a crab sandwich and pot of tea had been ordered and Rosa sat outside at the last remaining table and looked over the rim of her teacup at the waves rolling back and forth on the spit of a beach below. She tried to clear her mind and think of nothing. Karen, a friend at work, had once persuaded her to attend a meditation class a few months ago and one of the things they had been instructed to do was to replace thoughts with a white space - think of nothing. At the time, this proved to be an impossible task and all she could do was try not to giggle. Rosa had as much success this time. Even though she squeezed her eyes shut and imagined a white sheet in front of her eyes, the pattern of the man's face kept seeping through like some freaky image on a shroud.

'Mind if I join you?'

Startled, Rosa opened her eyes. In front of her stood a tall man silhouetted against the sun. 'Um …' Rosa shielded her eyes and tried to see his features, why the hell did he want to sit at *her* table?'

'I wouldn't normally ask, but all the tables are taken and I don't want to sit inside on such a lovely day.'

'Yes, I guess.' Rosa had no excuse apart from to say, 'Sod off I don't want company right now'. But as usual her polite upbringing wouldn't allow that. She eased her chair back so he could pull his out and shuffle the table towards her a bit. She took a sip of tea and bit into her sandwich as he sat down opposite. *Best get this eaten and get off.* There was no way she felt like pleasant chit chat. Luckily the guy poured his tea and kept quiet. She hadn't yet made eye contact and didn't intend to.

'Weren't you the lady who came down here when we were closed last night?'

Rosa took a mouthful of tea and looked up. She almost spat it right back out again and liquid slopped from her cup onto the table.

This couldn't be happening.

Could.

Not.

She looked away across the sea again to give her brain time to rectify its mistake. Rosa swallowed, blinked rapidly and looked back. No. Nothing had changed. While not quite identical twins, the man sitting opposite and the one she'd just seen in the castle could be brothers.

'You alright?' He wiped the back of his hand across his lips and swallowed a mouthful of food. 'You look as if you've had a shock.'

Rosa could only nod. Then she looked about her to see if the rest of the diners all looked like him too and she was trapped in some kind of crazy nightmare. Thankfully they just looked normal - unchanged. He asked again if she was the one from last night and she nodded, unable to tear her eyes from his face.

'I was sitting in the back of the Landy, my name's Talan,' he said holding out his hand across the table. She shook it briefly, pulling back when static shot along her wrist.

'Rosa.' Her voice sounded squeaky as if she'd just inhaled a balloon full of helium, and still she looked, carefully noting every inch of him.

His hair was parted down the middle, wavy, shoulder-length, where the other guy's had been to the collar. It was very dark brown but had some light-chestnut tones on the ends as if he worked outside. His face was angular with strong jawline. A dimple sat in the centre of his chin, and he had lots of dark stubble along the planes of his face, as if he'd been too busy to shave rather than by design. A straight nose, an eyebrow-ring in the left brow fashioned into an arrow-head, and a wide sensuous mouth which at the moment had curled into a nervous half-smile. Probably because she was full-on staring, she knew she was, but she couldn't help it. She couldn't help it because of his eyes. *Eyes as deep as the ocean, blue as an August sky and ...*

'Are you really okay, Rosa? You seem to be a bit ... Well, a bit out of it,' he finished shifting in his chair.

Someone dropped a cup to the stone floor with a clatter, which thankfully released Rosa from her stupor. 'Er, yes.' She managed, rubbing her eyes and looking over his shoulder at brightly coloured bunting flapping in the breeze. 'I didn't sleep well and I'm a bit tired. Sorry for staring.'

'That's okay. I'm just relieved that I don't have something unmentionable on my face.' He dabbed at his chin and wiped his mouth with his napkin anyway.

After the two strange experiences she'd had since arriving, and now with the third sitting across the table from her, all Rosa wanted to do was to run up the hill screaming like a banshee, but instead she forced herself to embrace the scientific and the rational. That's what her dad would advocate. *Act normal and try to find out as much as you can about him.*

Forearmed is forewarned or was it the other way around? Yes, it was the other way ar—'

'Are you here on holiday then?' Talan asked dipping a hunk of bread into his 'soup of the day' and demolishing it in one bite.

'Yes and no. I'm a travel journalist.' She allowed herself to look into his eyes and had to swallow hard. He was saying that her job sounded interesting, but she just randomly nodded at his eyebrow and said, 'What's that arrowhead thing made from?'

'This?' He touched it briefly and gave a short laugh as if dealing with an inappropriate question from a child. Given that she had been very direct and out-of-the-blue she couldn't blame him. 'It's made from Cornish slate. A friend made it for me. Why, d'you like it?'

'Yeah, it's lovely - unusual.' Like the rest of you she thought, but didn't say. She looked more closely at the rest of him while he turned his attention to finishing his soup. She already knew he was tall, at least six foot two, and he was muscular yet athletic, broad-shouldered, long-limbed. She watched his large 'artistic' hands break the last of the bread and his long elegant fingers place the soup spoon carefully in the centre of his empty dish.

'How long are you here for?' He put his head on one side and gave her that half-smile again.

'Oh, a good few days. I have booked a week, but not sure yet if I will stay that long.' She chewed thoughtfully on the crab sandwich which could have been charcoal for all the enjoyment she was getting from it. Her belly was churning and anxiety had provided a barrier to swallowing. 'And how did you recognise me from last night? You were rummaging in your bag the whole time.'

'Not the whole time. I noticed your lovely hair.' He hesitated and looked away almost shyly, then he looked directly back at her. 'And unusual eyes ... if you don't mind me saying.' His gaze never leaving her face, he leaned back in his chair and folded his arms. The muscles of his biceps strained the material of his short-sleeved denim shirt.

The heat of the blush spreading through her cheeks and down her neck did nothing to shrink the lump of anxiety in her throat, and whilst flattered, Rosa couldn't reply, just drained her cup and coughed.

'Sorry to have embarrassed you, but I'm known for plain speaking. I don't see the point in beating around the bush.'

'No. Neither do I … and thanks.' She picked up her rucksack and placed it on the table between them. There that felt better. 'I was hoping to find out more about the castle. Can you recommend a good book?'

Rosa smiled confidently, but inside, her heart and mind were racing. It was as if she was on the outside looking in at this other Rosa acting out a role or something, while the real Rosa just wanted to be hiding under a bed in a darkened room.

'I could tell you all you'd ever need to know.' He leaned his elbows on the table, laced his fingers together under his chin and fixed her with those eyes again. 'Can I take you out for a drink tonight … unless you are with someone?'

The real Rosa watched incredulously as the other Rosa said, 'Nope I'm single. And a drink would be lovely.' She looked at him from under her lashes and pouted. Then she deftly pulled her business card out of her purse and pushed it across the table. 'There's my mobile. Call me later, if you like…'

* * *

The real Rosa eventually caught up with the other Rosa halfway up the path to the village and started to hyperventilate. She leaned her hand against a wall and waited for her breathing to assume its regular rhythm. Just what the bloody hell was she playing at? Being rational and scientific hardly meant flirting outrageously and agreeing to go out on a date with a guy who looked like *Rain Man* did it? Damn it all.

She splayed her fingers out in front of her and noted they were trembling like aspen leaves. No wonder. No frigging wonder at all. Rosa needed a voice of reason. Thinking of which, perhaps that phone call to Jocelyn would put things more in perspective. Rosa blew heavily down her nose and set off for her hotel.

CHAPTER 6

'*And* how are you finding Tintagel, little one?' Jocelyn's familiar voice on the line moistened Rosa's eyes and sent a longing into her heart.

She coughed and took a sip of water. 'I can certainly see why you fell in love with the place. It is so beautiful.' Rosa plumped her pillows up and leaned back into them stretching her legs out on the bed.

'Have you been to the castle?'

'I have. I popped down last night but couldn't go round it as I was too late, but I went today. It is quite breathtaking.'

'Oh, it's that all right. I so wish I could be there again I don't expect it's changed much.'

'No, I doubt it has changed being pretty much a ruin for hundreds of years. I wish you could be here too … I do miss you.' Rosa took another swig from her water bottle and dashed at her eyes with the back of her hand.

'And I you. So, have you seen anything unusual and mysterious?'

Rosa frowned and sat up straight. How the hell could she know about *Rain Man?* 'Eh? What do you mean?'

'You okay? You sound a bit jumpy all of a sudden.'

'I'm fine. Just an odd thing for you to say.'

'Well not really. You *are* there because Jory asked you to visit after all. I thought he might have sent you a sign or something. He came to see me again last night, bless him'

Rosa sighed. She needed some straight talking. 'Gran, is Jory dead?'

'Hmm ... we-ll, I guess you could say so, yes.' Jocelyn sighed and Rosa could hear the wheeze in her chest.

'Either he is, or he isn't.'

'Okay, yes he is. But his spirit is as real as you or me. I'm no psychic, but apparently when you get to the end of life you're more open to the spirit world. The thing is, I know you are so against all this kind of talk. That's because of your dad's influence.'

The irritation in Jocelyn's voice came loud and clear down the line and Rosa didn't want her getting too upset in her state. 'Well I'm here aren't I? And is Mum looking after you all right?'

'You're there because I begged you to go, no other reason. And don't change the subject. Yes, Polly does her best, but let's talk about your adventure.' She broke off to have a coughing fit.

Rosa wanted to reach out to her down the line and hold her frail body in her arms. 'I think you need to rest. That cough sounds no better.'

'And why would it? I *do* have secondary lung cancer after all. Now, pin back your ears.' Even though she couldn't be seen, Rosa pinned them. 'As I said, Jory came to me last night and said that you are open to receive. He also said you should go to the church on the hill. You know, the one that I told you about?'

A shiver ran along Rosa's arms at that. 'Open to receive what? And what church?'

'I'm not sure about what he wants you to receive, but I know it is very important. The church that Jory and I walked past on that very last night and he said we'd marry in it? Don't you remember me telling you that?'

'Oh yes, sorry, it slipped my mind. Is it the one that you can see across the fields as you go down to the castle and from the island too?'

'It is indeed. Such a beautiful place ... I have walked down that aisle with Jory many a time in my imagination over the years.' Rosa heard a catch in Jocelyn's voice which started the prickle behind her own eyes again. 'Anyway, he said you should go up there as soon as you can.'

Rosa closed her eyes and lay her head back down on the pillows. As much as she wanted to, needed to, she wasn't going to say anything about *Rain Man*; or his 'little brother' whom she had foolishly agreed to meet for a drink. Until she had found out what the whole spooky experience was about, made some rational sense from it, there was no way she was going to encourage Gran in her beliefs about visiting spirits.

'Rosa, are you there?'

'Yes, I'm here. I would just like to know what this whole thing is about.'

'You and me both, love. When Jory visits he tells me he loves me and that we'll be together soon, tells me to tell *you* things because you have … never mind. He just never tells me what it's about either.'

In her heart Rosa felt that Jocelyn was hiding something. She remembered her saying about Rosa having 'something' since she was little before, but then she clammed up on the subject. Intuitively, Rosa realised that there would be no point in quizzing her gran further on it either. 'Okay, well I think that's enough chatting for you for one afternoon, you need to rest and—'

'It's not all in my head, Rosa, not a product of this morphine that I'm gobbling all day. You do believe me don't you?'

'Yes, Gran. Now get some rest and I'll call you tomorrow, okay?'

* * *

For the next few minutes Rosa lay on the bed and rolled the cold bottle of water back and forth across her forehead. Did she believe her? Just what was all this about? She went over the phone conversation again, and eventually, instead of fighting it she decided to allow her thoughts free rein, just for a while at least.

Alrighty, then. Was *Rain Man* Jory's spirit, or was he just a guy who'd happened to walk past in the rain and Rosa had somehow seen a finger of sunlight that had broken through the raincloud and caressed his hair?

Was the guy who she'd seen on the castle paths today just a guy who'd had a similar appearance and her imagination had filled in the gaps? Was Talan the fallout from her fragile state of mind? The fragile state of mind she was in because her gran was three-hundred miles away and fading fast? Had she imagined he looked like the other guy because she wanted to take something tangible back to Jocelyn. A present of the past, so she could take comfort from the fact that Rosa had experienced – no, *received* – a message in the form of Jory look-alikes?

The vibration of her mobile on the bedside table broke her contemplation and she picked up. 'Hi, Rosa? It's Talan.'

Talan's deep, rich, Cornish accent seemed to fill the silence in the room and she inexplicably felt heat in her cheeks and a few butterflies take up residence in her belly. 'Hi Talan, how are you?' God that was a bit inane. Rosa caught sight of her flushed reflection and sparkling eyes in the wardrobe mirror and shook her head. Looked like the other Rosa was back.

'Good, thanks. So where are you in the village?'

'Lewis's.'

'So the Tintagel Arms would be nearest. Shall I meet you there about seven-thirty?'

The sensible and rational thing to say would be, *I'm not sure that would be a good idea. I know I said we would go out, but I made a mistake, sorry.* She also didn't really want to see the waiter again from last night. What she did say was, 'Yes, that would be great. See you, then. Bye!' Ending the call, she looked at her stupid smile in the mirror and rolled her eyes. Exactly what was she hoping to achieve?

Yes, she'd been a bit tempted by the waiter last night, but Talan was in a different league; unusual, and certainly mysterious. She was kidding herself if she thought he could shed any light on everything though. She obviously couldn't trust herself around him and he'd just muddy the waters when she needed the pool to be clear. Still, he could tell her more about the history of the castle and maybe he could tell her what happened to Jory. It was a small village after all and perhaps he'd heard of him. Yes, that felt better. It had the semblance of a plan. Rosa liked those.

* * *

Indecision over what to wear had turned into a full-blown fashion crisis and the hands of the clock hit 7.45 before Rosa realised it. There was no time to try on yet another outfit and so the short black dress with the high neck and the red strappy sandals would have to do. If she looked over-dressed for a village pub, then bugger it. The alternatives all involved jeans or trousers with fairly ordinary tops, as Rosa hadn't planned on dressing up on this short break. She'd only shoved the dress in on the off chance.

The reaction from one or two people as she walked into the pub told her she'd made the right choice, though annoyingly she felt heat spreading through her cheeks. The blush wasn't solely because of the appreciative looks she was getting however; it was enhanced by the sight of Talan, his back to her ordering a drink.

As she made a beeline for the bar her eyes swept the length of his frame, the contours of his broad back outlined under a turquoise shirt, his long, long legs and his firm backside in close-fitting black jeans.

Rosa took a breath and tapped him on the shoulder. 'Sorry I'm late, Talan.'

He turned and looked down at her and she realised he must be more like six-four than six-two, as she was five-six and had to tilt her head back to look into his eyes, eyes which were inescapably as deep as the ocean, and all the rest of it. The gaze of these eyes had quickly appraised her outfit and now stopped at her mouth making her feel self-conscious and desirable all at the same time.

'That's okay, and wow, you were certainly worth waiting twenty minutes for.' He smiled and leaned in towards her.

As she felt his soft lips brush her cheek, Rosa took a breath and inhaled spicy cologne and the scent of his freshly washed, still-damp hair. Talan pushed his fingers through it and nodded at the bar. 'What will you have?'

Good question. Deciding that gin might be far too dangerous, she plumped for a white wine spritzer. The frazzled butterfly flitted about her business as usual, but so far she hadn't spotted the waiter. Hopefully it was his night off, because Rosa imagined that he'd have something to say after she'd unwittingly ruffled his feathers last night and then escaped before he could bring the coffee.

Seated at a cosy table in the corner, Talan smiled at her over the top of his frothy pint and took a long swallow. Rosa watched the muscles working in his throat and her eyes travelled downwards, noting a few dark chest hairs above the first few open buttons of his shirt. She wondered if he had a full-on hairy chest or just a smattering across his ...

'Penny for them?' Talan smirked at her as if he'd been reading her thoughts.

'I was just thinking what a nice shirt that is. Turquoise is one of my favourite colours.'

'Thanks. I like to be colourful. Though I must say you are certainly rocking the "little black dress" tonight.'

About to reply, Rosa spotted the waiter from last night appear from the kitchen and hurry a plate of steaming food to a couple in the middle of the pub. He hadn't seen her, but it would only be a matter of time. As if she wasn't nervous enough. Rosa took a few sips of wine, edged her chair more to the side and untucked her long curls from behind her ear to provide a curtain against possible recognition.

Conscious of the fact she was here to find things out, not to bat compliments back and forth all night, she said, 'So tell me about the history of the castle, Talan. What's truth and what's myth?'

He raised his eyebrows and the little arrowhead rocked slightly on its ring. 'Now that's something nobody knows with any absolute certainty.' He stroked his clean-shaven chin and continued. 'I'll give you a potted history, just jump in when you like, okay? Don't want to send you to sleep.' He flashed a wide smile, the first he'd given her, and boy had it been worth waiting for. His whole face lit up and his eyes sparkled - sunlight on a blue ocean.

'Oh I'm wide awake, I can assure you,' Rosa said quietly and took another sip.

'Okay. There have been bits and pieces of Mediterranean pottery found dating back to the Roman period and again between the fifth and seventh centuries. There was a settlement on the headland also. It is thought that a pretty important leader must have lived there as Mediterranean pottery was almost unheard of here then. The guess is this important person, let's call him a Cornish chieftain, exported precious tin from right where you stood by the beach the other day.'

'Really? So was this chieftain called Arthur?'

Talan shrugged. 'Could have been, but the whole Arthur legend kicked off with Geoffrey of Monmouth, a Breton who most certainly visited Tintagel in the twelfth century. He wrote the *History of the Kings of Britain*, completed in 1136, which was widely read and inspired others for hundreds of years.'

'Oh yes, I remember reading his name. So did he make the Arthur thing up, then?'

'That's where the legend started, yeah. But people believed it for years, some folk still do. The story goes that in the Dark Ages, Uther Pendragon, king of all England, invited every important lord of the land to London for Easter. That's where things got complicated for poor Gorlois, Lord of Cornwall, because old Uther falls head over heels for Igerna, Gorloi's wife and wants her for his own. Obviously Gorlois is having none of it and whisks his wife up here to Tintagel Castle, as it was a great stronghold being surrounded as it was by the sea on three sides.'

'Sounds like an ancient fairy tale crossed with a soap opera,' chuckled Rosa, thoroughly entertained by Talan's easy storytelling manner.

'Wait, it gets better,' Talan laughed and had a few more swallows of his pint. 'Uther summons Merlin the wizard and begs him for help. So the cunning old Merlin casts a spell and turns Uther into Gorlois - only by outward appearance of course, he is still himself inside. Then he gains entrance to the castle and to Igerna too, and low and behold Arthur is conceived!'

'What a great story.' Rosa smiled. 'What happened next?'

'Well eventually poor Gorlois is killed and Uther marries Igerna and they have a sister for Arthur called Anna'

'You know you really have a great way of telling stories. I wish my history teacher at school was as entertaining as you.' Rosa looked into his twinkling eyes and thought that if he'd been her teacher she'd never have been able to concentrate on her studies for long. 'Ever thought of it?'

'What, teaching?'

Rosa nodded.

'No fear. I am a history graduate, but I couldn't teach. I would want to ring their darling little necks. My mate's a teacher and he says teenagers are tough going these days. I do enjoy my job as a guide at Pendennis Castle though'

'Oh, you're not here all the time, then?'

'Nope, just part-time. I'm at Pendennis in Falmouth mostly.'

'Right. Great job, eh?'

'It is. Mind you, yours sounds pretty glamorous. Swanning about the world free of charge and then getting to write about your adventures.'

'It has its moments.' Rosa grinned. 'But it's not all swanning. To be honest sometimes it is plain boring, especially the long flights.' She was conscious of the way he was watching her mouth as she spoke and paused, losing track for a moment.

Okay, back to the story Rosa before you get tongue-tied. 'So who built the castle here in the end, Geoffrey of Monmouth?'

'No, it was Richard, Earl of Cornwall. It was built somewhere around 1230 and it is thought he was influenced by Geoffrey's writings and wanted to build on the legend of King Arthur. Kind of for show, really.'

A daft thought occurred to Rosa She smiled and said. 'It's amazing that historians can pinpoint the building of a castle all those years ago to a specific time of day.'

Talan frowned, leaned forward and folded his arms on the table. 'Time of day?'

'Yes, you said twelve-thirty. I'd like to know if it was am or p.m though'

Talan's frown stayed put, but then realisation dawned and his sudden guffaw turned a few heads their way. He punched her arm playfully and said, 'Hey that's not a bad joke, not bad at all.'

Happy that he'd found it funny she was just about to reply when the waiter appeared at the table. 'Hi Talan, and hello again' he nodded briefly at Rosa 'Not eating here tonight I see.'

The disapproving furrow of his brow and his arms-folded body language struck a note of anger in Rosa Why was he stating the bloody obvious and what had it to do with him anyway? She had expected a snooty look from him perhaps, but this was ridiculous. 'No, I had some delicious fish and chips from down the road, hope that's allowed?'

The cold edge to her voice raised Talan's eyebrows and he looked at the waiter. 'Hey, Dan You know Rosa, then?'

'Not really. She came in here for food last night and made fun of the village. Said we were all out to get money from gullible tourists and ridiculed me for believing in the spirit world.' Dan put his head on one side and stared a challenge into Rosa's eyes.

The anger already bubbling under in her grew into an indignant outburst. 'Hey, hang on a minute. I think you're twisting and exaggerating just a tad here. What's your problem, exactly?'

'Just don't like folk coming here and looking down their noses.' Dan huffed and narrowed his eyes.

Before Rosa could retaliate Talan said, 'That's enough, Dan I'm sure Rosa wasn't being nasty. Now please leave us in peace, we're *trying* to have a quiet drink here.'

Dan just snorted and marched off while Rosa gaped after him open mouthed. 'How rude! He was grumpy last night but this takes the biscuit.' Rosa drained her glass and sat back in her chair. She'd been so enjoying the evening and now Dan had put a damper on it. There was no way she wanted to stay there while he shot snide looks at her whenever she caught his eye. Talan asked what had happened last night and she filled him in

'I guess he's sensitive about all that. He used to get teased at school because his mother's a white witch. He's always been a bit of a prickly character, though I never had much to do with him as he was two years below me.'

'A white witch? Blimey. But that's no reason to be so rude to me is it?' The urge to cut the evening short there and then was growing more appealing buy the minute. Rosa was beginning to feel like an outsider at some cliquey party.

Talan held up his hands. 'No of course not. Now, would you like another drink?'

'I don't feel welcome here anymore, Talan, so no thanks.'

'Let's go to another pub, then We have quite a few to choose from' A hopeful smile spread across his face.

For a second or two Rosa almost said yes and then something stopped her. This was getting her nowhere and the idea of talking to him about Jory, without divulging her gran's business, seemed almost impossible. 'Perhaps another time, thanks.' She stood and hooked her bag over her shoulder.

Talan stood too, his eyes sorrowful. 'That's a shame. I was really enjoying our evening.'

'Yep. Me too. You are quite the storyteller.'

'I had hoped you were enjoying my company, not just my guide-speak.' He took a step around the table and encircled her wrist gently with his long fingers.

Rosa stepped back. 'Yeah, well …' That spicy cologne of his, his intense stare and the warmth of his hand on her wrist played havoc with her resolve. Nevertheless, she wanted to keep this all on a less personal level and then came up with the perfect solution 'I'm off to the church on the hill tomorrow, I expect you know all about that too?'

'I know some.' His smile faded and he removed his hand and shoved it into the pocket of his jeans. The other he ran through his choppy waves and then he sighed. 'Okay, if that's all you're interested in. Our Parish church, St Materiana is even older than the castle. It was built at the end of the eleventh century and the beginning of the twelfth. It was first built by the Normans but includes some Saxon features and was then added to in the fifteenth century or so. It has a graveyard outside - some graves are ancient and some say they feel real peace when they visit. That enough for you?'

Rosa nodded and felt her stomach twist. The lovely warm twinkle had left his eyes, turning them mercury grey, and his generous mouth had set in a hard line. There was no doubt she had upset him. But that couldn't be helped. She should never have come in the first place. 'Yes, thanks. You have been very helpful.' She gave a quick smile and hurried away before he could say more.

* * *

Once again in the solitude of her lovely room, Rosa contemplated her disastrous evening. She poured a second glass of wine that she'd grabbed from a convenience store across the road and though it wasn't the best in the world, it hit the spot. Rosa chewed the edge of the plastic cup and wondered how things had got so complicated. Complicated *and* surreal.

Into her hitherto normal and carefully planned life had come the spirit world, legends, unfathomable messages from a dead man, sightings of the aforementioned dead man, no idea about what was going to happen next, and of course the incredibly lovely Talan. Ah yes, the incredibly lovely Talan … the look-alike of the dead man.

Rosa stepped out onto the balcony and watched the last blush of the crimson sunset cool into a cobalt star-scattered sky. In the distance she could just make out the navy horizon of the sea and with it came a sense of hope and calm. There was absolutely no point tying herself up in knots about a situation she couldn't control. Objectively of course - in the end she was in control of the whole thing. Instead of doing Jocelyn's or should she say Jory's bidding and going to the church tomorrow, she could jump on a train and go home. But it was her choice to remain and try to solve the conundrum, and in doing so, hopefully fulfil her gran's wishes. Beyond that, she had to admit curiosity was getting the better of her. Rosa could no more leave the place now than jump off the balcony and fly to the sea

As the last drop of the wine slipped down her throat she felt a bit more positive. Tomorrow as they say was another day. But would it bring clarity or more of the same? A flutter of excitement tickled in her chest as she got ready for bed and she realised that in a way, she didn't care. Rosa would just face the day with an open mind and a pocket full of scepticism in reserve. The spirit of adventure that had arrived when she'd got out of the taxi yesterday was back and straining at the leash

CHAPTER 7

$\mathcal{I}$t was the kind of spring morning that had forgotten its place in the seasons. It was actually masquerading as a mid-summer afternoon and Rosa's brisk pace up and over the fields gradually slowed as she bowed to the heat of the ascending sun. The drone of insects filled the still air, and in her ears her heartbeat thumped a steady tattoo.

It had been much cooler at the start of her walk across a little wooden bridge. This led across a stream and along a rocky path over which trees bent from each side, entwining their branches to form a living green tunnel. Now Rosa set her rucksack on the grass, pulled out a bottle and tipped back her head. The cool water trickling into her mouth contrasted markedly with the hot rivulets of sweat trickling down her back, and she wiped the heel of her hand across her brow and took a look around.

The church sat squat and watchful over the graveyard, and to her left a path threaded through the tall grass. Behind, the village climbed up the hill in the distance, and on her right lay the calm hazy-blue ocean, like a chalk thumb-smudge left by an impatient artist. Picking up her bag she set off again and as she drew nearer to the church, the age of the place became apparent. Talan had told her it was ancient, but the 'It was first built by the Normans but includes some Saxon features' explanation had done nothing to prepare her for the beauty of the simple design.

Slate gravestones old and new flanked the path and Rosa stopped here and there to read an inscription and reflect on the tragic deaths and fleeting time on earth of some of the poor souls lying beneath One near the porch and entranceway was particularly poignant. Albert Graham here on holiday from Clapham apparently died aged twenty-four in 1894 whilst bathing in the ocean The despair of his loved ones must have been immeasurable. Beyond his grave, a huge tomb-like structure was the last grave before the path leading to the door and Rosa laid her hand on the sun-warmed stone.

Never a follower of traditional religious belief and custom, Rosa did however feel an affinity with the whole place. The church with its ancient tower and windows must have watched people pass in and through over the ages - their hopes, dreams, happiness, grief, longings, love and regrets alive in the stones. To Rosa it seemed as if perhaps these feelings were steeped into the structure of the building, through its foundations and deep into the very bedrock itself.

She leaned her back against the porch, closed her eyes and imagined her father's reaction to such thoughts. He would fold his arms, frown deeply and say something like,

Pure fantasy. Think about your feelings logically, for goodness sake.

But could everything always be explained scientifically? Could it be that human emotions were the essence of the spirit? If this was so, was it possible that part of the spirit remained grounded, long after the earthly body had turned to dust?

The sun went behind a cloud, a welcome breeze kissed her cheeks and heavenly voices sang in her ears ...

Heavenly voices?

Rosa opened her eyes, followed her ears and stepped through the arched door of the church In front of her on the floor was a tall vase of white lilies, their intoxicating scent heavy in the air, and peeping round the corner of the inner entrance she saw, not a host of angels, but a small choir at the end of the aisle.

Not wishing to intrude upon a rehearsal, she stepped back into the lobby and pretended to read the notice board whilst their voices lifted her spirits to the rafters. The song was unfamiliar to her, probably sung in Latin, but the next struck a faint chord somewhere deep in her memory. Snatches of the verse played the chord a little louder and then the chorus brought a huge smile.

Among the leaves so green-o ... to my hey down down ... to my ho down down ...

It was an old English folk song, one of Gran's favourites. She'd often sung it when Rosa had been little and Rosa had always joined in the chorus. The title escaped her, but not so the memories of the rope-swing days and lemonade on the grass. The song provided a soundtrack to the images of those times. Vibrant and tantalisingly real, they displaced the notice board before Rosa's eyes and then became blurred as the final notes died.

Unable to contain her emotions any longer she stumbled outside into the glare of the sun. Rosa brushed away tears and followed the path away from the church and out along the cliff tops.

A song far more ancient rushed in on the waves below and for a few minutes Rosa stood still and allowed the sound of the ocean to sooth away the sadness in her heart. There would be time to grieve after Jocelyn had gone. Memories of happy times should remain just that.

Once again the choir started up the same song and sent it drifting out of the church door and over the gravestones. But this time Rosa's eyes were dry. Standing looking out to sea, peace and well-being filled her. To her left across the water she could see Tingtagel Island, the ruin of the castle she'd walked around yesterday being explored by more tourists, tiny in the distance. It was almost like standing in the middle of a beautiful painting. Surrounded by a riot of spring flowers, the church behind, the Atlantic in front, huge cliffs jutting from unlikely angles, the artist's thick brush strokes defined the horizon and an azure ocean under a cornflower blue sky.

A woman carrying a tripod wandered by, and set her camera up facing the island just where the path curved. Rosa thought a walk down to the end of the path and then back to the church might be next on the agenda After that, she had no clue.

She was all too aware that although she felt a connection to the church and the emotions of the people down the ages who had passed through it, there hadn't been an earth-shattering revelation about the reason Jory had asked her to visit. Perhaps he had wanted her to consider the possibility of the existence of 'things beyond the scientific'. If that was the case, he had succeeded.

Rosa nodded to the photographer on her way past and the woman smiled in return. 'It's a lovely day isn't it?' Rosa said.

The woman took off her baseball cap and pushed her long dark hair from her forehead. 'Warm though I like it a bit cooler so I can concentrate. I keep drifting off, just staring, and then I come back into focus.' She smiled and Rosa noticed that her eyes matched the ocean behind and she found she couldn't look away. An irrational feeling of panic climbed along Rosa's spine, warm static ran along her arms and into her fingertips and she unconsciously took a few steps backward.

The woman looked a bit puzzled, perhaps because of Rosa's grim expression, and bent to take a lens from a sheet on the ground. When she straightened up and looked at Rosa again, her face had changed.

Immobilisation gripped Rosa's whole body again as it had yesterday on the cliff path over in the ruins of the castle; and as before, everything around her stopped. No sound, no wind, just a feeling of abject terror twisting her gut and sending her heart-rate into overdrive.

Jory looked out from the woman's eyes, but said in her voice, 'I loved a woman once; I told her we'd marry in that church behind you. But she left. It ripped the heart right out of me.'

Running wasn't an option, nor screaming, although the makings of an ear-splitting shriek was trapped somewhere between her chest and lips. In the vacuum, physical movement was impossible, but her eyes were fixed on the woman as she looked away and changed the lens on her camera When she looked back at Rosa she was her normal self, a frown deep-set as she jammed the hat down on her head.

'You allright? Your face has gone deathly white.'

A rush of noise followed the sound of the woman's voice; the singing of the choir, the scream of seagulls, and the pounding of the ocean against the rocks below. Rosa found she could move and talk … after a fashion. 'I … I … what did you say?'

'I said your face has gone deathly—'

'No, before that,' Rosa said and wiped a sheen of cold sweat from her forehead.

The woman put her hands on her hips and blew down her nose. 'I said nothing. I was just wondering why you were staring at me with that odd expression. Then the colour drained from your face.'

It was clear that Rosa was beginning to irritate her, so almost on autopilot she mumbled a sorry, and goodbye, before turning back to the church on legs that felt like they were borrowed from a newborn foal.

So that had been the earth-shattering revelation she'd been waiting for.

There was no question in her mind now that Jory had made contact, had been on the cliff top yesterday and no doubt had visited Jocelyn exactly as she'd said. But what was she supposed to do with such certainty? It still didn't explain why she had been asked to come here, or what she should do next.

Rosa stopped in her tracks to find that her feet had brought her to the edge of the graveyard. A sign just a few steps away said *Adders: Please Keep Your Dog On A Lead!!!* and beyond that, an inscription on an unkempt grave read:

Jory Marrack 1939 – 1968 aged 29 years. Gone too soon.

The shock of how young he'd been thumped hard in her gut and she had to lean against the stone, her breath coming in short huffs. She traced her fingers over the few words. Was that it? No, sadly missed by, daughter, mother, sister … anyone? And the year he'd died … that was the year that Gran had met him wasn't it? So how had he died? The last words he had just spoken through the mouth of the woman photographer came into her head again:

It ripped the heart right out of me.

Rosa put her shaking hand to her mouth. Oh my God. What if he hadn't been able to cope after Gran left? What if he'd taken his own life?

* * *

In the cool shade of a pavement cafe, Rosa watched the passers-by. From the churchyard she'd allowed her feet to take her back to the village, just as they had led her to Jory's grave. Any coherent plan had been abandoned in favour of instinct and intuition. Her dad would not be best pleased at the recent change in his daughter. So far she'd finished a much-needed coffee and ordered another while her thoughts had been given freedom to roam. There was no conclusion to any of the roaming however, and so Rosa was content to just sit at her table under a parasol letting the morning drift into afternoon.

Jocelyn would be getting a call later. Rosa had to know if Jory had taken his own life. If he had, there was nothing she could do to change it, but it had suddenly become very important for her to find out. Perhaps Jory had another task for her too. Intuition and logic both told her that she hadn't finished what she had been sent here to do in Tintagel. That last thought hung in the air. *Sent here to do?* That was a new concept. Rosa had never considered she would have to *do* anything really. The idea that she would find something out, experience something important to Jocelyn and latterly Jory, had been taken as read – but as for doing something?

A smiling waitress placed a second coffee and sandwich on the table before her and snapped Rosa back to the bustle of the busy street.

'Anything else for you?' the waitress asked, already moving to clear a table next to Rosa's. Why did they always ask that, when they were expecting an answer in the negative? Rosa tossed what she wanted to say around her head and smiled inwardly, *Yes, can I have an answer to the reason why I am here, bumping into a ghost, and having the living crap scared out of me? Oh, and a side order of time travel so I can go back to 1968 and stop my gran leaving him in the first place?*

'No thanks, I have everything.' Rosa wished that were true as she bit into her sandwich.

Two young women walked past a few moments later and one stopped, pulled a tea-towel from a plastic bag and shook it out. It had a picture of the castle and a knight in the middle. Across the top in gaudy writing was emblazoned 'The Legend of Kings'.

'Do you think Mum will like it? It's not a bit – you know - is it?' she asked scrunching up her nose.

The other one frowned. 'No. It's just a bit of something to take home isn't it?'

The woman bundled it back into the bag and they walked on. Rosa wondered if the few pounds the thing must have cost might have been better spent. She also wondered if a spot of shopping might make her feel a bit more normal and less like a ghost hunter.

Rosa looked in nearly every shop window on the High Street but didn't venture in. Too many questions without answers swam around her head which meant that she was staring at displays but not really taking any notice of them. She had a vague notion of going into the mystic *Willow Moon* that she'd seen on her first evening, but she was nearly at the end of the village and had evidently wandered past it.

Rosa stopped in front of a similar shop to *Willow Moon*. Its window displayed crystals, essential oils and handcrafted wooden ornaments, amongst other things. The sign over the door said *Heart's Desire* and Rosa realised that if she didn't go in this one, then she'd have to go all the way back the way she'd just come.

An old fashioned shop bell tinkled and Rosa got a waft of essential oils as she stepped into the cool interior. In the few seconds it took for her eyes took to adjust after the bright sunshine, her bag brushed against a display of wicker witches on broomsticks and nearly sent them flying. The surreal thought of them actually zooming around the shop above her head elicited a snort, and then she nearly went into orbit herself when a disembodied voice said, 'Anything you break, you pay for, my dear.'

A very tall, very sallow-faced middle-aged woman rose up from behind a counter like mist on an autumn morning and twisted her very obviously dyed jet-black hair into a clip at the back of her head.

'Oh, you made me jump,' Rosa said putting her hand over her heart and smiling politely, even though the woman's opener had been less than that.

'Yes. Lots of people say so.' The woman tried a smile; her angular features stretching her skin thinly over her chin and cheek bones. 'Are you looking for anything in particular?'

'Er ... something for my gran. No idea what though.'

The woman sat on a stool, propped her elbows on the desk and cupped her chin. Tawny eyes swept Rosa up and down and fixed searchingly on her face. 'Your gran isn't well, is she my dear? And you have recently had trauma in your life ... a shock perhaps?'

And you have just given me another one. How the bloody hell? Rosa looked away and tried to calm herself. 'Um ...' was all she managed.

'Look, take a seat over there.' The woman gestured to a small table and two chairs in the corner of the shop. 'I can tell you're in need of a reading.'

A *what?* Rosa looked at the sign on the wall next to the table and chairs. *Morganna Hardill - Psychic readings and Tarot a speciality.* 'Oh, no thanks. I don't believe in all that.'

'Yes, my son told me. But I think you might have warmed toward the spirit world today. Am I right?'

The name Hardill and the waiter's grumpy face floated simultaneously in Rosa's head to make the inevitable connection. So here was the white witch. And warming to the spirit world? Unable to define the border between fright and curiosity, Rosa wrapped her arms protectively around herself and watched as Morganna, taking her hesitation as agreement, came around the counter in one fluid movement, turned the sign on the front door to *Closed*, and seated herself at the small table.

Against all previous reasoning, Rosa seated herself opposite and swallowed hard when Morganna's eyes held her own. The white witch's gaze seemed to read every insecurity, every question, and every worry that was in her heart. To break the stare and to try to assert some kind of control over the situation Rosa said, 'So what exactly do you aim to do?'

'Firstly I want to tell you not to be afraid. I am into paganism, the power of nature, and allowing my gift to help people. In fact, that is my raison d'être – to help all who need it. The trouble is,' she leaned forward and smirked, 'most people's ignorance assumes the opposite is true.'

Indignance burned bright in Rosa's eyes. 'I hardly think *most* people are to blame if they aren't up with the latest practices and rites of white witchcraft. I mean, it's hardly commonplace is it?'

'No need to get grouchy, Rosa' Morganna smiled her stretchy smile again. 'So I think I'll forgo the Tarot for plain old palm-reading. Leastways that's the accepted name. I just call it "getting in touch".'

She held out her hand and after a moment's hesitation, Rosa placed her hand palm up in Morganna's. As she watched Morganna's concentration deepen, her long indigo nails stroking her palm periodically, a thought occurred. 'I presume your son told you my name, but how did you know me?'

Morganna looked up briefly and shrugged. 'He described you, I saw you coming out of your B&B the other day, and I knew it was your name as soon as I looked into your eyes. Just like I now know that your grandmother is called Jocelyn and you have encountered an unhappy spirit more than once since you arrived here in Tintagel.'

All pretence at being in control disintegrated under the impact of her words. 'But … how can you possibly know my gran's name and …'

'It's a gift I have had for many years. I can 'see' her in her bed, very ill, frail ...' Morganna looked into Rosa's eyes and spoke with genuine sympathy. 'Spirits also contact me from time to time ... Just as Jory contacted you today.'

Rosa pulled her hand free and swallowed hard. The walls were too close and there wasn't enough air. Everything she had ever known to be true was being pushed to the limit. Surety in the scientific and rational explanation was diminishing, shifting out of focus like the edges of a sepia photograph. She wanted to scream but instead out of her mouth came, 'I can't begin to understand how this all works, I—'

'No. It is rather full on all at once.' Morganna patted Rosa's shoulder gently. 'There is so much you need to know though about the past, and about yourself. There is one bit of crucial information I must pass on and then you should ask Jocelyn the rest. Ask her about your gift.' Morganna smiled, but this time it didn't look as stretchy.

'Gift?' Rosa felt a few bricks of resistance start to build a wall in her head. *Why don't I just get up and leave?*

'Yes, but as I said that is not for me to tell. The information I must impart is from Jory. He said he wants to see you at dusk tomorrow evening.' Morganna closed her eyes and cocked her head as if trying to hear something. Then she nodded. 'He says, at the spot where the photographer stood today.'

'But what for? Ask him!' Rosa leapt up, pushing over the chair with a clatter.

'Jory has gone. And I can't say more.'

'Can't or won't? The wall in her head laid down another row. 'Why can't you just come clean and speak plainly? All this melodrama is very clichéd.'

Morganna steepled her long fingers and sighed. 'I can see why you are angry. You feel threatened, unsure. Just go and phone your grandmother, we'll speak again.'

Rosa looked down at the white witch. Questions formed on her tongue but slid away before she could find the courage to open her mouth. Morganna's eyes were full of sympathy and then she stood and gave Rosa a quick hug. Rosa felt her whole body tense and then she grew calmer. Construction halted on the wall of resistance and it began to crumble, though it was only half-finished.

Outside *Heart's Desire,* Rosa blinked her eyes in the sunlight and hurried back along the pavement towards the B&B. All she could think about was asking what Gran knew about her past – this so-called gift. Jocelyn was ill, frail and needed careful handling, but the way that Rosa was feeling at the moment, if she didn't tell her granddaughter what she knew all bets were off.

* * *

Across the miles, silence settled into the gap left by the conclusion of the obligatory pleasantries associated with the conventions of polite British telephone manner. Jocelyn's laboured breathing broke the silence, along with anticipation, unspoken, yet sensed loud and clear by her granddaughter. But where should Rosa start? After her initial adrenalin fuelled determination to just blurt out everything that she'd experienced over the last few days - along with a barrel-load of questions - an image of her gran frail and ill and waiting for news made her more cautious.

Just when she could bear the impasse no longer, Jocelyn asked, 'So have you anything to report? Anything happen at the church?'

'Yes … but I need to ask you a few questions first.'

'Ri-ght.'

'Why didn't you tell me how Jory died and the fact that he was so young?'

A heartfelt sigh came down the line followed by, 'It was too painful for me to talk about I guess …'

Silence again. Rosa couldn't believe that Gran had left it at that. 'Okay, I see that, but I need to know. Did he kill himself?'

'That's the way it seemed at the time, but now …'

Again the sentence was just left floating in the ether. 'Please just tell me what happened.'

'Why do you need to know?'

Rosa had to bite the inside of her cheek to keep a lid on her temper. 'Considering I am here doing your bidding, not to mention following requests from a dead guy, just humour me, eh?'

'Okay, no need to get sniffy,' Jocelyn said and heaved another sigh. Rosa had to bite the other side of her cheek. 'Jory was distraught after I'd left him. A few weeks after I came back home, he … Jory got drunk and jumped from a cliff by the church you visited and … he died.'

So Rosa had been right. He'd killed himself because Gran had left him. No wonder she'd kept quiet. And he'd done it near to the church on the cliff path, where he'd asked her to go today. 'Right, I had guessed as much. I'm so sorry, I just needed to be sure.'

'At least that's what I and his family believed for years. I recently understand that not to be the case.'

'What? He *didn't* kill himself?'

'No.' Jocelyn sniffed and Rosa realised she was crying. 'But he wouldn't say more. He said he must tell you and nobody else.'

Rosa was torn between just winding up the conversation for now, or just getting it all out of the way in one. She wandered from the bedroom onto the balcony and looked out to sea. If she were to be effective, feel at least a little prepared, she had to get to the bottom of it after all. So it might as well be now. No point in upsetting her gran twice was there? Also this was the perfect opening to ask about 'her gift'.

'Are you there, love?' Jocelyn asked, her querulous voice pulling at Rosa's heartstrings.

'I'm here, Gran. Just wandered onto the balcony – you'd love the view of the sea.'

'Oh I would. I do miss the sea. Should have gone more often, when I had the chance.'

A knot of emotion swelled in Rosa's throat but she gripped the phone tighter and said, evenly, 'Why me, Gran? Why does he always need to communicate with me?'

'As I said, he wouldn't tell me.'

'That's as may be. But you know more, much more about my... my so called gift, don't you?'

The sharp intake of breath on the other end of the phone told Rosa that Morganna had been telling the truth. She could almost see Jocelyn, sitting up in bed, pale, wretched, her hand over her mouth in shock. 'But how ... have you remembered something?'

'Remembered?' A shiver of trepidation tickled the base of her spine. Just what the hell had she got buried in her subconscious? 'No. I have remembered nothing. A white witch kindly told me today that you knew stuff about my past, my gift. She also passed on the latest message from your dearly departed.'

'I ... I don't know what to say.' Jocelyn's voice sounded faint on the line as if the miles between them had increased tenfold. 'This whole thing is becoming harder to grasp.'

Rosa wasn't surprised as she felt exactly the same. Morganna's information about a dusk meeting tomorrow night was playing on her mind, tangling her thoughts. 'Seeing' Jory again had never been appealing, but now under these new circumstances, the very idea scared her witless.

What if Jory wanted to do her harm? What if he wanted to push her off the cliff even, just to punish Jocelyn for leaving him and driving him to his death? Because perhaps he *had* actually killed himself and pretended to Gran that he hadn't. Who knew? Malevolent spirits could be sneaky couldn't they? The craziness of that thought wasn't lost on her. Was he malevolent? And what the hell did she know about spirits, malevolent or otherwise?

'I promised your mother and father... especially him' Jocelyn said quietly cutting through Rosa's whirl of emotion.

'Promised what?'

'That I would never tell. I agreed, but wasn't happy. In the end I thought that you would remember all by yourself, but as the years went by you never did. Damn that woman for telling you now. What good will it do?'

'But she hasn't really *said* anything. Tell me what you know.' Rosa's tone made it clear this was an instruction not a question.

'I'm tired, Rosa. I need to rest.'
'Tell me.'
'Tomorrow, I will feel better and–'
'Tell me now.'
Jocelyn burst into tears and told her.

CHAPTER 8

$\mathcal{T}$he hands of the clock must be stuck. Talan swore that last time he looked they were in exactly the same position, and that was at least half an hour ago. He drummed his fingers on the desk and craned his neck to look through the open door of the shop. Still nobody around. If there was a customer or two, at least the time would go quicker. A model of a knight looked from a display at him, his beady black eyes missing nothing. Okay, if he were honest, the main reason he wanted his mind to be occupied was to stop it being filled with thoughts of Rosa.

'What's up with you today? You've not cracked a smile once.'

Talan looked up at his Aunt Clare who'd just come in the back door with more stock and felt his mouth twitch at the corners. She looked like she'd been pulled through a hedge backwards. The wind had blown her blonde curls into a miniature haystack, and having lost some of its adhesive, one of her false eyelashes resembled a drunken spider.

'I'm smiling now, aren't I?' he said.

'Hm. You look like you're smirking rather than smiling. Have I got something on my face?' She set down her boxes and touched her cheeks.

'No. You're just as gorgeous as ever.' Talan sighed and wondered what Rosa was up to today. Perhaps she'd gone home. Perhaps she'd gone home and he'd never get the chance to meet her again. Why did that feel so wrong? This mooning over a woman wasn't entirely new to him, but something he thought he'd left behind in his teenage years.

Aunt Clare's moon face thrust itself into his line of vision. 'Now I know you're not yourself.'

'Eh?'

'Saying I'm gorgeous.'

'Ah, yeah.'

'Charmin'! You're supposed to say, of course you're gorgeous, blah, blah.' Clare laughed and ruffled his hair. 'Let's have it then.'

'Oh it's nothing really.'

'I think you need the love of a good woman.' She took a small mirror out of her bag and poked at the drunken spider. 'Have you plucked up courage to ask Kate out yet? She'll be in this afternoon to take over from me.'

Talan loved his aunt, but she knew how to get right on his nerves lately. Of course he was grateful to her for getting him this part-time job here, but this constant matchmaking with their boss was becoming more than a little wearisome. 'I told you I'm not interested in her in that way.'

Another jab at the spider with a damp finger fixed it back in place and next she attacked the haystack with a tail-comb. 'But why? Now she *is* truly gorgeous, don't you think? Long dark hair, chocolate-drop eyes, lovely figure, what's not to like?'

'You ask her out, then.' Talan stood up and walked to the door. He needed air and a long walk by the sea. No chance of that until the end of the day though.

Clare went on as if he'd not spoken. 'She fancies you rotten, it's so obvious.'

'Is it?' Talan hadn't noticed. It was probably just a figment of Clare's over-romantic imagination. Since her husband had buggered off she veered between playing a snotty bitch on the one hand and cupid on the other. Uncle Harvey had a lot to answer for.

'Yes. Often asks how you are and what you've been up to when you're at Pendennis.'

'My God, you're right she's got it real bad.'

'Don't be facetious.'

'Moi, facetious?' Talan came back to the counter and grinned at his aunt's disgruntled expression.

She narrowed her eyes. 'Right, young man. I'm going to put the kettle on and you're going to tell me what the problem is.'

An hour later Talan could have committed aunticide. He suspected that wasn't a real word, but one thing was for sure, she was a real pain in the ass. For reason's best known to his subconscious, he'd eventually given in and told her he had a bit of a thing for a woman he hardly knew and now she wouldn't let it lie. For the past ten minutes she'd had to be quiet as there were people in the shop, but once they'd left, she started again.

'So if she lives in the village, you'd know her and I'd know her, right? So she must be a tourist?'

'I have told you I don't want to talk about it. God knows why I mentioned it in the first place.'

'You told me because you secretly want my advice. So what's her name?'

Talan threw up his hands. What the hell, he may as well spill it. 'Rosa.'

'Nice name. And where did you meet her?'

'In the cafe the other day. She was the one who walked down here the other night just after we'd closed.'

Clare's manner switched from indulgent maternalism to acid indigestion. 'That little madam? Oh, Talan, no. She is totally wrong for you. She'll break your heart and leave you high and dry.'

Talan wasn't expecting this. 'How can you say that when you saw her for all of five minutes?'

'Because she came in the shop the following morning didn't she, all stroppy and high and mighty.' Clare stroked the side of her face with a manicured talon and stared into the middle-distance. 'She's trouble that one – can smell it a mile off.'

A family of four walked in, so thankfully Talan was prevented from answering and for the next hour, folk came in one after the other. Relieved to see Kate walk through the door just as the last customer left, Talan made a big production out of gathering his aunt's belongings for her while chattering on to Kate about her morning. Clare couldn't very well question him while Kate was here, even though she was dying to.

Talan stifled a grin. If Clare had been a comic book character the artist would have drawn a huge grimace on her face and big clouds of steam coming from each of her ears. Clare said goodbye to Kate, shot a knowing look at Talan and left for home.

The afternoon idled, again allowing Rosa back into his head along with his aunt's misgivings. Perhaps she *was* trouble? She'd managed to rub his aunt and Dan Hardill up the wrong way after only a day here, and Talan could do without trouble. All he wanted was to meet a 'nice girl' as his mum would say. Rosa had certainly seemed nice, more than nice, but he could guess where she went from there. As far away as possible ...

'So what are you up to this evening? Carousing the flesh pots of Truro or Bodmin?' Kate's elfin face brightened with a smile as she set two mugs of coffee down on the desk.

Talan cracked out laughing despite his mood. 'If you can find fleshpots in either I will give you a medal.'

'So a TV dinner and a can or two of lager?'

Talan put his head on one side and considered the contents of his fridge. 'Probably, though I do have a nice bit of salmon I could grill.'

'A nice bit of salmon?' Kate pulled a face of disgust. 'You sound like my grandma, not a man in his twenties.'

'Thirty is on the horizon next year.'

'Really? My goodness – you'd better get your pipe and slippers sorted then.' Kate's dark eyes danced with mischief at him over the rim of her coffee cup.

Talan grinned and took a swig of his own drink and then his aunt's assertion that Kate liked him in 'that way' caught a tentative hold as she held his gaze and looked away shyly. But then he was never the world's best at reading signals from women. She was probably just being friendly.

'Well I won't sit back and watch you become an old fossil at twenty-nine. Meet me at the Tintagel Arms at seven and we'll have a bite to eat.'

Talan nearly choked on his coffee and picked at bit of thread on his shirt, anything to avoid Kate's eyes. How the hell was he going to get out of this one? He'd planned to go for a walk, but then if he said that Kate might ask to come with him.

'I'm a bit tired to be honest, think I'll just have a quiet one.' He added a fake yawn for emphasis and cringed inwardly.

'Oh for goodness sake,' Kate said colouring slightly, 'No need to be so horrified. I'm not asking you out on date, you idiot. I have a few ideas about reorganising this place that I'd like to run past you.'

Relief swept through him but when he grinned and looked back at her, he thought he noticed a shadow of hurt flick across her eyes. Not sure how to respond without putting his foot in it any further he said, 'I wasn't horrified. I *am* tired. Besides no way would someone as pretty as you be interested in me.'

Kate's colour deepened and she looked away. 'Oh please. Don't you realise most the women in this village married or single would give their right arm to be with you?'

Talan swallowed and wished himself far away. Why did he always manage to say the wrong thing? Clearing his throat nervously he said, 'I doubt that.'

'It's true. But I'm not one of them of course. Besides I am three years older than you – practically old enough to be your mother.' Kate flashed a perfect white smile and poked him in the bicep. 'Just come out for an hour or so. I promise to have you back at home in time for your cocoa.'

Knowing he couldn't back out of it without sounding rude, but wishing he could he said,' Okay, why not?' And anyway, at least it would be a distraction if nothing else. Rosa couldn't get into his head as much when he was distracted.

* * *

Sparks from the fire whooshed up the chimney like a flurry of shooting stars as a log shifted and crackled in the grate. Kate leaned forward in her chair and rubbed her hands together, the glow of the flames flickering orange and gold across her face.

'I love this time of year. Warm in the day, yet chilly at night. Nothing like a real fire is there?' She smiled across at him and then turned back to watch the fire.

'No. We used to have one when I was little, but we moved out of the tiny cottage when my sister was born and the new place just had a pretend one.'

Kate nodded and settled back in her seat and sipped her wine. 'That's why I've always loved this pub. Well, and because of the great food of course.' She rubbed her tummy and grinned.

It had been a lovely meal, and despite his misgivings about coming out tonight, Kate had been great company. They'd talked about rejigging some of the presentation displays and looked at moving the desk to a different area, and then they'd just talked about this and that. She was very easy to talk to and had a good sense of humour too. Because he'd only worked with her a few afternoons a week, Talan hadn't really got to know her much before tonight. As he looked at her delicate features lit up by the flames, her long dark hair swept into a chignon, he had to admit she was undeniably stunning. Then his heart lurched. And undeniably *not* Rosa

'So tell me about your family. There's just you and your sister, yes?' Kate asked, her dark eyes twinkling in the soft light.

'Yep. Sophie is a few years younger than me, works in a bank in Truro. She's due to get married next year.' Talan sighed and took a long pull on his pint.

Kate frowned. 'You seem sad all of a sudden'

Pretty, clever, good fun ... now intuitive. 'Not really. It's just that the time seems to have flown by; also it would have been nice for my dad to give her away. Our stepdad, Greg, is a really nice man, but I know she would have liked our dad to walk her down the aisle.'

'Oh I didn't realise Greg wasn't your biological father. I met him recently when he gave Clare a lift from work. He's her brother, right?'

'Yep he's her brother. Our 'real' dad left when I was five. He eventually married again and went to live in Canada.'

'So what went wrong between, your mum and ...'

'Look let's talk about happy things, hey? And would you like another drink?' Talan stood, noting the crestfallen look on her face, but there was no way he wanted to go over all the ins-and-outs of his parents' car crash of a marriage.

'Sorry, Talan ... but you did kind of bring it up.'

'Yeah, I know. Let my guard down, I guess.'

'Don't feel you have to be on your guard with me.' Kate smiled and held his gaze for longer than Talan thought she should if they were just friends. And when she gave him a slow smile, this time he was sure of the signal.

Talan swallowed and pointed at her glass. She nodded and he made a swift exit to the bar. He'd have one more drink and then leave in case Kate got even friendlier. There was no way he wanted more complications. One woman was already refusing to get out of his head; there was no room for another.

To his surprise when he returned with the drinks Kate turned the conversation back to work and seemed quite brisk and business-like. Perhaps he'd got it wrong once again. After all, Rosa had seemed pretty interested that day at the cafe and then later here in the pub. She obviously wasn't though, was she?

'Talan, are you with me?' Kate's face came back into focus across the table complete with a withering look.

'Oh, sorry ... miles away.' He'd not been miles away, but right there, just staring past her into the flames thinking how much the dark amber heart of the fire reminded him of the colour of Rosa's hair.

'I said are you looking forward to Sophie's wedding?'

Talan frowned. The last thing he remembered Kate talking about was ordering some more books for the shop. How did we get back to weddings? 'Um, yes I guess.'

'And when will it be your turn do you think?' Kate grinned and ran her finger around the rim of her glass.

'Oh God knows. I have to meet someone yet.' As soon as those words were out of his mouth he wished them back in again. Kate crossed her arms and leaned forward across the table giving him a good look at her ample cleavage.

'So have you had a serious relationship recently?'

Talan considered avoiding the subject but then decided it would work in his best interest if he told her the truth. She might back off a little then. 'Yes. It lasted five years and ended almost two years ago now.'

Kate put her hand on his forearm. 'Oh that's a shame, what went wrong?'

Given that he wasn't upset and just telling the story, Talan imagined Kate put her hand on his arm not out of sympathy, but to show him she was interested. He moved his arm slightly but her hand remained. 'We met at Uni and had a great time at first, but then she, Elaine, got obsessive about me, us. After two years she said she wanted to get married, and wouldn't believe me when I explained there was no one else but that we were too young. The relationship had become claustrophobic, stifling.' Talan moved his arm under her hand again, but Kate seemed oblivious. 'Anyway I finished it and she had a breakdown, ended up in hospital. I felt totally responsible and there's been nobody serious since. Happy to be single to be honest.'

Kate, her eyes full of sympathy put her other hand out and stroked his shoulder. 'Oh that's awful. Not all women are like Elaine though. You should give some lucky girl a chance.'

Putting her off went well then. Talan wondered what to say next, just as Dan Harthill whisked past with a tray of empty glasses and skidded to a halt by their table. 'Some guys have all the luck - out with two stunning women in as many days.' Dan gave a sly grin and picked up their empties.

Dan's comments soon shifted Kate's hands. She frowned, stopped stroking his shoulder and sat back in her chair. Talan glared at Dan. Damn it. What must Kate think of him after what he'd just said, and why had Dan said it? It was obvious he was being deliberately spiteful.

'So who was the other woman, Dan?' Kate said, not taking her eyes from Talan's.

'Rosa.' He rolled his eyes up to the left. 'Fernley, I think Mum said. She seemed a bit sniffy about the mystic elements of our town, but then according to my mum she's actually much more open to the spirit world than I thought.'

'So how did your mum meet her?' Talan asked.

'She did a reading for her today.'

Talan's heart rate picked up and he said, 'So she's not going back to London then?' Though he tried to keep his voice even, he heard a note of hope in it. Kate looked away into the fire, her lips pursed in annoyance.

'Nope. Think she's hanging around for a bit.' Dan noticed Kate's expression, jerked a thumb at her and pulled a face at Talan. 'Hey guys, I hope I haven't put my foot in it with my little joke. I know you two are work colleagues – not romantically attached are you?'

Kate whipped round on him, 'Of course we're not. Just having a drink and talking shop that's all.' Then she looked at Talan, her dark eyes now hard beads. 'No idea you had a girlfriend though, Talan. Thought you said you were happily single.'

Dan gave that sly smile and left. Talan could have throttled him on the one hand and kissed him on the other. Thank goodness Rosa was 'hanging round for a bit'. Now he had another chance to stop mooning about and try to see her again. He looked at Kate and sighed. 'Rosa isn't my girlfriend, just a girl who I had drink with.'

'You seemed pretty pleased to find she was still here though.'

'Surprised that's all. Anyway shall we drink up and go? I'm knackered now.' Talan picked up his pint. He was fed up with trying to please Kate. They'd come out as mates - if she had a different agenda, then that was tough.

'Yep, suits me.'

They both lived at the same side of the village, but hardly a word passed between them as they walked. Upon parting, Talan thanked her for the evening and said that the discussions about work had been productive. Kate nodded, said goodnight and then just walked off down her street. Talan shrugged and walked on to his own front door already planning how he would make contact with Rosa again in the morning. His key in the door, he paused, looked up at the full moon and made a wish.

CHAPTER 9

$\mathcal{F}$or a moment or two Rosa thought that she'd forgot to set the alarm for work and leapt out of bed, her heart drumming in her chest. Once her surroundings had registered in the insomnia induced treacle-pot of her brain she yawned loud and long. Nine-thirty. Damn. Not only did she feel like a stampede of elephants had trampled all over her, she realised she'd also missed breakfast. Great.

The bed looked so inviting, a warm cocoon, a refuge against the day and difficult decisions. She was convinced that she'd sleep now. It would be hard not to. After lying awake re-running Jocelyn's revelations, she'd eventually found the door to the Land of Nod only four hours ago. Still, hiding away wouldn't help, she must get up and get on with it. There might be time for a nap in the afternoon.

'Morning, Rosa. Didn't fancy breakfast this morning?' John's cheerful face popped round the corner of the kitchen as she wandered into the dining room.

'Morning. I overslept. I was awake all night until around five.'

'Oh, not ill I hope?'

'No. Just lots on my mind. I don't suppose I could have a bit of toast, could I?'

John came in and pulled a chair out for her. 'Look, I can see you are troubled, my dear. Have a seat and I'll cook you a full English, shall I?'

His simple act of kindness touched her heart. Rosa, already on an emotional knife-edge, could have kissed him. 'But are you sure, it's past ten?'

'Wouldn't have asked if I wasn't – now tea or coffee with that?'

John's full English and two cups of coffee had sent a much needed rush of energy through her body, and a firm decision into her mind. Morganna it was then. Rosa had already come to the conclusion that she had to share Jocelyn's news with someone and had considered Willa. She was fairly open to most ideas, and sometimes offered good advice. There was the worry that she'd keep harping on about it when she'd returned to London though. Rosa knew that her new discovery needed to remain with her and not all over the homeless shelter and beyond.

Mum and her brothers were out too. They would worry and demand that she came home for therapy or something. And Dad … well, the less she allowed him into her thoughts the better.

A shower, fresh clothes, perhaps another coffee, and then she'd pop over to see Morganna. Hopefully the shop wouldn't be heaving with tourists or she'd have to think again. John hurried over just as she was leaving the dining room and handed her an envelope.

'What am I like? This was hand delivered for you this morning and I forgot all about it until just now.' He smiled and cleared her table.

A bold hand had written across the envelope in black fountain pen – *For Rosa Fernley*. 'Who delivered it, John?'

'No idea. It was on the mat this morning.'

In her room she slid a nail under the flap of the envelope and pulled out the note.

Dear Rosa,

I really enjoyed the time we spent together the other night, before Dan came along and ruined it for you that is. I was hoping that you'd be willing to meet again before you go home. We could go for a drive down the coast on Saturday, if you'd like. There is a lovely walk along the cliff tops past Bedruthan Steps and we could have lunch in the Carnewas cafe too.

Please give me a ring and we'll go from there. I really would love to see you again,

Talan x

A feeling of lightness built in her chest, fanned up and out across her tired brain, and pushed at the heavy clouds left by sleeplessness. A business card with his phone number was attached and she ran her finger over the embossed lettering. Talan Kestle. So that was his surname. Appropriate, given he worked in castles.

Rosa caught her reflection in the wardrobe just as she had the other day when she'd been thinking of Talan. Sparkling eyes, flushed, and this time a big, daft, soppy grin because he'd gone to the trouble of writing and hand-delivering a letter. He already had her mobile number and she had his, but perhaps he wanted to make sure she responded after the way they'd parted company?

And would she respond? Rosa would be lying if she said she hadn't thought about him since the other night, despite all the weird shit happening. Talan wasn't just a lovely guy in every way; he was undeniably part of whatever was going on, unless the whole thing was some big coincidence. Being alike enough to be the brother of Jory was some coincidence however – a leap too far.

She re-read the note again. Saturday for a walk and lunch did sound just the thing she needed. As today was Thursday, it was far enough away to feel like she could look forward to it rather than get panicky about how it would turn out. Tomorrow would be soon enough to ring him, or even drop a letter into his address. That would be a fun thing. Rosa sighed, and remembered what lay ahead. She stopped smiling, a frown knitting her brow. Today was going to be a much more serious day.

* * *

The tinkling shop bell announced her entry to *Heart's Desire* as if she was a fairy in a play and had just flown on stage. Luckily the audience was singular, an elderly lady who hadn't even looked up as she flipped through some greeting cards in a rack near the till. Morganna sat behind it, and rolled her eyes towards the customer, pointing at her watch and indicating that she'd been there ages. Then she treated Rosa to a warm smile.

'Hello there, time for a cuppa? I'm just about to close up for lunch'

The lady looked at Morganna over her glasses and harrumphed. 'You never normally close for lunch?' Then she squinted at her watch. 'And it's only just eleven-thirty.'

'That's true, Gladys, but I need a chat with lovely Rosa here. So if you have decided on a card?'

Gladys stuffed a card back in the rack, her mouth pursed so tightly her lips were white around the edges. 'Forget it, I won't be hurried. They are ridiculously overpriced anyway.' Upon leaving, she slammed the door so furiously that the bell jangled on its spring as if a hundred fairies had fled at once.

'Oh dear, Gladys isn't a happy lady.' Rosa said with a giggle in her voice.

Morganna threw up her hands. 'Would you believe she's been in here half-an-hour picking up this and that, tutting at the price tag and then mostly flicking through the cards?'

She turned the shop sign on the door to *Closed* and then beckoned Rosa through a heavy purple velvet curtain and into a small kitchen-come-stock area

'Are you sure you have time for me in the middle of the day? You did it when I had a reading yesterday and again now. You must be losing custom,' Rosa said and seated herself at a little table in the corner.

'Of course. I can tell that your need is greater than theirs. Coffee?'

If a description of Morganna was required from Rosa last time they'd met, she would have said, prickly, scary and cold. Today though, her long black hair and indigo nails had lost their stereotypical witch-like characteristics and her angular face looked just thin, not skeletal. In fact, on reflection, she looked rather eccentrically elegant in her faded flares, purple tie-dye bat-wing top and sparkly flip flops.

'So what did your grandmother say about your past?' Morganna had to raise her voice over the noise of the kettle.

'That's what I'm here to talk to you about. It all came as a bit of a shock.'

'Yes it would. Choccie biscuit?' Morganna held up a packet of digestives.

Rosa's mouth dropped open. 'You know what my gran said to me already?'

'No, love. But I know by just briefly 'getting in touch' the other day that you have a gift, and of course Jory told me too. I also knew that Jocelyn was the one to ask about it all.'

Rosa sighed. 'This is mad. Here you are making coffee and handing out biscuits as if the whole thing was as normal as having a nice little chat about shopping, or the weather.'

Morganna laughed. 'In my world it is normal. It's just a dimension of life that not many of us experience, that's all.' She set down two mugs and the cafetiere between them on the table and through a mouthful of biscuit said, 'Okay, fire away.'

'My dad ...' There was a long pause while Rosa tried to get her words in order. She sipped at the scalding coffee and then said the words again. 'My dad ...' The repetition of these first words proved to be a catalyst – a trickle in the stream became a waterfall. 'Dad has always impressed upon me from a very young age that science has the answers to everything. Any suggestion of the paranormal, spirits or anything mystical was always ridiculed by him. Mum never really said what she thought, just kept quiet, so I don't really know her views, and my brothers always backed him. My eldest brother, Simon, was the most supportive of Dad's ideas. He said any dabbling into the paranormal messed with your head, was illogical at best and dangerous at worst.

'Dad once told me that if I wanted to be successful, get on in life, I must always trust in logical thought and explanation. Until I came here I did, I didn't really question it. You don't, I guess, not when you've had it drilled into you since you were small. And he is a well-respected professional too; I just assumed he knew what he was talking about.'

Morganna poured coffee and nodded. 'Of course you did. You mustn't blame yourself for not going against him. There would be no reason to, until like you say, you came here and your psychic experiences showed you otherwise.'

Rosa picked up a biscuit and felt a bit better. Morganna was easy to talk to once you accepted that she was just an ordinary woman with extraordinary abilities. After all, she was the same, wasn't she? Rosa wasn't up with the ways of white witchery, or plant or herbal lore, but she was in the way she could see and talk to spirits. All at once, Rosa realised that this no longer scared her, though the shock of her new knowledge was still sinking in.

'Are you ready to continue, or do you want to come back another time? I know this must be hard for you.' Morganna rested her elbows on the table, laced her long fingers together and rested her chin upon them.

'No. God, no.' Rosa rolled her eyes. 'I need to tell you this now, especially if I am to make a decision about meeting Jory this evening.'

'It's a daunting prospect for those unused to such things.'

'More so now I know what I know.' Rosa crunched into another biscuit and pushed a few crumbs around the table with her finger-nail, imagining going up to the church at dusk ... alone.

'Was Jocelyn shocked that you wanted to know about your past?'

'I think so. And she really didn't want to tell me as she's promised my parents.' Rosa looked across into Morganna's amber eyes; little flames warmly encouraging. 'Okay if you're ready for the rest?'

'Take your time, love. No rush.'

Rosa took a deep breath and let it out slowly. 'A huge thing happened when I was five. Well, actually some things happened before I was five now and then. Gran says I used to tell people that

I saw and heard things. Gran called it my sixth sense?' She looked at Morganna

'That's a good a name as any. I call it my gift, but it is a part of me like touch, taste and smell, etcetera – so yes that'll do.'

Rosa sighed and shrugged, 'I guess so. Anyhow, once when I was about four I think, I was visiting my grandparents and said that a man in a brown coat and hat was standing behind my grandfather – Jocelyn's husband, with his hand resting on his shoulder. I said that the man had spoken to me and said that he loved his family but had never told them.

'My grandparents just humoured me, but a few weeks later I was visiting at gran's again and I pointed to a photo on the mantelshelf of a man in brown trilby and long brown coat. I said it was the same man I saw last time. It was my grandfather's dad. He'd apparently died later the same evening that I'd seen him standing behind my grandfather. Jocelyn told my mum when she came to collect me as she was in shock, but Mum just told her never to speak of it, especially when Dad was around.'

Morganna smiled and patted Rosa's hand. 'I had very similar experiences as a child. My mother said that she expected I'd grow out of it, thought I was making it all up. She of course came to believe me, as proof will out. Took her a long time though. My dad died when I was little, but I had a few conversations with him growing up. It helped me no end.'

Rosa could identify with that. 'According to Jocelyn, Mum said she had heard of young people being more susceptible to the spirit world and that if it was encouraged, it would be harder to stop. Plus, the fact that my dad was so against it all.'

'You said something huge happened when you were five. What was it?' Morganna laced her fingers around her cup and took a sip.

Rosa drained her own cup and poured more coffee. 'After I had seen and heard my great-grandfather and been ignored really, or told to be quiet about these things as 'Daddy wouldn't like it and be cross', I did as I was told. But not long after I'd turned five, apparently I started talking to an old lady that nobody else could see in our house. This lady was very sad as her son never came home from the war and she died of broken heart.' She stopped and gave a wistful smile.

'I'm sensing that you see her in your mind's eye, now?' Morganna asked.

'I can see her.' Rosa grinned and felt her heart lift. 'After so many years of repressing her memory, she came back to me after I'd spoken to Jocelyn last night. I can see her lovely face now, just as I could when I was a kid. She looks happier now though, serene.'

'You must have helped her go to her rest then, Rosa.'

'I think I did, but not until after something terrible happened.' Rosa could feel her bottom lip tremble and she had to take a few deep breaths before continuing. 'The old lady told me one day that I must warn my parents that some of the floorboards in our attic were unsafe and they needed repair. I told my youngest brother, Ben, about the old lady and what she'd said, as I knew what my dad's response would be.'

'Do you remember doing this, or is it just what Jocelyn told you yesterday?'

'The whole thing is hazy – dreamlike. I kind of remember, but most of it is from what Gran told me … though I did have a weird dream about it when I was staying at Gran's house a few weeks ago … something about a toys' picnic.' Rosa ran her hands through her hair and continued. 'Anyway, Ben told Dad and he went ape. Told me never to speak of such twaddle again, told me it was unscientific and messes with the mind. There was no old lady and nothing wrong with the attic. He even took me up there and stomped all over it to show me it was sturdy, said that I had pretended there was an old lady and that I was too old for lies.' Rosa's voice caught in her throat and she found she couldn't speak for a moment.

'It hurts when someone you love and trust makes you feel small doesn't it? When they accuse you of lying?' Morganna blinked her eyes a few times and Rosa could see they were moist. 'It happened to me often when I was little.'

'It does hurt. It's fresh because I just found out … and also I am beginning to remember how I felt back then, I think. Obviously I, and thankfully Ben, stayed away from the attic, because despite what Dad had said, Ben wasn't reassured. Simon unfortunately wasn't as cautious. So later that week, the next-door neighbour's kid, Harry comes to play with my brother Simon and they go in attic.'

The atmosphere in the small kitchen seemed to grow thick and charged with electricity; it felt to Rosa as if Morganna was sending her strength to continue. 'They go in the attic and play with the train set up there ... Harry falls through the floor ... and ... he breaks his neck. He was nine, Morganna. Nine years old.'

Hot silent tears coursed down Rosa's face so she closed her eyes in a futile attempt to stop them She felt Morganna reach out and take both of her hands in hers. 'Oh dear God, child. You poor, poor thing.'

'And guess what?' Rosa's eyes snapped open 'Dad blamed me for dabbling in evil!' She put her hand over her mouth The scene played out in her mind again as clear as it had just happened. 'Yes ... I ... I was out on the lawn giving my toys a picnic. *That's* what my dream was about a few weeks ago when I was at Gran's. He ran over to me, grabbed my shoulders and screamed at me to never talk about it again, dragged me into the house.' The hurt and humiliation she'd felt aged five made her catch her breath

'Don't worry, love. It needs to come out. Take a minute, have a drink.' Morganna patted her hand.

Rosa sat in silence for a few moments and then said, 'Jocelyn said he warned my brothers not to divulge that I had mentioned the attic floor either. She also said that Mum had never seen him so angry, he was frightening apparently. Smashed stuff up, locked me in my room He said I must never ever mention anything like that ever again Block it from my mind, fight it with logic and science, or something bad would happen to me ... something bad like what happened to the boy from next door.' Rosa stared at Morganna and shook her head in disbelief.

Morganna's eyes flamed. 'That's despicable, putting the blame on you when all you did was pass on a message!' Then she frowned. 'But didn't you say your dad checked the loft – stomped all over the floorboards?'

'Yeah. But the thing is, the train track was set up in a circle in the middle of the attic. Dad didn't check inside the circle, that's where the weak floorboard was, and Harry was messing about on that exact spot, jumping up and down according to Simon' Rosa looked at the table. 'I just remembered something else. As I said, I was playing with my dolls in the garden … and I heard Mum scream and then the ambulance siren … I knew then that something very bad had happened.'

Morganna shook her head. 'And did you see the old lady again?'

'I remembered … or perhaps half-dreamed … something when I was tossing and turning last night. I think she was upset because Harry died, but said I had tried my best, and at least no other children would get hurt now. It would have been much worse if I hadn't believed her and not warned everyone. There could have been Harry, my brothers and me up in the attic and we could have all gone the same way. Therefore, she felt like she had at least done something to help.'

'That's why she looks happier now when you think of her.' Morganna pointed to the coffee pot and Rosa nodded. She pulled Rosa's mug towards her and filled it, seemingly lost in thought. 'Then afterwards, you did as your father asked, turned to science?'

'Pretty much. I know now that I did block out any further contacts. I have vague memory of a child dressed in Victorian clothes that my friend couldn't see, sitting at the back of my class at school. I think I was around eight. That's about it though. Dad did a good head job on me.'

'Stupid, stupid man. I have a feeling that he could have been frightened of something to have such a strong reaction against your sixth-sense.'

Morganna's intuition was right, but no longer surprising to Rosa. 'He was. His own mother, who died before I was born, was a medium. My grandfather hated it. He was a high flyer in his company and she was an embarrassment to him. Jocelyn said that she always tried to bury it, control it around him, as she loved him so much, but sometimes she just had to help a troubled spirit. She embarrassed my grandfather at some function, not sure how, and he left her – divorced her and left her without a penny.'

'Bastard!' Morganna slammed her coffee mug down so hard that the liquid slopped across the table.

'Indeed. The separation hit Dad hard, obviously, and to make matters worse, his father made him live with him and his new wife. His mother became a virtual recluse and died of breast cancer I think it was. She was only in her forties.'

A long sigh escaped Morganna's lips and her shoulders slumped as if she was miming a deflating balloon. 'Well, that certainly explains your dad's attitude. I'm not condoning it though, just trying to understand it.'

'Yes, that's my take on it too, but it doesn't help the hurt any less.' Rosa wrapped her arms around herself and wondered how she would even look her father in the face again.

'No. It will take some time for that to ease. Still, it must feel better to have spilled it all to me?' Morganna sat back in her chair and gave Rosa a huge smile. Obviously this was an attempt to cheer her up, but the smile just looked fake - the mouth was the odd one out in a face where both eyes brimmed full of sympathy.

It had helped, but there was still much to worry about. 'I do feel better, thanks, Morganna. But you know that Jory asked me to meet him tonight at the church?' Morganna nodded. 'Why does he want me to go there? You see, I'm a bit worried that if he killed himself because Jocelyn left him he might want to … to—'

'Harm you? Get his revenge?'

'Well, yes.'

'No way on this earth.' Morganna shook her head vehemently. 'And he didn't kill himself.'

'That's what Gran said. But how can I be sure? He might have told her that and be pretending to be benign, but what if he's a malevolent spirit?'

'I told you, he's not. I have had many years' experience and I know beyond doubt that Jory is just a sweet and sad spirit who needs your help.'

'I don't understand why I have to go up there again. Why can't he just talk to me, like he came to you yesterday? Now he knows I have been told the truth, accepted who I am … or beginning to accept it at least. What does he want to say?'

'I honestly don't know, love. But I do know that it is most important that you meet him there.'

Rosa rubbed the heels of her hands on her eyes and yawned. Despite two strong cups of coffee, her physical weariness was catching up with her. All the emotional upheaval, plus the sleepless night, was taking its toll. 'I'll probably feel better after a few hours' sleep. At least my head won't feel full of treacle and I will be able to think more clearly.'

'Good idea. And would you like me to wait for you at the end of the path tonight? I won't come up to meet Jory, that's something you should do alone, but I will be there to walk you back afterwards, if you like?'

Morganna's words were like the sun bursting through heavy rain clouds and a huge burden of uncertainty lifted from her mind. 'Oh thanks, that would be fantastic! I will feel much better knowing you're nearby.' Rosa almost jumped up and hugged the life out of Morganna but she thought giving her hand a squeeze would be more appropriate.

Morganna grinned. 'That's sorted then. I'll meet you at the church gates at about seven-thirty this evening. Now go and get some rest.'

Out on the street Rosa already felt more positive and confident about meeting Jory. With Morganna as support and a growing belief in her new abilities, she had a feeling her purpose for being in Tintagel would at last be revealed.

CHAPTER 10

*T*o add a kiss, or not to add a kiss? That was the question. Talan's note had included one, but if Rosa added one would that give him the wrong impression? Of course she liked him, but a kiss at this stage seemed a bit familiar, even if everyone did stick them on the end of text messages left, right and centre. She always thought it seemed a bit fake, and certainly meaningless, but if she didn't follow suit it looked as if she was a cold fish. Hmm, until she knew how he was involved in the whole thing, it was best if kisses were left out. Meaningless or not, best to be on the safe side. Rosa cast her eye over her note again.

Hi Talan,
I enjoyed your company too and yes I'd love a trip down the coast. I always like to see new areas. Must be the travel journalist in me! I'll give you a ring tomorrow (Friday). Best,

Rosa ☺

Was the smiley face childish? She couldn't cross it out, it would look too messy and she hadn't time to write it again as she wanted to hand-deliver it before she had to meet Morganna at seven-thirty. Rosa glanced at her clock on the bedside table. It was seven already. In the end it would probably just be a better idea to phone and forget all this stupid hand-delivery stuff. What was the point of it anyway if she was going to phone him? She was just being silly, indulgent really. Silly and indulgent sounded like they might be comfortable sitting on the same shelf next to intimate and romantic. That was no good was it? Kisses had been scrapped, so why not the note?

Rosa snatched up the paper and walked over to the waste bin. Her fingers curled round the note and began to crumple, but then she noticed the smiley face and stopped. It would be wrong to screw up such a cheerful little symbol wouldn't it? *Oh for goodness sake.*

The street-map of Tingtagel lay open on the bed and she checked the directions to Atlantic Road again. Less than five minutes away if she walked quickly. Lacing up her walking boots and shrugging her warm green fleece over her shirt, she left the room.

Three hours sleep, a shower and a light meal had done wonders for her clarity of mind. As the sea breeze blew off the Atlantic and tousled her auburn curls into a mess of ringlets, Rosa felt rejuvenated and ready for anything. If someone had told her a week ago that she'd be posting a letter to a mysterious and handsome stranger (well almost a stranger), agreeing to go on a day trip with him and then popping up to an ancient church to meet a spirit, she'd have laughed in their face.

She shoved her hands into her fleece and strode off down Fore Street smiling to herself about how surreal that sounded. The laughing in the face bit wouldn't have been her first reaction would it? No. She would probably have backed away very slowly and then made some excuse to disappear very quickly. Now the prospect of meeting Jory filled her with a little trepidation, but mainly with excitement. Not everyone had a sixth sense did they? Though she still didn't totally buy into that description, it felt a bit too Hollywood. Whatever it was called, she should embrace it and harness it for doing good. Damn her father for forcing her to suppress it for almost twenty-three years.

* * *

Atlantic Road, 35a, Flat 2 turned out to be on the end of a row of Victorian terraced houses. Some were guest houses and flats like Talan's, but Rosa imagined that in their heyday they would have housed large families, perhaps with servants. Looking round she realised that these were the houses she'd glanced at on her way back from the castle the other day. As she'd hurried in the rain up the steep path back to the village, she'd noticed the imposing buildings as she'd passed and thought how lovely it would be to have a view from the back windows over the Atlantic and the castle itself.

At the door she slipped the letter from the pocket of her jeans and shoved it through the letterbox. There was no way she was hanging about in case Talan was in and spotted her. On her way back up the path, she glanced at the view again and noticed that the church would be clearly visible from the back windows too. Lucky old Talan.

The previous route she'd taken to the church might be a bit tricky in the failing light. Instead Rosa opted to take the paved road marked with a wooden arrow sign – To the Church.

Morganna looked every inch the white witch as she waited at the end of the church path. She faced the sea, her hair billowing out behind in raven streamers, the hem of her long midnight-blue velvet cloak rising and falling to reveal pointy-toed boots under an emerald skirt of heavy linen. Rosa's heart fluttered and she felt she was walking into a scene from a film as she drew nearer. The church waited, dark against the vermilion-streaked sky, the navy ocean whispering a lullaby as it cradled the horizon.

'How are you?' Morganna asked as she looked down at Rosa, the light of the blushing sky softening her angular features and turning her amber eyes a burnt orange.

'I have mixed feelings. I'm a bit nervous about what he wants to tell me, worried that I won't be strong enough to help him, but strangely unafraid – calm even.'

'That's good.' Morganna placed her hand on Rosa's shoulder. 'There is absolutely no need for fear, and you are stronger than you think.' She slid her arm around Rosa and turned her in the direction of the church 'Right off you go, I'm right here if you need me.'

The path cut through the gravestones on either side like a grey ribbon and Rosa followed it up to and past the church. Before she went through the gate to the cliff tops she glanced back and was reassured to see the figure of the white witch standing sentinel. Morganna raised her hand and her cloak flew out behind, giving Rosa the weird notion that if she was indeed needed, she could just fly up over the church to be by her side.

Now standing more or less where the photographer had talked to her in Jory's voice the other day, Rosa wrapped her arms around her body and looked out to sea. The breeze at the edge of the cliff teased her own hair into streamers now, and she wondered how Jory's spirit would manifest. To her right, Tintagel Island jutted out, standing resolute against the tide; and to her left, a large flat-topped rock stuck out from the cliff like nature's diving board.

Rosa closed her eyes and inhaled a mix of salt air and damp moorland. Any remaining tension began to trickle away, and from the centre of her body, calm emanated to every part of her. After a few moments she knew she was ready and said in her head, *I'm here, Jory. Where are you?* Opening her eyes she looked to the island and then turned in a circle.

Nobody at all. She was alone.

A sigh escaped her lips and tumbled voices of uncertainty crowded into her calmness. She must have been kidding herself she was strong enough to just wander up here and have a chat with a …

On the large flat rock to her left where nobody had been seconds before, a man stood silhouetted against the damask sunset, his tangle of dark curls lifting on the wind. He tilted his head to the heavens and let out a cry of anguish that pierced Rosa's heart. Raising a bottle to his lips, he took a swig, then he let his arm fall, and with it came the sound of shattering glass. A strong smell of whisky blew back towards Rosa and the man staggered, put both arms out as if trying to right himself, but then he tripped, slipped … disappeared from sight.

Rosa's breath caught in her throat and sick to her stomach she forced her legs to take a few hurried steps along the path towards the rock. A voice inside her head whispered over and over, *Oh God, please let him be all right* though she knew already that he wouldn't be.

How could he be?

A few steps from the flat rock a bench provided support for Rosa's trembling legs and she gripped the back of it as she shuffled closer to the edge of the cliff. Bracing herself, she peered over, but saw nothing apart from a charcoal blanket of ocean tugged back and forth by white horse waves.

The bench took Rosa's weight as she slumped down, her legs refusing to hold her any longer, her heart thumping fit to burst. But somehow she needed to find strength, she needed to get to Morganna, they must raise the alarm, run and find help.

But of course they didn't have to do any of those things really, did they?

An icy chill ran through her from top to toe and Rosa finally admitted to herself what she'd known from the first time she'd seen the man appear on the rock. This hadn't just happened here in the present had it? No. Rosa had been granted a glimpse into that night back in 1968, the night where Jory had come up here in despair and ... she swallowed hard. She had just witnessed the end of a young man's life.

Under her bottom, the bench moved slightly as it took the weight of another. Rosa didn't have to look up to know who it was, but she looked anyway.

In profile Jory looked even more like Talan - the elegant straight nose, the strong jaw jutting like the island, his dark curls ruffling in the breeze as he gazed out to sea. This time there was no terror immobilising Rosa's senses or movement, no absence of sound, no vacuum, just an overwhelming feeling of sadness rolling up from her toes, enveloping her.

'So you see, I didn't jump after all ... though they all believe I did,' Jory said, still staring straight ahead.

'Yes ...' she began, trying to force the idea that she was talking to a spirit out of her mind. If she couldn't manage that, she would be of little use. 'Yes, you were so sad … you were drinking and then lost your balance.'

'Aye, I was sad, Rosa, sad and rotten drunk. But yes as you saw, it was an accident. I would have never abandoned my little daughter like that, no matter how much I missed Jocelyn … never.' His voice wavered and he drew a big hand down his face.

A moment or two passed with just the sound of the waves in her ears and she had no idea where to go from there. She tried the obvious. 'Why did you appear to me twice before and why did you want to show me the day you died, Jory?'

'I had to make sure you were strong enough – make sure you wouldn't just run. I am sure now. You're the only one who can help me. You must tell my daughter that I fell, didn't jump.'

'But why me? You could have asked Morganna, couldn't you?'

'It has to be you. You are Jocelyn's blood. You need to help right wrongs, and heal wounds.'

'But Morganna—'

Jory turned to face her, his eyes shining with passion, 'No. It is you. It has to be you.'

'Are you angry at Jocelyn because she didn't stay?' Although Rosa didn't feel frightened to be in his presence, a little voice of caution warned that he might be bitter about the past.

'No. On my last day on this earth I was just sad and desperate. Stupid to have taken solace in the bottle, but there we are.'

'So what can I do to help you?'

'You need to tell my daughter Daisy that I didn't take my own life.' Jory stared back out to sea as the first stars pinpricked the sky. 'She's been so sad all these years, believing that I abandoned her. It's affected her in so many ways.'

At last Rosa had the answer to why she was here. 'Does she live in the village?

'Yes, though I don't know where. I can't 'see' her anymore. She has closed her mind to me these past few years. I … am never in her thoughts.'

The sadness in his voice broke Rosa's heart and she wanted to touch his hand but instinctively knew she couldn't. 'I don't understand why you couldn't have asked Morganna to tell her—'

'Apart from what I have already said, Morganna's gift is not strong enough I could only give her short messages. Of course she is very helpful, but her power to receive is nothing compared to yours.'

Amazed, Rosa shook her head trying to comprehend. 'Damn my father. All these years I have been unaware, forced to bury my sixth sense...' Rosa paused, that term was still bothering her, then it came to her. '... No, not a sixth ... a special sense. I buried it and I might have been able to help so many.'

'Yes. But you have time yet.' Jory looked back at her, his eyes deep and sorrowful. 'I need release, Rosa But until my daughter knows the truth I am not at rest and must stay earthbound. I also want to be with Jocelyn...' His hand hovered over hers and static shot through her fingers. '... and her time is drawing ever near.'

This time it was Rosa that looked ahead and found that all the stars had blurred into one. 'You have to go together if you want to be reunited?'

'Sometimes, but all this isn't for you to know, not yet. For now, please do as I ask and all will be well.'

Rosa puffed air out of her cheeks and tucked her hands under her warm armpits, the cold fingertips sending a chill down her sides. The whole thing was crazy, wasn't it?

'So, Jory, what makes you think Daisy is going to believe me? I mean, a strange woman turns up at her door out of the blue and says her father wants her to know that he didn't commit suicide all those years ago? I know what I'd say if I was her.'

Jory smiled at her frustration and once again she was struck by his resemblance to Talan She was just about to ask him if he knew who Talan was, when he said,

'She'll believe you because you will tell her something that nobody could possibly know.'

'I will?'

'Yes. You will tell her that a silver locket that I gave to her after her mother died is in a locked red velvet box. Until she closed her mind to me I saw her take it out and look at it from time to time ... she used to cry such heart-rending tears. In the locket is a picture of me and her mother holding Daisy when she was first born. After I died, she locked it away ... locked me away I suppose.'

Rosa wiped her eyes and took a few moments. Eventually her voice was strong enough to say, 'That is one of the saddest things I have ever heard.'

Jory nodded. 'I don't blame her for hating me all these years. All the evidence pointed to a suicide, but it wasn't. I need her to know that, and that I love her.'

'I'll tell her; you can be sure of that. Morganna will probably know where she lives.'

'No.' Jory held up his hand, his palm flat towards her face. 'You mustn't mention what has passed between us this night. Daisy must be the first to know.'

'But, how will I find Daisy if I'm not allowed to say anything?'

'Sometimes these things aren't known. It will become clear. Just believe in your special sense as you call it, there may be an answer from a source unbeknownst to me.' Jory looked at her and his eyes twinkled in the light from the climbing new moon. 'You'll succeed, trust in your feelings. And thank you, Rosa.'

Rosa smiled and looked down at the sea, slate-grey in the moonlight. 'I hope you're right, Jory.' But when she glanced up, she was alone.

* * *

The wind had turned, and brought with it the damp ocean onto Rosa's hair and skin as she hurried back to the church path. Luckily the moonlight picked out the way and she could just make out Morganna, her cloak wrapped about her, still huddled against the wind at the main gate. Rosa waved both arms back and forth above her head and broke into a trot, 'I'm here, Morganna, bet you're freezing by now?'

'I'm not too warm' She grinned as she walked up to meet Rosa 'How did it go?'

'Well, I think. At least I didn't run off screaming!' She nodded to the road. 'Let's get back. Fancy a drink to warm up?'

'No, thanks, I have a good book I want to finish' Morganna slipped her arm through Rosa's as they walked. 'And don't think you have to tell me anything about what happened, I quite understand.'

That was a relief. Rosa had already been wondering how to broach that. 'The thing is, Morganna, I was told not to mention to anyone what Jory wants me to do'

'Ah, yes. That's not unusual; these spirits are quite secretive sometimes. I have learned not to ask questions over the years. There are things that we should know and things that we should not. Just remember I will be here if you need me. No matter what it is, big or small, Morganna's at your beck and call.'

Her raucous laughter sent a bird squawking from a bush as they passed and Rosa burst into laughter too. It felt good to laugh like that after so many days of unsettled anxiety.

'Well, that's good to know, Morganna I'm not sure I could have got this far without you.'

Morganna nodded and said without a trace of modesty, 'No, you wouldn't have, that's certain' Then she winked and squeezed her arm 'But now you have accepted who you are, you will have the strength to do what's necessary.'

Rosa squeezed back. 'I do hope you're right.'

Morganna tipped her head to the moon and cackled again 'Right? I am always right my dear.'

CHAPTER 11

$\mathscr{F}$riday morning found Rosa showered, dressed, well-rested and full of the joys. Except it was summer now, not spring. The days were barrelling along towards the end of May, and summer in Tintagel felt just fantastic. It had been August when Jocelyn had spent nearly a week of summer here all those years ago, but summer was summer, be it beginning or end. Her granddaughter liked to imagine that the season had a long memory. It helped her feel a connection to Jocelyn across the miles.

After all, most of the scenery in this ancient settlement would have been the same in 1968 as it was today, give or take. The summer magic could be found now as then, in the small colourful wildflowers along the cliff paths, the warmth of the ancient stones and in the sound of the waves caressing the island.

Jocelyn had sounded a little stronger last night when Rosa had phoned not long after she'd returned from seeing Jory. That thought was so surreal on the one hand, but kind of normal on the other. Bearing in mind what he'd said about not telling anyone what had passed between them, she'd just told her gran that they had met on the clifftop near the church and he'd asked her to help him. She'd also told her that she felt at ease with her past and her ability to do good in the future.

Jocelyn had been overjoyed that Rosa felt no anger towards her for keeping what had happened in the past a secret, and felt she could rest easier.

'And so you *should* rest easy. It wasn't your secret to tell. You were only doing what Mum and Dad had asked of you.'

'Thank you, little one. I hope when you have helped Jory you'll come for a visit?'

'Try and stop me. I'm hoping it won't be too long now.'

After Rosa had ended the call she knew it had better not be too long. Jory had said the end was getting ever closer for Jocelyn and if she missed saying goodbye she'd never forgive herself. Time, the elusive mistress that waits for no man. When she'd been little she thought that old saying had been 'Time waits for Norman'. She had a Great-uncle Norman and wondered why he was so important that time actually waited for him.

Time seemed to have flown by more quickly since she'd arrived here on Monday evening; she could hardly believe it was Friday already. Considering that she had to find Daisy and then figure out how to broach the subject of her deceased father, Rosa thought she'd better hurry up and book another week here, providing that John had the room. He'd already told her that in the tourist season she couldn't just book the odd few days. Of course it was unlikely that she would need another whole week, but it was only fair and couldn't be helped.

Rosa gave a little sigh of relief as she ended the call. Luckily for her, John had just received a cancellation or she would have had to go somewhere else and that would have been most unsettling. She turned a small circle in the bedroom and smiled. This place felt so calming and comfortable, just what she needed, given that the rest of her time here had been less than that.

Nevertheless, the excitement she'd felt since stepping out of the taxi a few days ago had been more than she'd had in years. Rosa had reached a huge turning point in her life, and though her special sense felt a bit uncomfortable and tight - like a new pair of shoes - hopefully it wouldn't take too long before she'd worn it in.

The phone still sat in the palm of Rosa's hand and as she looked at the screen, a mixture of excitement and nervousness bubbled in her stomach. Today was Friday ... the day she'd said she'd phone Talan. As she thought about what to say to him, the nerves whipped into a monster, towered over excitement and then gobbled it up until there was none left.

Perhaps if she took a few deep breaths and did a spot of logical thinking before calling him it would be okay. Although her father had been totally wrong to force her to suppress her special sense all these years, logical reasoning was still her friend and a valuable counter-balance to all this 'spiritual hoo ha' as he'd call it. Rosa walked up and down her bedroom for a few minutes reasoning with herself, but the nerves were still there, forcing her heart into a breakneck pace until her head swam.

Just letting her logical mind take over didn't really help, because it wasn't as if Rosa was just calling a nice guy she'd met to go out for the day tomorrow, was it? That would make her nervous anyway, but Talan, looking like he did and just happening to bump into her at the café, *must* have some link somewhere to Jory, mustn't he?

Rosa went over to her bed and flopped down on her belly. Her dad's frowning face left her memory and surfaced on the wardrobe door. She imagined his answer to that question. 'Not necessarily, Rosa. Coincidences just happen and they have no hidden worth. These kinds of instances only take on meaning if people force extraordinary significance upon ordinary circumstances.'

A little smile played at the corners of her mouth as she realised that her dad wouldn't even acknowledge the existence of Jory anyway, let alone decide if Talan was somehow linked to him. *Right, make a decision woman.* No more shilly-shallying as Jocelyn would say. Rosa grabbed her phone, sat up and pressed *call* on Talan's number. Just when she thought it would go to ansaphone he said,

'Hey, Rosa.' The smile in his voice did nothing to slow her heart rate, but this time excitement rather than nerves fuelled the race. 'Thanks for your note by the way.' The rich tones in his voice along with her memory of the rest of him had her tongue-tied. 'Rosa?'

'Oh, yes, sorry, I almost dropped the phone. Sorry, sorry.' God, apologising three times, how cringeworthy; and her voice sounded like a squeaky wheel.

'I'm at work at the moment, that's why I almost didn't answer. And my Aunt Clare is glaring at me.'

He gave a wicked chuckle and Rosa pictured his little slate arrowhead eyebrow-ring rocking to and fro, his face, lit by a smile and perhaps covered with dark stubble, and those eyes, those lovely eyes… All of a sudden aware that she had still said nothing, she snapped her mind back to the call and said, 'Your aunt works at Pendennis Castle?'

'No, I'm at Tintagel today. She works in the shop with me.' Rosa thought she could hear a woman's voice chuntering in the background. 'Um, you spoke to her the first night when we were all in the Land Rover and she says she met you in the shop the day after too.'

Really? That *awful* woman was Talan's auntie? 'Oh, yes … I remember.' There was no way she was saying that the woman was nice when she so wasn't, even if they were related. Talan must have noticed her less than enthusiastic tone.

'Yes, she does leave that impression sometimes,' Talan said and chuckled again. Then Rosa heard a door close. 'Don't worry I'm in the stock room now, she can't hear us. Clare's a lovely woman when she wants to be. It's just not often that she wants to be.'

Rosa laughed too. It was as if he'd read her mind. Then she stopped laughing and wondered if he had the same sense as her. That was the link? But no, mind-reading wasn't a part of it all, was it? The static on the line brought her back again. Talan must think she was a complete bozo just babbling, laughing and then falling silent all over the place.

'I'm sure she has her reasons for being … er … shall we say, a bit prickly?' She said, hoping that wasn't too disrespectful.

'Ha! A bit and then some. Listen, Rosa I have to go in a mo as she's alone in the shop and there's a coachload of kids just arrived. Can I pick you up from Lewis's tomorrow morning at around ten? Or is that too early?'

'That would be perfect. I can't wait.'

'Me either. See you then'

I can't wait? I can't bloody wait? Rosa groaned. What was she thinking? One minute she's dumbstruck, the next babbling, the next gushing like a silly schoolgirl. The fact that it was true, she couldn't wait to see him again, was neither here nor there.

* * *

Saturday morning and all was far from well. Nothing looked right. The meagre wardrobe that Rosa had hastily shoved into her small suitcase had been tried on, mixed, matched and then flung to the four corners of the bedroom. After the call to Talan yesterday, she'd felt in high spirits, in fact as soon as she'd heard his voice, really. And since her meeting with Jory, the burden of uncertainty had been lifted, so as a result she'd thrown caution to the wind. The rest of Friday had been spent wandering around Tingtagel spending money on clothes, knick- knacks and hand-made Cornish chocolate as if there was no tomorrow.

Rosa had grabbed things from the rail because she'd liked them, not for any other real reason, certainly not with any practicality in mind. But then none of those items were supposed to be worn while she was here. Jeans, a T-shirt and a warmer top for if the weather turned, should have sufficed for a day walking along the cliff tops, but the red, high-necked, no-nonsense top that Rosa had imagined would be fine last night, had somehow mysteriously covered itself in grease from the fish and chips she'd had the other day.

The offending garment was snatched up again and held to the light. No. There was no way she'd get away with that huge blob of fat the size of Jupiter splattered across the left breast. The trouble was, the other tops were dirty and the five new tops she'd bought were either long-sleeved (too hot for summer), sparkly, or low cut. One was all three. Why hadn't she checked on the state of her clothes more carefully?

117

An emerald, low-cut silky top that she'd flung on the bed caught her eye as she rifled once again through the pile of discarded clothes. Rosa held it in front of her and looked in the mirror. It certainly brought out the jade of her eyes and offset her burnished copper curls.

So, Rosa turned this way and that, *black jeans, this top and sensible walking boots should do it.* The top was frivolous, pretty and a little too revealing, but the boots ought to anchor her in the sturdy and non-flirtatious … shouldn't they? Talan mustn't be given the wrong impression; she needed to find out just where he fitted into all this 'spiritual hoo ha'. Her reflection raised an eyebrow and she quickly turned away.

* * *

Outside on the pavement for only five-minutes and Rosa had felt like fleeing back to the safety of her room. There were so many questions running around her head she could hardly order them into a coherent list. What if she got tongue-tied like on the phone, or conversely, what if she talked too much, babbling on about his appearance or something, like she had that very first day? Rosa felt heat creep up her neck as she remembered his expression when she'd asked him what the little arrowhead eyebrow-ring was made from.

What if he thought she looked tarty in that top? How would she approach his resemblance to Jory and if he knew of him, without giving away the fact that Jory was actually dead? Also, once she admitted that he was dead, but that she could talk to spirits, wouldn't Talan dump her on the side of the road and drive off in a cloud of dust?

She sighed and told herself that they'd had a lovely time at the pub until Dan ruined it, so why the heck was she worrying? It would be sensible just to see what happened, abandon any semblance of a plan and it would all work out…

Talan pulled up to the curb in a rather fetching silver Saab convertible and pushed his windswept hair from his forehead. He grinned and leaned across to open the passenger door and Rosa noted his subtle but appreciative sweep of her entire body. As she bent down to pick up her bag and fleece, she also noted his not so subtle look at her cleavage, but then what did she expect? He was a man.

Rosa on the other hand, certainly hadn't noticed the definition of his muscular body and arms under his light-blue shirt as he'd leaned across, or how his black jeans hugged his strong thighs. Nor had she noticed that his stubble was back, accentuating the dimple in his chin, nor the sparkle in those blue eyes, nor the tangle of dark waves tapering to chestnut on the ends ... nor his sensuous mouth which was now saying something.

'Sorry?' She said as she slid into her seat and clipped her seatbelt in place.

'I said you look lovely. The green brings out your eyes.' Talan smiled and pulled away from the curb.

'I know it's not really appropriate to go walking in, but I didn't have anything else.' Rosa knew she ought to shut up, just say thank you and leave it at that, but it seemed her babbling mode had jammed on high-speed. 'The red one I planned on wearing had a stain and the others were ... your hair seems even lighter on the ends today. Have you been out in the sun?' Lord, what *was* she saying?

Talan laughed. 'You do have a way of jumping around in a conversation don't you?' He turned at the roundabout and headed out of Tintagel. 'I have been out in the sun as it happens. Done lots of walking outside the castle in my Pendennis job.'

'Oh, that's nice. The blue brings out your eyes too. Though of course your eyes are darker than your shirt and ... so how long will it take to get to Bedruthan?' Rosa could hardly believe her own ears. Tongue-tied was much the better option.

Again he laughed and looked across at her. 'Thanks for the compliment. And it will take about forty minutes or so.'

For most of that time Rosa had been happy to let Talan do the talking. He'd talked mostly about his job, prompted by one short question after the other. Short questions were the way forward Rosa decided, and she'd just chipped in now and again with *Oh that's nice*, and *how interesting*, and once or twice with *remarkable*.

On fast stretches of road, they hadn't been able to say much anyway with the roof down Rosa wished she'd brought a hair band and shuddered to think what she'd look like when they got out of the damned car.

Overall it had been fairly easy to control her babbling, as she'd just pinch her arm when she'd felt the urge to say something daft, plus the fact that they had little eye-contact as he was driving. Eye-contact with Talan wasn't conducive to maintaining a level head. Perhaps she'd ask him to wear a blindfold when they were having lunch

They drove down a long narrow road and a guy popped out of a ticket booth at the end to receive Talan's National Trust pass. Then the car turned into a gravelly car park and pulled up outside a long barn-like building which turned out to be the cafe where they'd eat later.

'Here we are. Can't wait to show you the view from the end there.' Talan pointed to where a group of backpackers were headed.

The view was certainly spectacular. They wound down through a narrow path flanked by heather, knapweed and Cornish daisies, to find a panoramic vista of a coastline reminiscent of the stretch between San Simeon and Monterey, California Rosa had been there once or twice in her job and apart from a lighthouse (Trevose ,Talan had informed her) on the far peninsula, she could be looking at Big Sur.

Huge cliffs swept down to the ocean and jagged rocks poked from the surface like the spine of some ancient sea monster. 'This place is absolutely stunning, Talan I will definitely make some notes to add to my piece on Tintagel.'

'So you *are* writing a piece then?' He led the way down towards some steep steps.

'Not yet, but I'm planning to. I told my boss I'd combine business with pleasure.' It was certainly pleasurable watching Talan's bum in those jeans.

'And will I appear in the pleasure bit?'

Rosa wondered again if he was bloody telepathic but said, 'No. You might get too big for your boots and you need to be steady on your feet walking down there.'

It came as a bit of a relief to Rosa that the tide was in, as Talan had apparently expected to walk down the Bedruthan Steps to a tiny beach below. She had imagined that the steps they had just walked down along the cliff top were the ones he'd mentioned to her on the drive down, but no. There were more, beyond a viewpoint where tourists were having their photos taken against the backdrop of the wild coastline and impossibly blue ocean. Just looking over the railing at the sheer winding steps with the waves bashing at their foot made her stomach turn over. It had been a little hair-raising walking up the steps to the castle at Tintagel, but these steps were way beyond reason.

'Damn it.' Talan's little arrowhead rocked as his forehead creased into a frown. 'I was going to check the tide times but then got distracted. What a shame you won't get chance to go down to the little beach. It's lovely down there. There are caves and rock pools to explore, you'd have loved it.'

'I'm sure I would have loved it once I was down there, but getting down there is quite something else.' Rosa nodded at the steps and shuddered.

'The steps are quite safe.' Talan smiled.

'Oh I'm sure they are. But don't feel disappointed for me; I can live without seeing the beach. Why don't we take a walk along the cliff path?'

'Which way do you want to go? There's a nice beach in both directions, but I think walking to our left is better as it won't take as long to get there and back. Thought we'd eat at the cafe around one?'

'Sounds good to me.' In fact, anything he said sounded good.

He could be reading the phone book and Rosa would be rapt. Thankfully though, her crazy babbling and relentless questioning had given way to a more relaxed conversational manner. Rosa smiled to herself and followed Talan's long easy strides along the track. It must be because of the sea air and the calming effect of nature.

Once or twice as they walked, Rosa wondered how she would broach the subject of Jory, but mostly she just gave in to the moment and enjoyed how being outside by the ocean continued to lifted her spirits. Being with Talan had a similar effect she was beginning to realise. This at once thrilled and worried her. It had been a long time since she'd felt like this; in fact, she wondered if she ever had enjoyed being in a man's company so much But then, once she'd found out how to contact Daisy and passed on Jory's message, London and work would be calling.

There was no way she could have a relationship with Talan, even if it was something they might both want. London wasn't on the moon, but coupled with all the travelling for her work it would make seeing Talan almost impossible.

He had stopped a little way ahead and lifted his arm to beckon her to the edge of a cliff. Rosa realised she'd dawdled behind, her mind idling over something that would never happen Such thoughts about this man were fantasy and belonged in a happy-ever-after type novel. A thought of beloved Jocelyn, leaving before her time and never having lived it with Jory, brought a lump to her throat. Life wasn't a novel – far from it.

Catching up to Talan, she looked to where he pointed and was delighted to see far below a stunning expanse of yellow sand and blue ocean, headed on each side by green-topped rocky promontories. Rosa shielded her eyes to watch little ant-sized people walking along the cliff path, winding behind and before like an ochre ribbon.

She nudged Talan and pointed across the beach 'See those people on the hill, Talan? They look so tiny, like little ants.'

'Well, duh,' he said playfully, nudging her back. 'That's because they're far away and we look just the same to them'

Rosa gave him a withering look. 'I do realise that you know.'

'Really?' Talan's face showed no emotion 'I thought you actually imagined they were ant-people.' He laughed at her bewildered expression and added, 'God, you are so easy to wind up.'

'No, I just refuse to laugh at such a lame response.' Rosa smiled and shifted her gaze to the beach below.

'What's this beach called?' Rosa asked

'Mawgan Porth. There's a few nice cafes and shops here too. It's a great little place.'

'Shall we go down to it?'

Talan looked at his watch. 'There's not much time really if we are going to eat back at Bedruthan We'll come here another time if you like. Come on, I'm starving.' He turned back up the way they'd come before she could respond, and that was a blessing because she could feel her tongue attempting to tie itself in a knot. Another time implied that he was planning a future date. But was that a good thing or a bad thing? *Just wipe it from your mind, Rosa and take things as they come.* She took a deep breath and hurried after him along the path

CHAPTER 12

$\mathcal{A}$ whole egg, half an apple, tomatoes, cucumber, radishes, lettuce, a pickled onion, a huge home-made roll and butter, a pot of relish and enough ham to service a supermarket deli sat on the plate in front of Rosa She smiled at the waiter and then once he was out of earshot hissed to Talan, 'My God, I chose a simple ham-salad not the last supper!'

He laughed and looked at his own towering plate. 'I forgot how generous these portions were.' Then he took a big bite out of his burger. 'Delwishious, poo.'

Rosa nearly spat a mouthful of cider out. 'Delicious poo? That's disgusting!' She laughed and dabbed a napkin to her mouth.

Talan nearly choked too, stifling a laugh while trying to swallow his food. 'No, not poo! I actually meant to say—'

'Too, yes, I knew that. You are SO easy to wind up' Rosa flashed a smile and felt a giggle in her belly.

Talan raised an eyebrow, made his face blank and said, 'I will not dignify that with a response.'

Rosa looked into his twinkly eyes full of mischief and felt her heart pick up a pace. She looked down at her plate and wondered whether she was about to babble or become mute again. 'Do you know, I think that the radish is one of the most underrated vegetables on the planet? I never buy them, but when I do eat them I always wonder why not.' She pointed over his shoulder at the wall surrounding the lovely garden of the cafe they were sitting in 'Wow, that seagull is massive!'

Talan turned to look at the gull, put his head on one side, shrugged and turned his attention back to his burger. The gull was just the same size as any regular gull and Rosa knew it. Her brain apparently had decided that it would be a perfect distraction however to give its owner time to regain her composure after being caught in the sweep of Talan's debilitating gaze.

Taking a forkful of the ham, Rosa looked over Talan's shoulder to the lovely view beyond the garden wall. In the distance, Trevose Lighthouse stood sentinel on the headland and a tumble of farmland stretched down to meet it. Perfect. The sun, now high in the sky, was hot, though not oppressive, and a fresh sea breeze caressed her skin maintaining a perfect temperature for eating al fresco. Rosa swallowed and smiled across at Talan. Just at this moment everything was perfect ... the view, the food, the setting ... the man.

'So when do you go back to London?'

Oh great. Put a damper on the whole thing why don't you, Talan? Though he did look a bit sad when he said it she thought. 'Erm, not sure.' *What the hell should she say next?* On this perfect day, this was a perfect time to mention Jory, but it felt so wrong. 'Let's say it depends on a few things.' *Even greater, why was she being so enigmatic? Now he was bound to ask more awkward questions.*

'Sounds mysterious.' Talan dabbed at his perfect mouth and smiled. 'Am I allowed in on these "few things"?'

Now he was looking at her with those eyes, those eyes that seemed to be able to reduce her to a babbling mess one minute, or a mute the next. Eyes which could reach into her soul and draw her feelings out like a magician pulls coloured hankies from his mouth. Rosa pretended to choke on a bit of boiled egg and took a long drink of cider. Valuable thinking time. 'No mystery, Talan. Just things I need to get straight in my head, you know?'

'Perhaps sharing them might help.' Talan folded his arms, leaned them on the table and added, 'I'm a good listener.'

Panic poked her in the ribs. What would she say to that? Like a life-line, Jocelyn's image passed through Rosa's frantic mind on the end of a succession of jumbled thoughts and Rosa grabbed at her.

'It's to do with my gran mostly. She spent a wonderful summer week here many years ago... and I ...' A tightrope presented itself. On one side was the whole truth and a drop to a possible very sticky end, on the other was partial truth and a nice fluffy landing in a marshmallow cloud. 'I'm here to have quiet time to think about her, to relive her memories in a way.' The marshmallow cloud slipped under Rosa's bottom. 'You see ... she's terminally ill.'

Talan reached out for her hand, his lovely face growing immediately serious. 'Oh, you poor thing. Sorry for prying. I didn't mean to upset you.'

The marshmallow cloud disintegrated as Rosa's conscience stabbed her in the gut. The poor guy looked genuinely mortified. 'Oh please, don't feel bad. I didn't want to mention it as it tends to put a damper on a conversation. Just thought you should know why I'm not sure if I'm ready to leave yet.' She gave him what she hoped was a winning smile and squeezed his hand.

'Thank you. And I promise for the rest of the afternoon we'll just talk about nice things, eh?' Talan lifted her hand to his lips and placed a soft kiss on the back of it.

Though an innocent action, Rosa felt a tingle of excitement in a place she'd forgotten about, it had been so long. 'I think that would be a good idea. I like nice things,' she said, and this time dared to look him straight in the eyes.

* * *

As the afternoon turned to early evening, Talan's car came to a stop at the traffic lights in Tintagel village. Inside it, the atmosphere felt light and full of expectation. Like a needy child, the happy day the occupants had spent together hugged them close, reluctant to leave their sides.

'Would you like to go for a drink later? Or you could pop into mine for a coffee now if you like?' Talan's voice was calm, measured, though Rosa could sense a tumult of emotion running just under the surface. Was 'in for coffee' the old cliché for sex? If it was, what did she think about that?

She heard herself say, 'Coffee would be grand, thanks.'

As he pulled away from the lights she immediately regretted her answer. The reality of a long-distance relationship pushed at the edges of her mind for the second time that day. Admittedly, she was extremely drawn to him and her body had sent her brain not too subtle messages all day, but she was and never had been a quick fling type of girl.

Rosa watched Talan's long fingers manoeuvre the gear stick as he eased his car into his driveway, then the silence without the hum of the engine became almost palpable. Talan leaned over and kissed her on the cheek, his breath warm, the salty smell of the outdoors on his skin.

'You know, the invite for coffee wasn't meant in a crass way. I felt the tension in you immediately afterwards.' He twirled one of her curls around his index finger and added, 'I would hate such a lovely day to end awkwardly.'

Gorgeous, clever, fun, and now super-sensitive … Was there no flaw in his attributes? Those eyes held hers like a magnet until she forced them to look at the floor. Rosa could see herself falling quickly and hard if she allowed it. So she mustn't. She was here to find Daisy and go. In fact, a straightforward question about her was an excellent way to snap the invisible rope of desire winding itself from her and around Talan - a perfect emotional shield. Jory said she would know who to trust and Talan was almost certainly that.

'No, problem I was wondering though; do you know someone in the village called Daisy? Must be in her fifties now?'

Talan's finger stopped winding her curl and his hand dropped to his knee. He drew back and narrowed his eyes. It was her turn to feel tension rise up like a fortress between their seats.

'Daisy who?'

The cold slate-grey colour of the sea she'd seen the other night had somehow seeped into the blue of Talan's eyes and his look of utter contempt made her forget Jory's surname for a moment. Then it came to her. 'Marrack was her maiden name. No idea if it still is, but I guess she might have been married given her age and—'

'What do you want with her?' Talan's question cut across and jabbed sharp and threatening into her emotional shield. To her horror she felt the suggestion of tears. Where had the lovely warm, sweet Talan gone? He reminded her of a lone wolf; dangerous and angry. Suspicion hooded his eyes.

Telling the whole truth about Jory in this new situation was unthinkable. 'A friend told me she had a sad past. It was to do with her father's death, but recently new evidence has come to light to suggest that her father didn't die in the way she imagined.'

The frown that furrowed Talan's brow deepened for a few moments as he scanned her face, then he removed it with a slap of the heel of his hand on his forehead. 'So *that's* your angle. How could I have been so stupid to think you were interested in me? You're a journalist after a tearjerker of a story and you want Daisy to tell it.'

'What?' It was her turn to frown and she felt her face grow hot with indignation. 'I'm a travel journalist and—'

'Yeah, course you are.' He leaned across her and threw open the passenger door. 'Get out. For once my Aunt Clare was a good judge of character, and I should have listened. Scum, the lot of you!'

'Now hang on a minute …' Anger swelled in Rosa's breast as he ignored her, popped her seatbelt and threw her bag onto the driveway.

'Out. Now.' His voice rasped as if he was choking back tears or fury.

Rosa looked at the loathing in his eyes and guessed it was the latter. 'Don't worry I'm gone.' She leapt out of the car and yelled as she slammed door. 'You have it all wrong; I would never do something like that!' She watched him slam his own door and stalk away towards his flat, his back ramrod straight. Damn it. How could he even think she was some kind of unscrupulous newshound?

Rosa took a few tentative steps after him, threw her arms wide and shouted, 'Hey, you obviously know Daisy … please believe me when I say I genuinely just want to help her!'

Talan wheeled round his face contorted with rage is eyes aflame and jabbed a finger at her. 'Help? Ha! Yes, that's what you lot said when it first happened. Don't you *ever* speak her name again, and if you don't piss off *right* now I'll call the police.'

Left stunned in the middle of his driveway, she stared at his closed front door and noticed a few passers-by staring at her and talking behind their hands. Rosa picked up her bag and blindly ran up the road towards Lewis's. She wanted to lock herself in, crawl under the duvet and protect herself from the confusion of feelings that hooked claws in and tore at her heart and mind.

Rosa hated him for the way he made her feel – he thought she was a dirty cheap parasite, when in fact she was wronged, terribly wronged. God knew who Daisy was to him, but he should have at least heard her out. It was obvious that Talan didn't know Rosa at all. This romantic attachment she'd imagined - a bond, affinity, an understanding - was all false.

It seemed that there was no flaw in Talan's attributes after all. The damage had gone way beyond that – not a flaw but a gaping hole.

CHAPTER 13

$\mathcal{U}$nable to cope with the relentless bombardment of questions, thoughts and blow-by-blow reliving of the showdown with Talan, Rosa's mind had shut down and cocooned in her duvet she'd slept. Now a tapping at the door nudged her mind into consciousness again and still wrapped in the duvet she shuffled across the floor.

'Hello?'

'Surprise!'

Rosa leaned her forehead against the wood and sighed quietly. She wanted to wave a wand and make the person outside the door disappear, but not even Morganna had one of those. Buggeration and bollocks, there was nothing she could do about it. Flinging open the door she drew a smile from the bottom of a deep well and splashed it across her mouth.

'Willa! What the bloody hell are you doing here?'

A beaming Willa pushed past and bounced onto Rosa's bed like an unruly puppy. Rosa half expected a wagging tail to suddenly appear from the back of her jeans. 'I decided to pop down for a few days and I'm in the room just across the landing.' Willa's voice bubbled with excitement.

'But how did you find me?' Rosa asked through a rictus smile, wishing with all her heart that Willa had not.

Willa giggled. 'I hardly had to be Poirot, darling!' The upper-class accent was often allowed free rein when speaking to Rosa as she knew the truth of her background. 'You had doodled the name and number on that little pad by the phone in the kitchen. I expected that there would only be one Lewis's in Tintagel.'

'When you say a few days—'

'Yep, this weekend and Monday. If I want longer, I'll just ring up my boss.' Willa noticed the balcony and went to have a look at the view. Over her shoulder she asked, 'Why, aren't you pleased to see me?'

Rosa wanted to say, *No, please leave. My state of mind has no place for a twenty-six-year-old teenager*. Instead she said, 'Of course, but I don't know how much longer I will be here, that's all—'

'No matter. I expect I'll be surfing most of the time anyway. You know me, where there's a Willa there's—'

'A wave … yes.'

'And guess what? I bought an old V Dub camper and a new surfboard to put on top!

'Slumming it again I see,' Rosa muttered into the duvet.

'How cool is that?' Willa waved an arm at the view. 'My God, this is heavenly.' She looked Rosa up and down only now taking in the dishevelled appearance and the tightly-wrapped duvet. 'Why were you asleep at six in the evening?'

Rosa shrugged and sat on the edge of her bed. If only she knew. 'I have been busy these last few days.'

'But it's only six o' clock, woman!' Willa bounded over and knelt at her feet. 'It looks like I turned up just in time. Get showered, dressed and we'll hit this town!'

Willa's shining eyes and 'kid-at-Christmas' expectation managed to splash a real smile across Rosa's mouth this time. 'This is Tintagel, not Las Vegas.'

'There you go with your old woman attitude. You have to make things happen Rosa, not wait around for things to happen to you.'

Rosa really wanted to shock Willa by spilling everything that had happened to her since her arrival, but instead she just smiled. There was no way she was breathing a word.

'Now you look like the bloody Mona Lisa with that enigmatic

little smile.' Willa put her head on one side and lightly rested her hand on Rosa's cheek. 'You okay, hon?'

Rosa stood and walked to the bathroom. In her vulnerable state if Willa was nice to her she might cry. She paused, her hand on the door frame. 'I'm fine, just had an emotional time.' *True.* 'Seeing all the places that Gran loved has drained me a bit I guess.' *Also true.*

'Oh you poor, love.' Willa got off her knees and puffed out her cheeks. 'Did you find out anything, you know, about why Jocelyn wanted you to come here?'

'No, nothing. I think it was just so she could feel like she was here again, through me, you know?' *Big fat lie.*

* * *

Against her better judgement, Rosa had allowed Willa to persuade her to go out for a drink. If only her better judgement had been a bit more forceful she wouldn't be sitting on a wall in the middle of the town, bemoaning the fact that the chip shop was closed and feeling decidedly squiffy.

She had enjoyed allowing the booze to numb her nagging brain though and Willa had been very good fun. It had been bliss not to talk about spirits, special-senses, the past, how to track down Daisy and of course, Talan. His name was the last thing she wanted on her lips – it would leave a bitter taste. Willa had asked if she'd met anyone interesting and she'd skimmed over Morganna but that was all.

The only pub they'd not visited was the Tintagel Arms, much to Willa's puzzlement, but she'd been happy with a story about poor service. Right now, her platinum blond crew cut was sticking up in spikes due to the continuous raking of its owner's fingers. Willa put her forefinger to her lips and wobbled back up the road from where she'd been peering into the chip shop window.

'Shh. Stop going on about food. I just looked again and there's no light on, so no ships.' She giggled. 'Chips not ships! Anyone would think I'd had a drink.' She raked her hair again 'I need food and my head feels like it's up there floating with the moon'

'Mine is right next to yours, can you see it?' Rosa pointed to the silver crescent, its space shared with a myriad diamonds in a navy sky.

'Yep.' Willa slid down the wall and lay prone on the pavement looking up. 'Jeepers the sky down here is magnif... magnifish ... bloody marvellous!' she finished with a guffaw.

Rosa copied Willa's earlier gesture and put her finger to her lips as she noticed a column of light shine from behind a lifted curtain in a nearby house. 'Shh It is indeed. Now come on, we should get back. I think I have some biscuits in my room'

Willa remained where she was and folded her arms across her chest. 'Oscar Wilde was a clever bloke wasn't he?'

Rosa sighed. 'I love his work, but I fail to see what he has to do with this particular converslation'

'Converslation? Anyone would think that you'd had a drink too.' Willa struggled to her knees and pointed at the sky. 'He wrote that brilliant poem about the gutter and the stars didn't he? I always dug that one, but I really get what he meant now.'

Rosa laughed and made a V with her middle and index fingers. 'Peace man, you really dug it, man Faar out.'

Willa held on to the wall and heaved herself upright, her face poker straight. 'Are you mocking me, fair maiden?'

Rosa could tell she was barely holding back a torrent of laughter and her eyes danced with mischief. 'Seems that way,' she said and took a few steps in the direction of the B&B.

Willa pounced, swinging her round by the arm. 'I demand that you apologise for mocking me forthwith, otherwise it will be pistols at dawn!' she yelled and pretended to slap Rosa on both cheeks with an imaginary handkerchief.

The sight of Willa's sticky up hair and ridiculously silly expression set Rosa off laughing. After a few seconds she became worried that she might not be able to stop and struggled to get her breath and control her hysterics. Just as she managed it, Willa adopted a boxer's pose and danced around the pavement jabbing the air.

'Stop, Willa!' Rosa begged, holding her stomach as the giggles burst forth again

'Pud 'em up and fight me, damn you!' Then Willa also collapsed in a laughing fit and the two women leaned on each other for support as hysteria claimed them

A man walking his dog huffed and tutted as he stepped around them on the pavement and Rosa looked up to apologise but the man had hurried on Another man watched them from across the street however, a man with a look of disgust on his face. Rosa put her hand over her mouth but the laughter was long gone. Nothing was funny anymore and she suddenly felt very sober. Talan turned up the collar of his jacket, turned on his heel and walked on

'Who was that? Do you know him?' Willa said wiping tears of laughter from her cheeks.

Rosa shook her head and slipped her arm through Willa's. 'No. I don't know him at all.' *True.*

CHAPTER 14

$\mathscr{A}$fter the deluge overnight, the newly-showered shrubs hugging the path that wound down to Tintagel Castle stretched their vibrant blooms to the calm blue sky. Willa kept stopping to alternately inhale the heady scent of the flowers and then the fresh salt air. She adored everything to do with the coast and wanted to whoop her joy to the heavens. Convention wouldn't allow it however and so she contented herself with a skip in her walk and a merry tune in her head.

Proximity to the sea wasn't the only reason she felt so joyful this morning. What fun the two of them had had last night! Willa couldn't remember Rosa ever really getting drunk before. Yes, she'd seen her tipsy, but the way she'd thrown back her head and laughed out loud in the middle of the street had shown a crazy side that Willa liked. But then Willa liked everything about Rosa

Being apart from her this past week had been intolerable and even this morning when still in bed Rosa had declined a visit to the castle, dark circles under her eyes, her auburn hair a nest, her breath sour with alcohol, Willa still thought she was the most beautiful woman in the world. Of course she knew such worship was futile, but there was nothing she could do to alter her feelings. God knows she'd tried. Just to be close to Rosa was enough A sad little smile passed across Willa's mouth Okay, it wasn't, but it would have to do

At the end of the path, the sight of the ruined castle clinging to the cliff top, the sunlit waves and the gulls screaming into the wind was just all too much. Willa bounced on the balls of her feet, punched the air and whooped at the top of her lungs. A few knots of visitors gingerly climbing the steps to the castle grabbed the rail and swivelled their heads as one towards her. She laughed and waved enjoying the bubbles of excitement popping in her belly. An elderly couple sipping coffee outside the cafe shielded their eyes and regarded her as if she was something distasteful they'd found on their shoes. Willa laughed and waved at them too.

'Isn't this a marvellous place? Makes you feel so alive!'

The couple looked at each other and the woman shifted her chair slightly putting her back to Willa. Willa didn't mind though. Nothing could bring her down today.

A rather stunning woman with dark silky hair looked up from behind the counter inside the gift shop. Her nutmeg brown eyes alert and intelligent and a half-smile graced her full mouth.

'Hello, my name is Willa and I am delighted to be here! Can I get a ticket for the castle please?'

The woman raised an eyebrow at this less than orthodox entrance, but when she smiled Willa could tell it was genuine. 'My name is Kate and we are delighted to have you.'

Willa paid for her ticket and wandered around the shop picking up this and that. Perhaps Rosa might like a little gift to make her hangover feel better? Nothing seemed appropriate though. A display cabinet caught her eye across the room and placing her hand on the glass door, Willa looked at the small selection of jewellery inside. A pair of jade teardrop earrings just shouted *Rosa* and she asked Kate to open the cabinet.

The earrings nestled against the velvet black of the box looked just perfect and Willa took it from Kate's palm. 'They are lovely. I'll take them.'

Kate nodded. 'They are beautiful. Not sure how much they are I'll just have a look—'

'Don't bother; I want them for a special friend of mine. They match her eyes exactly.'

Kate looked at the price tag and walked back to the till. 'Lucky friend. Are they for her birthday?'

'Nope.' Willa scrubbed her knuckles across the top of her hair and grinned sheepishly. 'Just to cheer her up. Rosa and I had a boatload of booze last night.'

Willa noted the warmth leave Kate's eyes and her hands quickly slapped the box into a bag as if it was too hot to handle. 'Rosa? She's the one up from London?'

Taken aback by both the change in Kate and the fact that she knew Rosa, Willa said quietly. 'Yes, that's right. You know her?'

'No. I met her briefly when she first arrived but she *has* made quite an impression on my work colleague.' Kate held out her hand for Willa's credit card and shoved it into the machine as if it had offended her.

Nausea tickled the walls of Willa's stomach. Perhaps it was a delayed reaction from overindulgence, perhaps not. She grew hot and wanted to take a few deep breaths of cleansing sea air but she wanted to know more about this work colleague of Kate's more.

'Did she? Is your work colleague here?'

'No, he's off today.' Kate waved a hand at the machine.

Willa punched in her PIN with the same amount of force as Kate had inserted the card, her gut twisting. 'What kind of an impression?' She tried to make her voice light but she was fooling nobody.

'I'm not entirely sure, but if I had to bet on it I'd say that Talan is well and truly taken with her.' Kate handed the card back and folded her arms, the warmth of her original persona forming ice around the edges. 'He took her for a drink apparently and was very relieved to find she'd not yet returned home the other night.'

Willa swallowed and felt jealousy like a pit of vipers writhing within her, spitting venom, poisoning her lovely morning. Rosa had never mentioned this, this Talan or Talon, whatever he was called. Stupid name. Who did he think he was, a bird of prey?

Willa could tell Kate had more for her and could practically see the woman's own vipers flick their tongues behind the nutmeg eyes. The poor woman had obviously got a huge thing for this Talan guy.

'Funny, Rosa never mentioned going out for a drink with anyone since she's been here.'

Kate gave her a look and snorted. 'According to his aunt, your friend and he were out together yesterday too.'

The way that Kate had said the word friend was full of innuendo. Okay, Willa had perhaps given a clue when she'd said Rosa was a special friend and her short cropped hair and make-up free face could have helped Kate form a stereotypical opinion about her sexuality. Nevertheless, there was no need for rudeness.

A wave of nausea rippled again and instead of going to the door for air and leaving the whole thing at that, a particularly large viper sank its teeth into her heart. 'Well, she wouldn't be interested in him in 'that way' of course. Rosa is my partner.'

Relief quashed the vipers in Kate's eyes and she nodded twice as if internally congratulating herself on her assumptions. 'Romantically, I take it?'

'Yes.' Willa said quietly. At the door she turned and added. 'Sorry to disappoint your colleague, but Rosa would have gone out with him as a friend, nothing more.'

Kate all smiles nodded again and raised her hand in goodbye. 'I'll be sure to put him straight.'

Willa stepped out into the wind and muttered to herself, 'Oh, I know you will.'

* * *

The blood draining from Rosa's face and yell of protest as Willa wafted a hot pasty under her nose helped her mood a little. At that precise moment she wanted Rosa to suffer; after all, learning of her dates with this Talon had made Willa feel pretty bloody dreadful. Her trip had been ruined, just when she thought they were getting

138

on better than ever. Willa's walk around the castle had been taken with a head full of Rosa, her eyes blankly staring ahead, oblivious to the sights at every turn and the history under her feet.

'For God's sake, take that disgusting thing away from me!' Rosa wrinkled her nose and opened the doors to her balcony. Willa noted that her hands shook as she grasped the railing outside and sat down on a stool.

'Oh, dear. Still feeling a bit worse for wear, sweetcheeks?' Willa flashed a smile and took a big mouthful, rubbing her tummy in exaggerated enjoyment. 'My goodness, that is so yummy!'

'Seriously, Willa, if you keep this up I swear I'll vomit.'

'That bad, eh?' Willa took another bite, moved away and adopted a cross-legged position on the middle of Rosa's bed. 'But then I guess you don't drink much, do you?'

'Not like I did last night.'

'So you haven't been out for a drink the whole time you've been here then?' Willa cracked open a can of coke.

A hand to her head Rosa said,' Um … not really. I had a drink with a meal once or twice.'

'So you haven't met any strapping local men to whisk you off for a night of cider and sex?'

Rosa gave her a withering look. 'I told you I hadn't met anyone and even if I had, sex wouldn't have been on the cards. Well, not until I got to know them better.'

Eyes shut Willa tipped back her head and took a long swallow from the can. This denial was killing her and she wondered how much longer she'd be able to keep up the happy-go-lucky act. If there was nothing behind Rosa meeting this guy for a drink, then why was she hiding it? Willa belched and wiped her mouth on the back of her hand. In fact, she was more than hiding it, she was blatantly lying to her bloody face, wasn't she?

Rosa glanced across at her. 'What's up? You look like you want to do murder.'

'Do I?' Willa mustered a smile. 'No, just thinking about catching a few waves. You wanna come with?'

'I can't surf, as you well know.' Rosa managed a watery smile in return.

'Then it's time you learnt.'

'Yeah, right. Can you imagine me on a surf board today in this state?'

'It would do you good and you need something to eat.' Willa got off the bed. 'Okay, if not a pasty, then a sandwich or something? It's past noon.'

'No I couldn't face it. I'll just sit here and sip my water. Perhaps if you stop by this evening I will be better.'

Willa detected a note of irritation under the polite reply that set her teeth on edge. So now madam wanted her to go, she was dismissed – an inconvenience. Just when Willa imagined they were the best of friends she realised that Rosa couldn't really give a shit about her. Friends don't lie to each other do they? A pang of guilt about what she'd told Kate earlier nudged her. Friends don't tell lies about each other to strangers either, do they? She scrubbed her knuckles over her hair. Perhaps she was being a tad unreasonable.

'I won't hear of leaving you alone, oh poorly one.' Willa walked over and put her hand on Rosa's shoulder but she flinched under her touch and shifted position.

'No. I really *would* feel much better if you did. I need to sleep.' The irritation in Rosa's voice was clear now.

A lump of anger and hurt burned in her chest and Willa knew she had to leave before she gave the game away. Coming here had been a bad idea. It was time she grew up, faced facts, stopped reading things into situations that weren't there. Last night when they had held each other weak with laughter, Willa imagined that Rosa had brushed her lips against her cheek when she leaned her head on her shoulder. When she'd flinched and shrugged off her hand it put paid to that notion. And it was just a notion wasn't it? The kiss hadn't happened. It was wishful thinking - fantasy.

Willa loved Rosa yes, but there was no way she would ever feel the same way about her. She knew it before she came, knew it last night ... had always known it. So why then did she continue to torture herself with futile hope on the one hand, and ideas that friendship would be enough on the other? *Because you're a bloody fool, Willa, that's why.*

Suddenly aware she was staring into Rosa's puzzled eyes, she said in a small voice, 'Sorry, sweetheart, miles away. I'll go and blow my cobwebs away down the coast. Might see you later.'

'Okay, have a nice time,' Rosa said and turned her face to the view.

Willa placed a kiss on her palm and blew it toward the balcony. Then she stepped out and closed the door.

CHAPTER 15

$\mathcal{D}$awn submerged her darkest hour beneath the waves and spread her grey cloak along the western horizon, a fireball of sunrise at its clasp. At Rosa's feet a drowsy bee already bumbled amongst clover and primroses, while four gulls hung in the air screaming for the day.

In this light, if she half-closed her eyes, she could almost pretend Jory was sitting next to her on the bench as he'd been the other night. But this time she was quite alone. Having stayed in her room most of yesterday (apart from popping downstairs for a light sandwich in the evening) sleeping and licking her wounds, she'd woken completely refreshed in the early hours and decided to walk up to the church and the bench beyond.

Never had the world smelled so fresh and new. At five-fifteen when dawn had been just a suggestion of light over the hills, Rosa had zipped up her fleece, donned walking boots and revelled in the smell of damp grass underfoot, the occasional birdsong from the hedges, the salt-tang on her lips and the light breeze running its fingers through her hair.

The compulsion to see the church and sit on the bench again had been just one of those intuitive feelings that Rosa had allowed to blossom since she'd rediscovered her special sense. The idea that she'd actually 'see' Jory again in the daylight hadn't occurred to her, though she knew she wanted to be near where he was last on the earth and where they had spoken. Rosa needed guidance and comfort from his remembered presence.

As the sun rose higher, turning the ocean from navy to cobalt and the burnt cinnamon of the rocky crags to yellow ochre, she hoped her mind would find inspiration At the moment she was stumped as to what to do next. Though comforted by being in this spot, Jory had remained quiet, even though she had asked him silent questions.

Talan hadn't been so quiet however. His words crashed in on the waves and in the cry of the gulls. Harsh words and hurtful words. It was hard to believe that he could have imagined her to be an unscrupulous journalist after a story, but Daisy was obviously someone he cared about, someone he didn't want hurt, wanted to protect – someone who had suffered at the hands of journalists in the past judging by his comment 'that's what you lot said last time'. Who was she to him? A friend of his family? An aunt? His mother?

Yesterday her mind had shut down almost, hunkered into the comfort-blanket of sleep, and refused to let her think properly, but now, rapier-like intuition sliced through the fog, delivering clarity and an answer. Her heart thumped in her ears and her mouth grew dry.

Yes. Daisy *was* his mother.

The now familiar rush of adrenalin, static and heat along both arms plus the tingling in her fingers when she sensed something, followed this unspoken statement. So she was certain Daisy was Jory's daughter and her son resembled his grandfather. That's why Talan's eyes were so alike; perhaps they were a family trait?

Rosa took a moment calm herself and absorb this new information Not all questions were answered, nor in which direction she should go next. If Talan had been introduced into her life to lead her to Daisy, then why hadn't he? If he wasn't meant to help her, then why did she bump into him and become so attracted? It didn't make sense.

The sun grew warm on her face and the bee in the clover was shortly joined by others. Glancing at her watch, Rosa was amazed to find that it was eight-thirty. Time had been absent from her life over the last week in as much as she hadn't really checked her watch or had to worry about deadlines. Nature had become her clock, the minutes and hours marked by bird's voices, the wind in her hair and the pull of the tide. Bliss.

All good things had to come to an end however and soon she'd be heading back to London and normality. Rosa stretched her arms above her head and yawned. What was normality though? Everything had changed since coming here – she'd changed. Now she had a special sense, always had of course, but now it was as much a part of her as the other five. Intuition, strong and powerful, was as natural as breathing to her. The tingle in her fingers and heat rushing through her veins when she allowed her sense to guide her actions made her feel alive – useful.

Rosa stood and flopped forward shaking the aches from her body caused by sitting on the hard wooden bench for over two hours. A bee, alarmed at her hair brushing its wings, buzzed in irritation and settled again a little way off. From this upside-down position, the sea became the sky and Rosa wondered what it would be like in a world where the sky rolled in and out all day while the clouds passed over the face of the sea

Time enough for procrastinating and surrealist thoughts once she'd finished her task here. But how to finish it? Jory had said not to ask Morganna about Daisy and to trust her feelings. Hmm, look where that had ended. Perhaps Jory had got it wrong – spirits weren't infallible where they?

To talk to Willa would be as much use as a chocolate tea pot - sensitivity didn't appear to be in her remit. Besides, she'd not popped back to see her last night. Maybe she had taken umbrage after Rosa's not too subtle indication that she wanted to be left alone yesterday.

Standing upright again she unzipped her fleece and set off back past the church and towards the village. Intuition told her to go and see how Willa was and then pop into *Heart's Desire*. After that, there was no road-map or flashing arrows pointing to how she should approach Morganna or the slightest hint of what came next.

In the hallway of Lewis's, she paused to take off her wet boots. John whisked into the dining room opposite with a plate of bacon and eggs, mushrooms, sausage and beans and the delicious aroma had her salivating. Intuition didn't have to tell her that she was hungry and needed her own full-English. Sitting down at her table she waved at John and he came over.

'You look much better than you did yesterday if you don't mind me saying,' John said and gave her a friendly wink.

'I feel it.' A flush of embarrassment tinted Rosa's cheeks. 'Thanks for making me that sandwich out of hours and being so kind.'

'We've all been there, my dear.' John smiled and pulled a notebook out of his apron. 'Now, what can I get you? Your usual?'

'Yes, please, I am starved.'

'Coming up in ten.' John pocketed his order and hurried away but then he stopped at the door. 'Oh, I almost forgot. I have a note for you and a gift – this is becoming a habit.' He grinned. 'I'll bring them with your breakfast.'

Excitement flipped her tummy into a somersault. Talan had written again. And a gift? Did this mean he must be okay with her? She really hoped so. And if he was, it might mean that he was happy to introduce her to Daisy. Perhaps she was getting ahead of herself, but it would be fantastic if she could pass on Jory's message soon – even today maybe!

Rosa's eyes followed John on invisible strings as she demolished her breakfast. He hadn't had chance to grab the note from his study as there was a sudden rush of breakfasters. If he didn't bring it by the end, Rosa would ask politely if she could retrieve it as the suspense was eating her up quicker than she was eating the food. At last he came in holding a lilac envelope aloft and propped it against the coffee pot. By the side he set a tiny black box, complete with a blue bow.

Disappointment flipped her tummy this time. She had seen this handwriting before on countless post-it-notes stuck to the fridge, toaster and kitchen table at home. Willa had written *Rosa* in her flamboyant hand across the centre of the envelope and embellished the *R* and *a* with two tiny rosebuds just as she always did. Chewing the last bit of sausage, she slid a knife under the flap and pulled out a note

Dear Rosa,

Sorry I didn't pop in again yesterday but I got carried away catching the elusive perfect wave – you know how I am! ☺ Anyway, it turns out that my boss can't do without my invaluable services for one more day so I have set off home already. We had a great time the other night, didn't we? What larks!

See you when you get back, much love, W xxx

Rosa sighed and stuffed the note into her pocket. Well at least she didn't sound grumpy, one less thing to worry about when she returned to 'normality'. She lifted the lid on the box and looked at a pair of jade earrings. Pretty, but she wished Willa hadn't. It wasn't Christmas or her birthday, a gift like this made her feel uncomfortable. Rosa drained her cup, went to her room to freshen up and then set off in the direction of *Heart's Desire*.

* * *

Morganna looked a little on the flustered side as Rosa pushed open the door. Her raven mane resembled tangled tree roots in some enchanted forest, her eyebrows had been drawn on unevenly and the top buttons of her orange grandad-collar shirt had been fastened higgledy-piggledy. The atmosphere in there felt thick with despair, even the shop bell sounded less like a fairy's entrance and more like a toll by a plague doctor.

'Oh thank God it's you. I couldn't bear anyone else at the moment; it's been all go in here since I opened an hour ago.' Morganna hurried over, flipped the sign on the door to *Closed* and took Rosa by the elbow. 'Come through and we'll have a cuppa.'

Rosa wondered how on earth Morganna ever made any money given the number of times she appeared to shut up shop, though she hadn't locked the door - perhaps hedging her bets. She watched her flap about making the tea, noting that her socks sticking out from under her red silky Indian type trousers were odd. A red and a green one; no shoes.

'What's up? You seem a bit distracted today.' Rosa sat at the kitchen table and shrugged her coat off.

'I am. I barely slept a wink all night, dropped off around four and then slept through the bloody alarm.' Morganna set mugs and a plate of biscuits in front of Rosa 'I didn't even have time to put my make-up on properly.' She touched her eyebrows self-consciously and turned back to the boiling kettle.

'Nor time to put the correct pair of socks on or button up your shirt either, eh?' Rosa raised her eyebrows and bit back a giggle when Morganna noticed her mistakes.

'Bloody hell! No wonder old Tom Hegarty kept looking at my chest when I wrapped up that gift for his granddaughter. I thought my luck was in for a minute!' Morganna hooted and put a pot of tea between them.

'Thank goodness you laughed. I'm not used to this frazzled version of Morganna.' Rosa dipped a biscuit in her tea.

Morganna twisted her tangled roots into a claw-clasp and sighed. 'I'm not normally like this but I've been invited to a birthday party.' Noticing Rosa's puzzled look she added, 'Yes I know that's not normally a problem, but Clare Leadon asked me. We were at school together. We were friends, still are, but we always played a game of one-upmanship.'

'A little old for that now, aren't you?'

'Yes, but it's her that carries it on. She always has to go one better. We've been out for a drink quite often over the last five years since my husband died and hers buggered off. We are good company for each other, but she always gets a new outfit, has her hair and nails done and makes a huge production out of the event.'

Rosa thought about the clothes that Morganna normally wore and put her head on one side. 'Forgive me for saying so, but I wouldn't have thought you would have been bothered about conventional dress and appearance.'

'I'm not. But because of her antics I always get a new outfit too, the more flamboyant the better. Then when we're out, people invariably notice me and not her.' Morganna had the good grace to flush at this and paid particular attention to a knot in the wood table top.

Rosa snorted, nearly choking on her biscuit. 'Sounds like you are as bad as each other!'

'I expect we are.' Morganna conceded, a twinkle in her eye. 'The problem is everyone we know will be at this damned party and I got the dates wrong. I thought it was next Monday but it's tonight and I haven't had time to get anything new! I realised late last night, and that's why I couldn't sleep.'

'But I'm sure you have lots of nice things, you always look stunning, don't worry about it.'

Morganna brightened. 'You say the nicest things. I wondered if you'd come with me … for moral support. I was going to come to find you later but you saved me the bother.'

'Me? Um, I don't really think I would fit in at your friend's party. I mean I don't know anyone and—'

'It's not her party, it's her sister-in-law's. She's turning fifty-five or six I think, so I need someone nearer my own age to be around!' Morganna hooted again.

'I'm twenty-eight, and you are?' Rosa asked raising a brow.

'Fifty-four, but who's counting?'

At the moment Rosa thought Morganna looked more like twelve, her eyes full of mischief, a giggle in her voice. 'Okay, I'll come,' she said shaking her head. 'I haven't anything better to do this evening anyway.' As Morganna yelled her thanks and hugged her across the table, Rosa wondered if there might be someone at the party who knew Daisy. It was certainly possible if 'everyone' was going to be there.

'Brilliant! I'll come by for you at seven?'

'Okay. I'd better get this sister-in-law a card hadn't I? What's her name?'

'That would be nice. Her name's Daisy. She was a year above me and Clare at school, so I don't really know her apart from to say hello to'

The shop bell tinkling sent Morganna scurrying from the kitchen before she could see the shock and surprise register in Rosa's eyes. As she let out a long slow breath and tried to calm her heart-rate, Rosa thought that the phrase *saved by the bell* had never seemed more appropriate.

CHAPTER 16

'So what was your weekend like?' Kate put a cup of coffee down on the counter in front of Talan. He stared out of the shop door at the sheeting rain and fiddled absently with the little arrowhead eyebrow ring. He had heard her question but didn't feel inclined to answer it. In fact, to describe his weekend accurately wouldn't be easy. How would he find the words to describe the fantastic time he'd spent down the coast with Rosa on Saturday, and then the crushing blow of disappointment she'd kicked into his gut as they'd parked outside his flat upon their return? Even if he could put it all into words, he certainly didn't want to share it with Kate.

Kate moved closer to him, pinched her nostrils between her thumb and forefinger and said, 'Earth calling Talan.' She giggled and leaned her forearms on the countertop. She was so close that he could feel her breath on his arm and he knew she was staring right at him. He crushed a sudden urge to tell her to piss off and took a sip of his coffee.

'I said Earth call—'

'Yes, I heard you.' Talan knew his voice was sharp but he didn't care the mood he was in. Saturday was hell, he couldn't even get drunk that evening though he'd tried hard, and Sunday he'd spent in bed comfort eating, watching back-to-back DVDs and licking his wounds. The last thing he wanted was a discussion about it.

'Oh, sorr-ee. Must have been a bloody awful weekend then.' Kate walked round into the shop turned her back to him and began tidying an already tidy display of knights and dragons.

Talan sighed. It wasn't her fault was it? She was just being polite, making conversation with a colleague on this wet Monday morning. 'It wasn't the best, but nothing I want to talk about, thanks.'

Kate turned to face him, folding her arms across her chest and adopting a sympathetic expression. 'Now come on, Tal, you'll feel much better if you get it all off your chest. You've been like a bear with a sore arse since you got here.'

Tal? He hated the shortening of his name and he was beginning to hate this excessive nosiness. 'No. No I really wouldn't and to be honest there's not much to say.' He willed someone to walk through the door but, given the weather, that was unlikely.

The sympathetic expression shifted a little and a knowing look edged into her eyes. Turning slightly, she ran her fingers down a row of greeting cards and said lightly, 'It's obvious that your date on Saturday didn't work out. Shame, I could tell how much you liked Rosa the other night when Dan said she was still in the village.'

Talan felt his neck grow hot and a quiet anger begin in his chest. How the shitting hell did she know about Rosa? And she sounded more gleeful than sorry. 'What do you mean, date?' There was no way he was giving anything away.

Kate looked back at him, her chocolate-brown eyes aflame with curiosity and something else. Something he couldn't quite identify. 'Clare told me she saw you drive past with Rosa on your way out of the village on Saturday.' She tapped a pen against her teeth and added innocently, 'Was she mistaken?'

Talan registered the look in her eyes now. It was a mixture of jealousy and triumph. Damn her to hell, she was enjoying this. 'No. We went out, had a nice time, then it ended in fucking disaster. Is that enough information for you?'

Kate flushed and snapped, 'Okay no need to get nasty. I was just concerned for you that's all.'

Talan sighed and ran his hands through his hair. 'Look, it's no biggie; let's just leave it alone, eh?'

'Suits me … I'm just puzzled as to why she went out with you in the first place.'

Jeez what was this woman playing at? 'Oh thanks very much, Kate. Kick a guy when he's down, why don't you?'

She put her hand over her mouth and flushed. 'God that sounded awful. No I don't mean it like that.' A shy smile. 'As I said the other day, lots of women round here would give anything to go out with you.'

It was obvious to Talan since the other night when he and Kate had gone out and again just now that she counted herself amongst them. He gave her a withering look. 'What *did* you mean then?'

'Well,' she said, running her tongue along her lower lip obviously relishing the whole damned situation. 'I was in here yesterday morning and in walks someone called Willa, short blonde hair, upper-class accent and very dramatic. She buys a ticket and then announces that she'd like to buy some earrings for a special friend.'

She paused and searched Talan's face. He stared back, his forehead furrowed in a frown. The woman he'd seen drunk in the street with Rosa on Saturday night after the pub had fitted that description. And why didn't Kate just get to the bloody point? 'Yes, so?'

'I'm sorry, Tal, but Rosa is her partner. You know, her partner-type partner.' She raised her eyebrows and nodded knowingly.

'Partner-type partner?'

'Do I have to spell it out? They're lesbians.'

'Lesbians?' Talan couldn't believe it. He was a bit out of practice on the girlfriend front, but surely he would have known. 'You certain?'

'Yes. She told me.' Kate's sympathetic expression had made a come-back but her eyes still held a spark of triumph.

Talan put his head in his hands and thought back to the scene on Saturday night. Rosa and this Willa one in the street, laughing … holding each other. It could be true. In fact, it would corroborate his idea that Rosa pretended to get close to him so she could get a story about his mum. If she was a lesbian then there could be no other reason, she certainly wouldn't be romantically interested, would she?

He felt a hand on his shoulder. 'Gosh, she has really hurt you hasn't she?' Kate soothed. 'God knows what she was playing at.'

Talan stood and walked over to the door and looked out at the river of rainwater rushing down the path in front of him to rejoin the mercury-grey ocean.

Mercury-grey, that's how he felt.

Kate came up behind and put her hand on his shoulder again. He wanted to shrug it off, tell her to leave him alone, that he wasn't remotely interested in her, but he hadn't the heart. In the end what did it matter?

'Well at least there's your mum's birthday party to look forward to tonight,' she said tightening her grip on his shoulder. 'We can let our hair down and have a drink or three. It will all look better in a few days.'

'Yep.' Talan considered telling Kate that Rosa was a journalist here to reopen old wounds, but decided against it. With any luck Rosa would have pissed off now anyway. He'd tipped his mum off yesterday over the phone, warned her not to speak to Rosa if she tracked her down somehow. It was time to take a deep breath and put the lying little cow out of his mind and heart. She clearly didn't care about his feelings, laughing her head off in the street with Willa. They'd probably been laughing about him. He turned to face Kate. 'And for the record, I'm really not that upset. Just hate it when people lie to me.'

Talan walked to the back of the shop and ripped apart a cardboard box that had held the latest delivery of King Arthur snow globes now gracing the middle shelf. That felt better. He picked up another.

* * *

Morganna had assured Rosa that black velvet trousers, a red halter-neck top and those lovely, but inappropriate for castle-path-walking, red strappy sandals would be grand for Daisy's party. She looked at herself in the wardrobe mirror, her curls tumbling about her shoulders, a peppering of freckles across the bridge of her nose - or sun's kisses as Jocelyn called them - her eyes bright green against her lightly-tanned skin, and had to admit she looked good. Now and again however, the butterflies in her belly made her screw up her face in the most unattractive manner.

The party was to be held in the private rooms of the King Arthur's Arms where there'd be a buffet, bar, a disco and possibly even karaoke. Morganna seemed thrilled with the prospect, which didn't ring quite true to Rosa. Here was Morganna, white witch extraordinaire, fortune teller, spirit talker and soothsayer, shrieking with excitement at the idea of hanging on to a microphone and belting out *I will survive*.

Rosa herself was far from thrilled. Of course she wanted to talk to Daisy but the miserable Aunt Clare and Talan would obviously be there too. There was no doubt in her mind that he would cause a scene before she could get to her, and what would everyone make of that? Would they believe Talan's mistaken view that Rosa was here to cash in on Daisy's traumatic past? If Talan was as angry as he'd been on Saturday evening, there was a good chance. He was a local after all – she was a journalist from up country ready to dig dirt. It didn't look good.

The edge of the bed took her weight and she sighed. Jory had certainly sent her a mountain to climb. Why did it all have to be so complicated? If she'd asked Morganna about Daisy in the first place she would be on the train home by now, but Jory specifically told her not to tell Morganna about what he'd asked her to do for him. He said trust your feelings and she had, with disastrous consequences.

Then a thought occurred to her. Jory hadn't actually told her not to mention Daisy to Morganna, just that she shouldn't tell her or anyone else what Jory had asked of Rosa - because he wanted

Daisy to be the first to hear it. Besides, it couldn't all have been just coincidence could it, Morganna asking her to the party out of the blue? This had been tumbling around her head all day, and the more she thought about it the more she suspected that Morganna knew about Daisy somehow. She had to know, it stood to reason. Rosa grabbed her mobile and pressed call on Morganna's number.

'No I haven't changed my mind about the party,' Rosa said listening to the sigh of relief on the end of the line. 'But I do want to have a chat with you before we go. Can you get here a bit earlier?'

'I'm just getting astride my broomstick and will be with you in a trice!' Morganna laughed.

Rosa ended the call and wondered if she'd done the wrong thing once again.

CHAPTER 17

$\mathcal{W}$hat do you think?' Morganna twirled around Rosa's bedroom like a dervish in a crimson medieval-type dress. Beaded sleeves, long and cut on the bias whipped centimetres from Rosa's nose as she perched on the edge of the bed, and around Morganna's neck hung a chain of blue crystals heavy enough to weigh down the Empire State. Rosa took in the blue sparkly shoes, heavy make-up and intricately plaited side tresses of hair threaded through with silver stars and didn't know how to respond.

'You certainly will have all eyes on you tonight,' she said and meant it.

'Yep! I forgot about this dress, it was in an old box on top of the wardrobe. Clare has lost this game of one-upmanship!'

'You're incorrigible.' Rosa had to laugh despite the nerves in her chest.

'I am, aren't I?' Morganna panted and sat down in an armchair to catch her breath. 'Now, what's this chat about? I got a sense of anxiety across the line just now.'

Rosa took a moment to catch her own metaphorical breath and said, 'Correct me if I'm wrong, Morganna, but I think you asked me to this party for a reason. The stuff about you worrying what to wear and wanting me along for moral support was just bunkum, wasn't it?'

The flush on Morganna's cheeks and her reluctance to hold Rosa's gaze told her she was right. 'We-ll, I suppose you might have something there,' Morganna said to the blue sparkly shoes on her feet.

'What exactly do I have?' Rosa heard echoes of her father's voice in her own when he'd put his 'teacher's head' on when they were kids. Morganna sitting across the room looking like a naughty child completed the picture.

'It was just something Dan said about Talan. Well, that's what started me thinking at least. It was later when I got a definite image of you and him together that I thought I'd help things along a little.'

'Hold on. Let's go back a bit. What did Dan say?' Rosa's memory of Morganna's sharp-tongued son wasn't pleasant.

'Dan said that he thought that Talan was smitten with you. He saw him last when he was having a drink with his 'work colleague' Kate. Dan reckoned that she wanted to be much more than that to him and looked most put out when Dan said that he'd seen Talan with you. On the other hand, Talan looked over the moon when he realised that you hadn't gone back to London.' Morganna paused, looked up from her shoes her eyes trying to read Rosa's expression.

Rosa deliberately kept her face blank even though her stomach was churning and said, 'Go on.'

'Since then, I have had a few clear images of Talan and you happy together. In one you were walking along a cliff path the other day, and another where you were curled up together on a sofa in front of roaring fire, and another where you were looking at an emerald ring on your finger.' Morganna's eyes sparkled with excitement.

Rosa looked away from their gaze towards the open balcony door and the delicate brush strokes of peach and lemon sunset beyond. The stomach-churning turned into a washing machine on final spin and her thoughts went into free fall. Talan and her, happy – engaged even? Ridiculous! Morganna must have got this so wrong and she'd not even mentioned Daisy or Jory's quest.

Rosa looked back at Morganna and noted a look of satisfaction – a-cat-that-got-the-cream look slip across her face. 'Morganna, that is impossible. We met a few times and the last time ended very badly. I won't go into details, but there is no way we would ever be together.'

'I saw you with a ring.' Morganna folded her arms and smirked.

'But did you see him there too?'

'No, but—'

'So that could be me looking at Jocelyn's ring. She has an emerald ring and I have always liked it, she's leaving it to me in her will. You could have seen me with it after her death.'

'No. It wasn't her ring. I know how you felt when you looked at it on your finger. Your head was full of Talan.'

Rosa felt irrational hope and understandable annoyance vying for leadership in her mind. 'And you have never been wrong with your predictions, eh?'

A frown dampened Morganna's excitement and she sighed, 'Once or twice, but I'm not wrong this time.'

'But they were just a few random images—'

'At first they were, so I did a few readings to make sure.'

'You did readings without my permission?' Rosa said exasperated.

'Yes, that's not dishonest. I do readings for people all the time – it's part of my life.' Morganna huffed and narrowed her eyes. 'And I think the lady doth protest too much if I'm honest. I can tell you have feelings for him, so what's the problem?'

'I have feelings for him yes. They are not fit for your ears though. Suffice to say he has as much chance of marrying me as King Arthur!' Rosa could feel her face aglow and her heart thumping. She must try to get this conversation back on track before she said how she really felt, or tried to, given that she didn't really have a clue.

Morganna laughed. 'I think that King Arthur would be no match for you, my dear, not now you have your dander up!' Receiving a black look from Rosa she hid a smile and said, 'Anyway, I asked you to the party because you never mentioned that you had been out with him or even liked him and when you've carried through Jory's wishes you'd be off back to London. I wondered if things had gone awry between you and knew he'd be at the party of course and—'

'You thought you'd do a spot of matchmaking?'

'Yes.' Morganna shrugged.

'So you don't know what Jory asked me to do?'

'No. Though I guess it could be something to do with Talan – that's another reason why I thought I'd help.'

'So you know that Talan is Jory's grandson?'

'Of course, yes.'

'And that Daisy is his mother?'

'Yes. What a tragic life she had as a girl, losing both parents. My mother told me about Jory's death when I was younger. Everyone assumed he'd killed himself because of a lost love – I now know that was your gran. But we are a close-knit lot here, we closed ranks. Nobody mentions it now, not even Clare.'

Rosa let out a long breath and with it most of the pent-up emotion and irritation caused by Morganna's revelations. Leaving the preposterous idea that she and Talan would be together aside, she concentrated on the reason why she was still in Tintagel, her quick mind formulating a plan.

'Okay, Morganna. For reasons I can't go into, I need you to keep Talan away from me tonight. In fact, could you go in a few hours before me, wait until everyone's had a few drinks and distract him. If he sees me turn up, all hell will break loose.'

Morganna raised her eyebrows in surprise and then turned them into a frown. 'Eh?' She held up three fingers complete with green sparkly painted nails and counted them down with her other finger. 'One, how on earth am I supposed to distract him? Two, why will all hell break loose if he saw you? And three, what are you going to be doing?'

'You will find a way to distract him I'm sure. And the other two questions must remain unanswered I'm afraid.'

A sad little smile curled Morganna's lips and she leaned forward in her chair. 'You know you *can* trust me, Rosa. I only want what's best for you.'

The warmth and compassion in the other woman's voice

brought a small lump to Rosa's throat. She had been so lucky to have Morganna's help and support and she wished with all her heart that they'd keep in touch once this was over. 'I know you do, and I'm so grateful for everything you've done.' Rosa went over and rested her hand on her shoulder. 'But I can't tell you, it has to do with what Jory wants.'

Morganna covered Rosa's hand with her own and flashed a smile. 'Well that's different, my girl. Of course I'll distract Talan for you.' She stood up and undid the zip on the side of her dress. 'Do you think me walking in starkers should do it?'

* * *

Outside the pub, Rosa listened to the thump of dance music escaping through an open window, pulled the hood up on her short black jacket and looked up at the moon. Still a crescent, it had grown slightly fatter since the other night and the white threads of cloud snaked over its tip as they drifted by. Since the rain this morning they had enjoyed a sunny afternoon and a relatively clear night sky which brought a chill to Rosa's skin.

The job she had to do made her feel even colder and she checked the time on her phone. A white 9:30 flashed up and Rosa took a deep breath. This was the time that she had arranged for Morganna to distract Talan. It shouldn't be too hard with the party in full swing, folks would be a bit tipsy, the conversation and music would be loud and then Rosa would just wait for her chance. She swallowed her nerves, reminded herself that she was doing this for Jory and shoved her hands into the pockets of her coat.

Warm air laced with the smell of sausage rolls, alcohol, perfume, and undertones of sweat hit her cold face as she slipped into the noisy pub. Rosa hurried to an unfeasibly overladen coat stand in the corner which gave her good cover and a vantage point from which to scope out the room.

The multi-coloured lights flashing in time to the music and

across people's faces made identification more difficult, but eventually she saw Morganna across the room flapping her sleeves at Talan, and a little knot of people sitting at a table near the dance floor. Judging by their amused faces, she appeared to be telling a funny story and punctuating each section by treating them to banshee shrieks of laughter.

Talan looked incredible as usual in a white shirt, a leather strap around his neck with a larger arrowhead than the one in his brow suspended from it, and newly-washed rich brown hair waving to his shoulders. The strobe lights picked up the white of his teeth when he smiled and turned his eyes alternately turquoise and navy.

To her surprise and shame Rosa felt a pang of raw jealousy when Talan leaned in to a very attractive brunette next to him to whisper something in her ear. She put her hand on his arm and laughed out loud. Though she wasn't entirely sure, as she'd only seen the woman once in the Land Rover that first night, she guessed it was Kate. Dan had said she wanted to be more than a work colleague to Talan, and watching her body language now, little brushes of her fingers against his when she lifted her glass, a squeeze of his bicep when she laughed at something Morganna had said, her eyes all over him, Rosa knew that Dan was correct.

It looked like Talan was enjoying her company too and it was surprising how much that mattered to her. With an effort she dragged her gaze from them and looked around the room. She had to finish what she started and then slip away before she was seen lurking amongst the coats like some weird stalker. In order to do that, she had to find Daisy.

Rosa scanned the room looking for Daisy, and though she had no idea what she looked like, she thought there might be an obvious woman surrounded by friends giving her cards and presents. Though there was a small pile of presents at the end of the buffet table, no recipient was nearby.

A middle-aged blonde woman sang to herself as she passed the coat stand, not drunk, but obviously merry. Rosa could see she was headed for the ladies and seized her opportunity.

'Excuse me,' she said stepping out in front of the woman.

The woman put her hand to her heart and stepped back. 'Lord, you nearly scared the pants off me popping out like that.' She laughed self-consciously and flapped a hand at her face.

'Sorry. I just wondered if you could give this birthday card to Daisy for me and tell her I want to see her outside. I have a surprise for her, but I want it to be in private.'

'Oh, okay. I have to go to the loo first though, I'll give it to her afterwards.'

'I know you must think I'm a bit mad jumping out and all, but I really need to see her as soon as possible. Is there any way you could do it before?'

The woman sighed and took the card. 'If you insist. Outside the front, or in the beer garden?'

'Beer garden?'

The woman nodded and hurried back through the bar. Rosa followed a sign for the beer garden and stepped out into a neat, lawned area scattered with wooden bench tables and colourful shrubs. Lawn lights dotted amongst the shrubs gave the garden a cosy feel. It wasn't though. The nip in the air grabbed her cheeks after the warm atmosphere inside and Rosa pulled her hood up again and fastened her coat up to the neck.

'Hello? You wanted to see me?'

Rosa took a breath and turned to face the owner of the voice. Involuntarily she took another as she looked into a pair of curious eyes as deep as the ocean, blue as the August sky and yet green too, like the sea-green depths under an anchored boat. 'Um … yes, I did, thanks for leaving your party to see me.'

'Thanks for your card by the way. But there's no signature and I'm sorry but I have no clue as to who you are.' Daisy ran her hand self-consciously through her shoulder length dark waves and gave a sheepish grin.

It was uncanny how alike the three generations looked. Daisy was tall, slim, had the strong chin, high cheekbones and straight nose, and of course the eyes. She was a striking woman and even in her mid-fifties Rosa guessed she'd still turn heads.

Daisy looked around and then back at Rosa, a question in her eyes. She was clearly beginning to think her behaviour was a little odd and Rosa didn't blame her, asking her outside and then clamming up. 'I'm a friend of Morganna Hardill's. She asked me along.'

'Oh right.' Daisy looked a little more relaxed but added, 'I didn't see you come in with her.'

'No I was late.' Rosa needed to cut to the chase before someone else came outside. Someone like Talan. 'Look Daisy, I know you will think I'm mad when I tell you why I'm here, I would if I were in your shoes. Morganna and I share certain ability; we can communicate with the spirit world.'

Daisy pulled the sleeves down on her black velvet top and rubbed her arms. 'Okay. I'm not really into all that stuff to be honest.'

'No. I didn't think I was until I arrived here. Well, that's not strictly true, I have always had the ability but my dad ...' She was rambling and the look in Daisy's eyes was less than encouraging. 'Sorry, you must be freezing and I'm not making a lot of sense.'

'No, I can't say you are.'

'Right. What I wanted is to arrange to meet you for coffee tomorrow so we can have a chat about ... things.'

'Things?' Daisy's forehead furrowed into a deep frown.

'Yep. We can't talk about things, personal things, out here now.'

Daisy narrowed her eyes and took a step back. 'Wait a minute, you're not that journalist Talan warned me about are you? Rosa someone?'

Shit! Rosa hadn't thought of that. Now what should she do? 'Yes. I am a journalist but not —'

Daisy was already walking away her hands raised above her head. 'Leave me alone, I have nothing to say to you!'

Rosa put her hand to her mouth. *Damn it, do something before she goes back inside and everything goes tits up.* 'Daisy, my grandmother is Jocelyn, the woman who your dad was in love with!'

Daisy stopped and turned around a look of pure hatred on her face. 'Just what evil little games are you playing at? If that's true, why on earth would I want anything to do with you after ...' her voice faltered and tears stood in her eyes. '... After everything that happened?'

'I can explain, just not here. Can I come to your home tomorrow? We need somewhere that we won't be disturbed. What I have to tell you is for your ears only.'

'So you can get a nasty little story eh? What's the title, Return to Tintagel? We meet brave little orphan Daisy again nearly fifty years on since her father's plunge to his death?'

'No I promise you I—'

Daisy snorted, 'Oh please, I'm going in now. I suggest you leave, pronto.'

Just as Daisy pulled back the door to step back inside, Rosa decided she had little choice but to shout, 'I have a message from your father! He saw you with the silver locket, the one he gave you after your mother passed away.'

Daisy turned and stared at Rosa, her face drained and she leaned her back against the door, her mouth working but uttering no sound. Rosa took a few steps towards her but then Daisy recovered and held up the flat of her palm 'Get away from me,' she hissed. Then pulled the door open and stumbled back inside the pub.

The strains of *My Way* being murdered could be heard clearly as the door swung shut behind her, probably Morganna dutifully carrying through her distraction to the letter. She might as well have not bothered. What a bloody mess! The look on Daisy's face had been one of shock and horror, obviously frightened to death. There was no way she'd ever get near her again. The poor woman was probably telling Talan all about her right now. She'd failed Jory, failed him miserably. Failed Jocelyn too.

Utterly dejected and miserable, Rosa decided that there was nothing else she could do apart from leave. Raucous drunken laughter filtered out into the night air and Rosa decided that she too could do with a few glasses of something after this debacle.

Perhaps the Tintagel Arms would be a good bet, given that half the village was in here.

Noticing a side-gate, Rosa walked through it and round to the front of the pub, then she stopped short. Just when she thought her night couldn't get any worse, it did. Under the fairy lights strung across the main entrance, two figures leant against the wall kissing passionately.

The woman's hands wound themselves through a shock of lustrous chestnut waves, her body pressed tightly against the man's. His hands ran up and down her back and caressed her bottom over tight white jeans. For a second Rosa's brain refused to acknowledge what her eyes had seen, but then it all became too real. Rosa ducked back into the shadows before either Talan or Kate saw her and ran blindly along the street, desperate to put as much distance between herself and the happy couple as she could. The thump of her feet on the pavement kept time with the thump in her chest. She had no idea in which direction she was running, and at that moment, she really didn't care.

CHAPTER 18

$\mathcal{R}$osa drained her second glass of red wine within half-an-hour and contemplated another. Then she remembered how vile she'd felt the other night after being out with Willa and pushed the empty glass to the middle of the table. Dan had nodded to her as she'd stood at the bar and then busied himself wiping down tables and rearranging chairs. He was obviously at a loose end in the more than half-empty pub.

He came out of the kitchen and made a beeline for her glass, a real job for him at last. Rosa looked up at him, uncertain of his reaction, but to her surprise a generous smile lit up his handsome face. 'I've been hanging about in the kitchen trying to pluck up courage to come over,' he said, a slow flush creeping up his neck.

Rosa caught his flush and folded her arms. What the hell did he want? If he asked her out she'd probably say something she'd regret the way she was feeling at the moment. 'Why's that?' she said casually.

'I wanted to apologise for my awful behaviour the last few times we've met. Mum has filled me in on your … similarities … and I feel such a fool now about the way I spoke to you.'

'Ah, right.' Rosa said with a smile, relief dispersing the tight feeling in her gut. 'To be fair, at the time I *did* think the spirit world was a load of hoo-ha as my dad would say.'

'Even so, I shouldn't have been so nasty, especially the next time when you were here with Talan.'

The mention of Talan wiped the smile off her face. 'Not to worry, apology accepted.'

Dan picked up her glass. 'Might I ask why you're here alone? I thought you were going to Daisy's party with Mum.'

'Yeah, I went but it was a bit noisy, full of folk I didn't know, so ...' Her voice tailed off and she stood up. 'Anyway, I'll get back now. Night.'

'Sure you won't have another? I could join you.' Dan waved his arm at the handful of people. 'As you can see I'm hardly run off my feet.' His cool blue eyes twinkled and he held Rosa's gaze a little too long.

She looked down and made a production out of buttoning her coat, reluctant to look at him again. 'No. I'll pop off now, need an early night.'

Dan shrugged and stuck his bottom lip out in exaggerated show of disappointment. 'Okay, perhaps another time.'

Rosa just smiled and hurried for the door. There would be no other time, and if she couldn't find a way to somehow pull triumph out of the ashes of failure in the morning, she'd be at home this time tomorrow night. Just as she was closing the door behind her, Dan grabbed her by the arm. 'Rosa, wait!'

For God's sake, why didn't he just piss off? 'What?' she snapped and shook his arm off.

That raised his eyebrows and he said quietly, 'It's Mum on the phone, she's been trying to contact you, but your mobile's switched off. She wondered if I'd seen you.'

Rosa took his mobile and stepped back inside. 'Okay, sorry,' she said to him. Then she listened to Morganna talk at ten thousand miles an hour and trying without success to get a word in. 'Morganna! Can I say something please?'

'Jeepers, you'll make me deaf shouting in my earhole like that!'

'It was the only way I could get you to listen.' Rosa moved away from Dan and sat down at the furthest table. 'So, Daisy was upset in the Ladies when you walked in, and she grabbed you and demanded to know if you knew me and if I was a white witch?'

A sigh on the end of the line. 'Yes, I just said all that.'

'Yes, but you said it so fast I couldn't make it all out. So what happened next?'

'I said I knew you, that you weren't a witch, but that you did have certain paranormal abilities.'

'Paranormal? Bloody hell, Morganna.'

'What would you call it, then?' Morganna huffed.

'I don't know, psychic?... It just seems a bit dramatic. Was she freaked out?'

'She was already freaked out when I walked in and saw her dabbing at her eyes in the mirror. She nearly jumped up onto the washbasin.'

'Great. I was responsible for that. I met her in the garden and had a word or two.'

'Yes, she said that you'd talked but didn't say what about.' Morganna's tone implied that she expected Rosa to clarify.

'I can't say what it was about, sorry. What did she say next?'

'She asked me if you were trustworthy.'

'What did you say?'

'I said no and that you were an evil backstabbing spawn of Satan.'

Rosa couldn't believe her ears. 'Did you?'

'Of course not, you lemon! Just trying to lighten the mood a bit.'

Rosa giggled. 'You are so not funny.'

'I said I thought you were one of the nicest, most trustworthy people I had met in a long time.'

'Aw, really?'

'Yes, really. And then she took a scrap of paper out of her bag and jotted down her address, and said would I ask you to pop round tomorrow about ten-ish for coffee and a chat?'

'Really?' Rosa felt a light feeling settle in her head and a weight lift from her belly.

'Yes, really!'

'Oh Morganna you are brilliant! I thought I'd blown it all, failed Jory and—'

'Don't say any more, I'd hate you to spill the beans to me in your excitement if you didn't mean to. Now have you got a pen and paper to jot down her address?'

Ending the call, she walked over and handed the phone back to Dan.

'Everything okay?'

'Yeah, thanks, Dan I really think it might be now,' she said.

* * *

Tuesday morning and at last the world looked brighter again. Still in her nightshirt, Rosa folded her arms and leaned on the balcony. The garden was bathed in early morning sunshine, the tips of the pine trees waved in the breeze and the ocean drew a hazy blue line along the horizon. She exhaled, drew in a deep breath of country fresh air and released it slowly. How she adored this place, and how sad she'd be to leave it. But leave it she must. One more night here and then tomorrow she'd pack up and head back to the big smoke.

Daisy's address was about ten minutes away according to the little street map. As the morning was so warm, she slipped on a black vest top, tan crop trousers and walking sandals. Because her tummy had a bag of nerves jumbling inside it she decided she'd miss breakfast much to John's disapproval. 'You should never miss breakfast, young lady. It's the most important meal of the day,' he said as she pretended to run away from his admonishment. John really seemed to care, she would miss him too.

Daisy's bungalow was at the opposite end of the village to Talan's, and at the end of a cul-de-sac of similar dwellings - neat, tidy and though not to Rosa's taste, pretty in a quaint sort of way. A huge and very beautiful pink magnolia tree stood in the garden outside Number Eight and behind it a picture window looked out onto the street. A quick movement at the window told Rosa that

Daisy had been looking out for her and the front door opened just as she lifted her hand to knock.

'Hello, there. Come inside,' Daisy said, her voice pitched a little higher than last night, an obvious sign of nerves. She led the way down a short corridor, through a living room and into a bright and sunny conservatory. Daisy pushed open double doors which looked out onto a patio and garden, small, but full of colourful pot plants and shrubs.

She ran her fingers through her hair and adjusted the neckline of her lemon blouse. 'I thought we'd have coffee out here?' She gestured to a white wrought-iron table and four chairs on the patio and the stuck her hands in the pockets of her grey linen skirt.

'That would be lovely,' Rosa said, giving Daisy her warmest smile to try and put her at ease. Her own nerves settled a bit now that she realised that she was actually in a better position than poor Daisy. At least Rosa knew what was coming next. She also had a few minutes breathing space while she waited for coffee to formulate her opening sentence. Once that was out of the way, she hoped that the rest would flow after.

With a tremor in her hands Daisy placed a tray of biscuits, a cafetiere and two mugs on the table and drew up a chair to sit opposite Rosa In the morning light her eyes looked even more similar to Talan's. Rosa swallowed and forced his face to the back of her mind.

'Let's not dance around the subject. You're probably as nervous as I am, so I'll just pitch right in and we'll see what happens, okay?' Rosa smiled and patted Daisy's arm Daisy nodded, gave a sigh of relief and poured the coffee.

'Last night I told you I have a message from your dad. Without going into the ins and outs of my history, I didn't realise I had a sixth-sense, or as I prefer to call it, my special sense. Anyway, your dad's spirit appeared to my grandmother, who has a terminal illness by the way, and said that he wanted me to come to Tintagel. That's all I knew until I came here and almost immediately I made contact with Jory. Well, not direct contact you understand—'

Rosa stopped and shook her head. Daisy looked tearful already and totally bemused. 'Sorry, this isn't going very well. I'll stick to the main message and then you can ask questions as you wish. I met your dad up on the cliff top near the church the other night.'

Daisy pulled a damp tissue out of her pocket and dabbed at her eyes. 'That's where he jumped from.'

'That's the thing, Daisy. He *didn't* jump. He was drunk and he slipped. He told me he would never leave you alone, no matter how much he missed Jocelyn.' Rosa was aware that she was speaking quickly but she had to get it out instead of waffling.

Daisy strangled a sob and blotted her eyes again. 'But what was he doing up there drunk at night? No. I think you might like to believe he didn't take his own life, what with your gran being involved and all, but it's obvious why he was there that night.'

A deep sigh escaped Rosa's lips and she said, 'He was up there remembering a lovely evening he'd spent with my gran and he took a drink and lost his footing. I … saw it happen.'

'You did what?' Daisy's lips turned down at the corners and her eyes flamed. 'Do you think I'm that gullible?'

'I know how it sounds but it's the truth. Last night you knew I wasn't lying as soon as I mentioned the locket. That's how Jory knows that you'll believe me. He told me to tell you that he didn't jump, that he never would have left you alone and that he loves you very much. You were his world. He needs to go to his rest in the knowledge that you know what really happened and that you don't hate him.'

Daisy's tears followed down her face unchecked now. 'It all seems too crazy to take in. How do I know that you didn't just guess about the locket – most women have jewellery belonging to their mother?'

Rosa knew that Daisy's mind was just trying to clutch at rational straws in the midst of processing totally irrational information. 'This is the locket that your dad gave you after your mum died. Inside it is a photo of the three of you and you used to look at it from time to time. You kept it in a red velvet box. You locked it away after he died. Over time you closed your mind to Jory, you hated him for abandoning you. There is no way I could have guessed all that, now is there?'

A wail of despair escaped Daisy's mouth and then she hid her head in her hands rocking back and forth, sobs wracking her body. 'My poor dad! My poor, poor dad! He never left me … thank God.' Daisy sobbed some more and Rosa handed her some tissues she'd noticed on a table inside the conservatory. She wiped her eyes and gave a short bark of laughter tinged with hysteria 'That sounds really pathetic doesn't it? Because he died anyway, but he loved me, still does. If only I had known … my life would have been so…so different.'

Rosa struggled to keep her own tears at bay and patted Daisy's hand. 'It's not pathetic. It makes perfect sense. Now here, have a sip of coffee.' Rosa handed her a mug and took a big drink from her own which helped to dislodge the lump of emotion in her throat.

Both women were a little more composed ten minutes later. Rosa had told Daisy all about Jocelyn's life and dilemma over Jory. Daisy listened, a slow tear running down the corner of her face. 'What a bloody mess. Poor Jocelyn didn't have a lot of choice did she? All these years I have hated her too because I thought Dad loved her more than me.' She closed her eyes and turned her face to the sun 'After I was orphaned at the age of eight I lived with my aunt Meredith She took care of me when Dad was working and so it wasn't so much of a shock to her to take me on permanently. I was a mess though, obviously and wouldn't leave my room for weeks.' Daisy opened her eyes. 'Sorry you don't want to hear all this.'

'No, do go on If you want to tell me I will be glad to listen' Rosa realised how far she'd come from that woman who didn't like to face up to life's woes. The kitten had left for different pastures. She felt like she'd grown up so much over the past week or so, in fact she felt changed beyond all recognition

Daisy nodded and continued. 'Not long after Dad died we had the local press in the town and one journalist managed to get a story from my unsuspecting cousin, Sue, as she walked home from school. It was picked up by a tabloid and the poor little orphan Daisy story was everywhere then. They cashed in on the mysterious Tintagel angle too. One of them made Dad out to be a mystic Merlin-type, up on the cliffs spurned by his true love and trying to cast a spell to bring her back. One day it all became too much and he jumped when it was clear he'd lost her forever.'

Rosa's heart went out to Daisy. What she must have gone through as a girl. Not only did she lose her mother, but lies in the paper about her father - coupled with the idea that he thought so little of her that he preferred death to living without Jocelyn - must have left deep wounds. She struggled for appropriate words but only found, 'I'm sorry, so very sorry, Daisy.'

'Thanks, and I'm sorry I didn't know that my dad's death was an accident years ago.' Daisy sighed, picked up her empty mug went to drink and then just looked at it. 'Because of everything that happened I found it very hard to trust anyone, especially men. My first husband, Jack, bore the brunt of it. I didn't believe he really loved me, you see?' Daisy poured them more coffee. 'Even after he had given me two lovely children I was convinced he would leave me. It ate me up inside, but I never really let him know how much I loved him either. I would always hold this bit of me back, you know?'

Rosa didn't, but she could guess. The look of anguish on Daisy's face spoke volumes. She nodded and leaned back in her chair.

'I was terrified of being hurt again, but in the end I made what I feared most happen. I was always questioning him if he came in from work late, wanted to know who he was talking to on the phone, criticising his every move - the list went on. I sometimes told him I didn't love him and wished him far away. I hated myself but I couldn't stop.' Daisy let out a slow breath. 'In the end he went to Canada when his company opened a new branch there. I broke the poor guy's heart. Eventually he met someone else, had more children.' Daisy's voice cracked with emotion and she dabbed at her red puffy eyes with a fresh tissue. 'I also deprived my children of a loving father. I married again years later and Greg is wonderful, but he's not their dad is he?'

An ache in Rosa's chest and a lump in her throat made answering impossible. She took a moment and said, 'I can't begin to imagine how you all must have suffered. So are you happy with Greg?'

A sunny smile brightened Daisy's face instantly showing Rosa how much she loved her husband. 'I am. He's a counsellor – that's where we met believe it or not. As his client he helped me to put things in perspective, showed me that I had trusted friends and family who would be there for me come what may. He also helped me to close my mind to the hurt Dad had caused me. I suppose when I did that, I closed my heart to him forever, it was too painful not to.'

'Thank God some good came out of so much heartache. Did you fall in love right away?'

'No. It was a good eighteen months after I finished my sessions when I bumped into him in Truro. It wouldn't have been ethical for us to get together while I was seeing him professionally. I had always liked him, but never imagined anything would come of it romantically. Anyhow, we went for a coffee and the rest is history.'

She laughed then and Rosa noticed shades of Talan in her smile. Talan and Kate replaced Talan's smiling face in her mind and so she focussed on a crack in the patio until it had gone.

Daisy shielded her eyes against the sun, fanned her face and twisted her hair into a ponytail. 'It's getting hot out here, shall we go inside?'

'Yes. I'd better get going now anyway. Mission accomplished.' Rosa grinned and stood up.

'Oh must you? I have enjoyed having your company and of course I'm overjoyed at what you've told me.' Daisy gave her a warm hug.

Hugging her back, Rosa said with a tremor in her voice, 'I am overjoyed that I managed to tell you it. It took me long enough. Yesterday I thought I'd failed your dad ... my gran too.'

'Don't beat yourself up.' Daisy picked up the tray and led the way into the cool of her lemon and white kitchen. 'You did your best to find me through Talan, but because of the past and the fact that he is very protective of me you didn't manage it. And last night I was in total shock and not a little scared to be honest. I'm not used to all this spirit stuff!'

'Believe it or not, neither am I!' Rosa quickly summed up her recent history and her past while Daisy washed up the cups. She was a good listener, so easy to talk to and said all the right things. Even though they had only just met, Rosa felt as though she had made another friend.

Daisy dried her hands on a tea-towel, looked Rosa in the eye and said hesitantly, 'I can't pretend to understand everything you have just said … as I have never been one to believe in those … kinds of things. Though after today I guess I must … but I do feel it was very wrong of your father to behave like that. I know he was worried because of his parents' situation but I think you and he need a chat about it, sooner rather than later.'

'I'm not sure he would want to hear anything I have to say about what happened here this past week or so. He is very set in his ways and stubborn.'

Daisy sniffed and she blinked moisture from her eyes. 'You only have one dad, Rosa as I well know. You have brought mine back to me today – please do your best not to lose yours.' Rosa found she had to blink then too and the two women smiled across the room at each other. No words were needed.

'Well, I must be off, Daisy.' Rosa said walking to the front door. 'I need to book my train, taxi and of course say goodbye to Morganna. I will so miss her and this magical place. It's been fabulous to meet you, too.'

'Likewise, I feel like I have known you for ages. It would be great if you could come back again so we could have a longer chat.' Rosa nodded her agreement and then Daisy sniffed again and held her finger up. 'Before you go, would you like to see the locket?'

'I'd love to.' Rosa smiled and got a tissue out of her pocket in readiness. She'd be a blubbering mess if she didn't get out of there soon. Strangely enough, as she looked at the lovely photo of Jory,

Daisy and Daisy's mother set into the locket, tears were far away. Only pure unadulterated joy filled her heart and her smile was so wide that her mouth began to ache.

Daisy said, 'I really feel like Dad can see us now and he's overjoyed.'

Rosa nodded and handed the locket back.

Daisy looked up at the ceiling to her left and right. 'Can he see us ... is he here?'

'I can't see him, Daisy. But I'm certain you're right. I have a warm feeling in my arms and tingly fingers, a sure sign'

On the doorstep the two women hugged again and Rosa promised she would come back one day. At the bottom of the path she turned and waved. Waving back, Daisy's face suddenly lost its smile and her hand fell to her side as she looked beyond Rosa's shoulder.

'What the fuck are *you* doing here?'

Rosa turned to see an irate Talan racing up the road towards them His face flushed, eyes blue chips of anger, he stopped inches in front of her and yelled, *'I said what the—'*

'Talan stop! Rosa isn't after a story, we got it all wrong!' Daisy called, running down the path towards her son

'Oh really?' he growled, his top lip curled in a snarl, his eyes never leaving Rosa's.

Though her pulse rate set off at a gallop and she felt very intimidated by this mountain of fury standing over her, there was no way Rosa was letting him know that.

'Yes, really! Now if you don't mind I was just leaving.' She side-stepped him but felt his large hand firmly encircle her wrist.

'Not until I find out exactly what you have been doing here.' He spoke quietly, but his voice sounded all the more menacing for it.

Daisy brought her hand down sharply on his. 'Talan! Let her go this minute you have it *all* wrong!'

Rosa stepped away, horrified to feel tears of frustration pricking her eyes. Damn it, he might see this as a sign of weakness. 'Sorry it had to end like this, Daisy. I'll keep my promise.' She raised her hand to Daisy in farewell. A quick glance at Talan's furrowed brow and set jaw told her he wasn't in the mood to be placated, and then she hurried away down the street.

'Hey, what promise? Come back!' he yelled after her.

Rosa sped up and when she turned the corner she ran. It occurred to her that lately she always seemed to be blindly running along the streets of Tintagel close to tears. She silently cursed and wished that she'd never set eyes on Talan Kestle.

CHAPTER 19

$\mathcal{R}$osa slowed her pace as she arrived in the High Street and decided that she'd pay Morganna a visit sooner rather than later. After the encounter with Talan she could *so* do with a friendly ear. It was a shame that would be her last impression of him after the great time they'd had together.

Her mind drifted back to the day when they'd first met in the castle cafe. He had scared the life out of her as he looked so much like Jory, but his easy manner and adorable smile had soon won her over. Then that day at Bedruthan she'd fleetingly contemplated a relationship, how stupid was that? Even if Morganna were to do a hundred readings there was no way forward for them now. Besides, he had Kate.

A host of fairies announced Rosa's arrival as the shop bell tinkled merrily. A pang of sadness that this was the last time she'd be stepping through the door of *Heart's Desire* for a good while caught her unawares, and she heaved a deep sigh. This was the place where she had been told she had a gift and soon after her life began to make sense for the first time in a long time.

Morganna resplendent in a gold and green kaftan leapt from her seat behind the counter, locked the door and practically flung herself at Rosa 'So did you meet Daisy? Did it go well? And can you tell me anything about it now?'

Rosa laughed and followed Morganna's beckoning finger into the familiar little kitchen 'Yes, yes and yes,' she said, nodding as

Morganna held up the kettle.

'Well go on then, spill!' Morganna gesticulated with a tea-bag. 'Don't keep me in suspenders.'

Rosa spilled. Morganna's eyes grew moist and she had to blow her nose a few times on an enormous multi-coloured hanky. Rosa had to hide a smile. Morganna couldn't even have anything as normal as a tissue like the rest of the world.

'Oh I am so relieved for poor Daisy. What an awful time she's had. And I am over the moon for our Jory too.' Morganna patted Rosa's hand. 'You have done an incredible thing, my dear. You should be so proud.'

Rosa hadn't really had time to think of it like that. She'd been so worried about not failing Jory and Jocelyn that she'd not really considered the importance of her own role. Now that Morganna had mentioned it, she guessed that she did feel proud and hoped that she could help others in the future. 'I am actually. Wonder whose spirit I will bump into next?' She laughed and bit into a huge piece of chocolate cake that Morganna had placed in front of her.

'I expect there will be an orderly queue forming!' Morganna hooted. Taking in Rosa's look of delight as she munched, she said, 'It's good isn't it? Made it myself with my own hands.'

'It is incredible! I missed breakfast this morning as I was so bloody nervous about meeting Daisy. She had biscuits but I thought I might choke on the crumbs I was so emotional. This is so hitting the spot.' Rosa looked at Morganna and wanted to hear her signature hoot again so she could commit it to memory for use on grey winter days. 'And you could hardly have made the cake with anyone else's could you?'

Morganna furrowed her brow and wiped cake from her lip. 'Eh? Anyone else's what?'

'Hands.' Rosa twinkled. The hoot she was hoping for was loud and long - the essence of Morganna.

'You are completely mad. In a nice way though,' Morganna said, then her eyes grew serious. 'You've come to tell me you're leaving haven't you?'

'Yes. Tomorrow morning …' Rosa swallowed the cake and emotion. 'I will really miss you.' She waved her arm expansively. 'This place too. I never did get that gift for Gran. I must do that before I go.'

'I'll miss you too. But you'll be back before long. I can feel it in my crystals.' Morganna shot her a bright smile. 'Have you told Jocelyn about it all?'

'No, not yet. I will pop up and see her this weekend and tell her face-to-face. I'll phone her to say things have gone to plan though before I leave here.'

'It's not quite all gone to plan though has it?' Morganna's tawny eyes regarded her keenly over the rim of her tea cup.

'Er, yes. Unless you know something I don't.'

'Talan.'

'Oh, not this again, Morganna. There's nothing going on there and never will be.' Rosa sighed and told Morganna all about the fact he'd gone crazy when he'd thought Rosa was after a story, the way he'd been today, and that she'd seen him kissing Kate outside the pub the other night. 'So you see, your readings were wrong after all.'

'No. No, they weren't.' Morganna put down her cup and stared unwaveringly at Rosa. 'But if you put a mental block up against it, you will have to wait far longer than you need to for him.'

'Ha!' Rosa snorted. 'You should see who had the mental block this morning – he looked like he wanted to rip my head off.'

Morganna raised a brow. 'That's because he thought you'd been hassling his mother. Hopefully Daisy will have put him straight by now.'

'Be that as it may, he looked more than happy with Kate, and I really do have to go back to my life. London isn't on Neptune but it would be difficult in the extreme to maintain a relationship, particularly with my job sending me here there and everywhere.'

'Where there's a will there's a way.'

This reminded Rosa of Willa and she wondered how much longer she'd be able to put up with her strops. She shook her head at Morganna 'But I don't think there is a will on mine *or* his part. Sorry to disappoint you.'

'There are journalist jobs in Cornwall you know, perhaps not in travel, but I'm sure you can turn your hand to other types of writing.'

Rosa was getting tired of this now. She didn't want to spend the last few minutes of her time with Morganna fending off flights of fancy, no matter how well meant they were. 'Haven't you been listening, Morganna? I keep saying—'

'I have been listening, but not believing a word. You have strong feelings for Talan and they are reciprocated.' Morganna held up her hand as Rosa opened her mouth to interject. 'But I'll drop it for now.' She smiled and stood up. 'Come on. Let's go and find something for that wonderful grandmother of yours.'

* * *

The wonderful grandmother's voice sounded much stronger than it had for some time and the happiness coming across the line was almost palpable. 'Oh, my little one, I'm so pleased that everything worked out. Jory's not visited for a day or two, but I expect he'll pop by soon.'

'I hope he doesn't tell you what's happened because I want to do that in person!'

'Does this mean I'll see you soon?'

'Yes! Hoping to be with you on Saturday morning. I'm back to London tomorrow, a few days earlier than I told my boss I would be, so that should earn me a few brownie points.'

'Fantastic! Your mum has been here but I know she wants to get home and sort a few things out. I'll tell her you'll be here over the weekend then?'

'Until Sunday afternoon, yes. Sorry it couldn't be longer but I expect I have a mountain of emails to wade through and—'

'Don't apologise, my love. I think you have done more than enough for me this past week or so don't you?'

'Oh, yes. It has been so dull here in this awful place. No scenery to speak of, or fresh air, or exciting meetings with spirits on cliff tops and crazy white witches. It's been *such* a hardship.'

Rosa was treated to a wheezy chuckle across the line. 'You do make me laugh Rosa, and not much does nowadays I can tell you.'

* * *

Supper over, train ticket and taxi booked, suitcase packed apart from toiletries, Rosa decided to have one last walk around Tintagel village to say goodbye. The heat of the day had left reminders in Lewis's stone arch as Rosa trailed her hand over its warmth on her way to the street beyond. The village was still quite busy for nearly eight o'clock, but then the tourist season was hotting up. Down the street on the opposite side, folk peered through the window of Granny Wobbly's Fudge Pantry – somewhere she still hadn't managed to visit – and a group of women laughed raucously as they walked into the Tintagel Arms.

Unbidden, a picture of Talan appeared laughing at one of her daft jokes that night they had been in there. He'd been telling her about the history of the castle and she'd twisted something he'd said into a joke. For the life of her she couldn't remember what it was now. Right now that lovely evening seemed as far away as childhood to her, yet it had been only last week. She shook her head – no room for him in there.

Further down the street she walked past the old Post Office, yet again somewhere she'd not had time to visit. She underlined it in her mental list as an excuse to return to visit in the future. Not that she'd need much of an excuse, she adored everything about the place. Talan's angry face from this morning popped up from behind a cloud. Well, almost everything.

At the little wooden signpost Rosa paused and looked out over the cobalt sea nestling in the green valley in front of her. One last look at the beach, or one last look at the church? The church stood sentinel on the hilltop, its ancient stones golden in the last rays of evening sunshine. Her feet moved in the direction of the church before her head had properly decided, so allowing her intuition to run free, she picked up her pace.

By the time she reached the entrance to the churchyard she was almost running. Something about this spot drew her, calmed her, anchored her to the past and all the people who had passed through over the centuries. Rosa wanted to run up to the doorway of the church and press her hands and face to the stone, breathe the hopes and fears of those who were now just dust in the graves in front of her; touch their dreams and see their lives.

A few weeks ago that idea would have seemed totally preposterous to her, alien even. It would to most people. Now though, it seemed as natural as seeing the sun rise in the morning. Moreover, most people weren't here to see her. The only sounds were her quick footfall on the path, the chatter of a jackdaw and the light breeze tousling her hair and kissing her warm cheeks.

At the church, Rosa tentatively checked that there was no one inside, visiting a grave or wandering past along the cliff top. At nearly half-past eight in the evening it would be surprising if there was. The warmth of the stone under her hands immediately connected the past to her soul, her mind and heart. Lightly resting her cheek next to her hands she closed her eyes and stilled her thoughts. A distant call of a seagull, the smell of meadow grass and the song of the ocean connected her to nature. Her spirit soared and she immediately felt truly at peace.

Reluctantly Rosa moved away after a few minutes and once again her feet governed her direction. Jory's bench watched over the reflected sunset turning the ocean a shimmering red and gold. It was suddenly clear that her feet had been leading her to the bench as soon as she'd left Lewis's. Static tickled the back of her arms and her heart grew full.

Jory needed to say goodbye.

Silhouetted against the tangerine sky the bench looked lonely for company and Rosa, eager to provide it, hurried down the coast path and across the spongy grass. She didn't sit immediately, but stood on the edge of the cliff and marvelled at the beauty of this spot once again. To her right, rising from the crashing ocean, the ruin of Tintagel castle hugged its walls around the island and to her left, the crag from which Jory fell jutted out dark against the sky.

Without turning round she knew that he was behind her sitting on the bench. Rosa's heart thumped under her ribs and she turned to look at him, a big smile on her face. Though she knew he was a spirit, he looked more real somehow, more ... alive. The madness of this thought wasn't lost on her, but there he sat a picture of relaxation in jeans, his right foot resting on his left knee, his hair and face bathed in the last gasp of the sunset, and his eyes indistinguishable from the navy of the ocean in front of him.

Jory smiled too, a smile that crinkled the corners of his eyes, a smile that told her he was truly happy. Rosa swallowed and walked to the bench and sat next to him.

He stared ahead at the sea. 'I have come to say goodbye, and to thank you, Rosa. Thank you so much.'

'I was glad I could help you, though it was trickier than I imagined,' she said with a little laugh.

'How so?'

Rosa looked at him and found that he was staring at her, puzzled. Surely he knew? 'As you know it took me a while. I asked your grandson as you said I should trust my feelings when asking for help ... he was less than helpful.'

'I didn't know any of what you have done. There are only certain times I am able to see the living. I have no knowledge of day-to-day actions – I *can* read feelings however.'

Rosa's heart jumped as he held her gaze, he seemed to be reading hers right now. She wanted to shield her mind from his, but instead felt it open up to him, and she drifted trance-like deep in the ocean blue of his eyes. A jackdaw chattered nearby and broke the connection.

'Tell me what happened between you and Talan,' he said quietly and looked up at the sky.

Rosa gathered her thoughts. 'I had been seeing Talan a little before I knew that Daisy was his mother. I trusted him, trusted my feelings like you said, and asked him if he knew a Daisy. He thought I was a journalist after a juicy story and went crazy, practically threw me out of his car. How could I have got it so wrong? How could my instincts have got it so wrong?'

Jory smiled at her. 'As I said, I only know some things; other things appear as suggestions or impressions. When I told you to trust your feelings I didn't know who you would trust. I know that you trusted my grandson because you love him. He was just the wrong person to talk to about Daisy. I didn't know it then, but I can feel it in you now.'

Reeling from his words Rosa closed her eyes and tried to get a handle of her emotions. None of it made sense. The way Talan made her feel when she thought of him was a big mixture of happiness and despair. It couldn't work, she didn't want it to. It could have worked at the beginning, maybe, but surely now it was too late? And what about Kate? Besides, there was no time in her changed life for chasing 'what ifs' and 'maybes'.

She opened her eyes and said, 'Morganna seems to have the same impression as you. But I don't think that Talan and I getting together is likely. Perhaps I thought so for a while once, but not now.'

'You have free will and only you can decide to follow or reject happiness. My Jocelyn, for reasons that were right for her, made the wrong decision years ago. That ended in tragedy for us both in different ways. I hope you won't make the same mistake. I believe that you meeting Talan is fate's way of putting right the past.'

Before Rosa could order her feelings and her mouth to respond, he stood and gave her a beautiful smile. 'Will you see Jocelyn soon?' he asked.

'I will.' A prickle of tears made her pause. 'Does this mean you and she will be reunited soon?'

'If that is her wish, and I think it is.' Jory's eyes twinkled.

'I hope you will be … even though I will miss her so …' Rosa's voice faltered.

Jory nodded and took a step forward, his hand hovering above her shoulder, so close she could feel the static needling her skin. 'She is waiting for you. And now I must leave. You have much to do in the future, many to help. Be happy, Rosa.'

Rosa wanted to ask him so much more, get answers to so many things, but through her tears she saw him fade and then there was nothing between her and the ocean, save the soft descent of twilight.

CHAPTER 20

*T*he clock said 8:15 but Rosa felt as if she'd only just closed her eyes. Jory and Morganna's words had resounded in her head all night as if someone was continually hitting pause and replay. She yawned loudly, her tired eyes adjusting to the bright room. Then remembered that there had been a weird dream in amongst it – so she must have slept at some point.

In the dream she was accused of treason in King Arthur's court. Apparently she hadn't replaced the sacred ancient arrowhead in the alcove of learning. When challenged, she had said that King Arthur spent too much time walking on the beach instead of governing and Rosa would be a much better ruler. Alcove of learning? What the mind comes up with when left to its own devices beggared belief.

Rosa threw back the covers and sat on the edge of her bed. There was no mystery about the arrowhead though, was there? Talan had one in his eyebrow and he had taught her much about the history of Tintagel, so that's where the learning connection came in she guessed. Before she'd gone to bed last night she had paced the room, anxiety settling over her like a cloak, going over and over what Jory had said about fate and not making the wrong choice. His words had hit home – she didn't want to repeat Jocelyn's mistake and end up living a life without love.

But then she wondered what was she *actually* supposed to do about it? Run round to his house and say that his dead grandfather and Morganna thought they should be together? She didn't think so. He was the one who had made it perfectly clear what he thought about her. Okay, the first time he could be excused to an extent given the journalist thing, but now Daisy must have told him the truth and he was hardly beating a path to her door was he? No. The more she thought about it, the more she believed it was up to Talan to get in touch with her.

That was last night, and this morning her opinion hadn't changed. In the wee small hours, she had asked her heart an honest question. *Do I love Talan?* The heart had been non-committal. She'd gleaned that she found him very attractive, intelligent, funny, sexy and she liked being in his company, but did that constitute love? As she'd never been in love before, that was hard to gauge; and her objective, logical, scientific upbringing said that the whole thing was far too complicated.

In the shower she leaned her forehead on the tiles and let the hot water wash away the tension in her shoulders and fully wake her. Logic piped up again that if Talan wanted to see her he would have been round by now, texted, phoned, even sent a hand-delivered note. But he hadn't and that should be the end of it. Added to that, as she kept telling herself, was the fact that he had Kate.

Now dressed, packed and out on the balcony for the last time, Rosa tried to absorb as many sights, sounds, smells and tastes of the scene before her so they would be held forever in her memory. In a few hours she would be back in her flat with just the row of Victorian houses to gaze at from her bedroom window.

Talan belonged in her memory too, in a locked box of memories, because she couldn't have them popping up unbidden, it would be too painful. Perhaps when she was an old woman she'd take them out from time to time and remember summer in Tintagel.

Rosa picked up her bag and looked one last time around the lovely bedroom and checked that she had her keys and phone. Phone? Where the blue blazes was that? A five-minute panic-fuelled search in drawers, under the bed, in the bathroom and under the bedcovers proved fruitless. But it *had* to be here, she'd spoken to Jocelyn just before she left for the church last night and she'd checked it before she went to sleep.

Rosa put her hand to her head. *Think, woman.* Where had she last been? Of course, there it was out on the balcony seat. Snatching it up she noticed that she had a text message. Funny she'd not heard the tone - must have come when she was in the shower. Walking to the door she thumbed the screen aside and then froze with one hand on the handle, one foot inside and one outside the room, unable to believe her eyes. The message was from Talan.

Rosa, I'm letting you know that I have left a letter with John to give to you at breakfast. I was going to phone but I was worried that everything I had to say would come out wrong, and a text would take too long. I'm texting now to make sure you know about the letter. Hope to hear from you once you've read it.

Talan x

Rosa watched her fingertips trace the little kiss, adrenaline rocketing through her veins. Then she watched her feet thumping on the stairs and into a full dining-room of breakfasters. Heads swivelled at her bull-in-a-china shop entrance and some seemed amused at her excited appearance. 'John! You have a letter for me apparently?'

John glanced up from his notepad in surprise. 'I do. Would you like your usual on your last day with us, my dear?'

'Yes please, but could I have the letter first?'

'Of course, but if you don't mind I'd like to finish taking Mr and Mrs Dingle's breakfast order.' He smiled in amusement.

'Of course, sorry ...' She sat down and rummaged in her bag for an imaginary something to hide her scarlet face.

At last, after what seemed an hour but in fact was five minutes, John brought her a pot of tea and a white envelope. The speed with which she tore open the flap nearly damaged the damn thing and then with a galloping heart she read :

Rosa,

I want to apologise for behaving like a brute yesterday. In my defence, I truly thought you were using me to get to Mum, which both infuriated and hurt me. I of course now know the whole truth and I hope that since my mum explained what happened to her with the press when she was young, you can forgive me, just a little bit?

What Mum did tell me about your visit took a hell of a lot of swallowing. Like her I have never been one to believe in spirits. In fact, I haven't really thought about it too much before, so it has taken a sleepless night for it all to really sink in. Your story is incredible, but nevertheless I believe it to be true … There is no other explanation.

Mum is wearing her locket proudly and seems happier than I can ever remember. John tells me you are leaving for London this morning. I wonder if I could ask you to pop round to my home before you do? I would like to say a huge thank you in person for setting us straight on Grandad's death.

I have taken this morning off, so come round when it's convenient for you. I couldn't bear if we parted like this. And at least you know that I won't try to jump your bones now! (Kate told me that she spoke to Willa who explained your situation).

Once again, Rosa, I am truly sorry and want to make sure you know just how much.

See you soon?

Talan xx

Key points stood out for Rosa. He was profoundly sorry, he wanted to see her in person to make sure she realised just how much, and he couldn't bear it if they parted like this. This news made her stomach giddy with excitement and she had to sit on her hands to stop herself picking up the letter again and reading it for umpteenth time.

John placed her breakfast in front of her and she began to eat on auto-pilot. But what also stood out, and served to bamboozle rather than excite, was the line about Kate speaking to Willa. What situation had she explained about? As far as Rosa knew there was no situation. And the line about him not jumping her bones? *No point in puzzling, Rosa, all will be revealed very soon when you see him.* When you see him ... that thought made her stomach flip and brought a blush to her cheeks. Until now she hadn't realised how much she longed to do just that.

Rosa hurried down the High Street towards Talan's flat, smoothing her hair and checking in a little handbag mirror that she didn't have the remains of breakfast in her teeth. Damn it all. Why hadn't she booked the later train? She had to be at Bodmin station at 11:30 for her noon train and it was almost 9:15 now. The taxi was due to pick her up in an hour, so she would barely have time to say hello and goodbye to Talan. Hindsight was a great thing. Trouble was, it was bloody useless in the here and now.

Outside his front door she took a few deep breaths and hoped that her rush hadn't caused any damp patches on the clingy low-cut green t-shirt dress she'd hastily changed into after breakfast. A surreptitious glance under both arms told her that the claims made by the adverts for her deodorant had been thankfully telling the truth.

Just as she steeled herself to press her finger to the doorbell, the door swung open. The sight of Talan's head popping round it, his beautiful eyes twinkling as his stubbly face stretched in a huge smile, made her mouth copy it.

'Rosa! So glad you came, come in, come in!' He pulled the door fully open, she stepped into the hallway and then her heart, already beating a tattoo in her chest shot into hyper-drive.

There he stood bare-chested, the modesty of his 6'4" frame barely covered by a short fluffy white towel around his waist. Tucked in at his right hip, his muscular tanned thigh was partly revealed and before she quickly averted her eyes, Rosa noted that his wet hair curled along his damp shoulders, and in the smattering of dark hairs on his broad chest water droplets clung like diamonds. Rosa knew her face was on fire and her tongue clove to the roof of her dust-dry mouth. *What the hell was he playing at?*

Talan led the way down the hall. 'I've just jumped out of the shower and put the coffee on. I was on my way to get dressed when I saw you hurry down the drive so I just grabbed a towel. No cause for embarrassment now though, eh?' Talan took two mugs out of a cupboard and turned to face her. 'Well, there is on my part. You must think I have been such a dope for not realising you couldn't be interested in me – romantically that is.'

Still unable to look at his face even though what he was saying made no sense, Rosa just laughed nervously and made a big show of looking around his kitchen. It was neat, functional and clean. Nothing fancy. An L-shaped counter supported all the usual appliances and the overall impression she had was of fresh lime and light wood.

It was difficult to form an impression however, when all she had in her mind was an image of his almost naked body. 'What a lovely kitchen you have,' she managed, and perched on a high stool next to the counter. She pushed a coaster around with her fingernail and realised she couldn't spend the whole time looking down. He would wonder if she had a stiff neck.

'It's not bad is it? I'll give you the grand tour in a bit if you'd like?'

Rosa forced herself to look at him without turning crimson. 'That's not going to be possible I'm afraid.' Damn it. She could feel the heat in her neck already. But then what did he expect looking at her with those incredible eyes and revealing himself like that? 'I have to leave for my train in less than an hour.'

'Oh that's a shame.' He stroked his hand across his cheek thoughtfully. 'I suppose I could take you so we could chat on the way. It's the least I could do in the circumstances.'

'You'd have to put some clothes on first.' She gave a little laugh and took a mug of coffee from his hand, a shot of electricity tickling along her wrist as his fingers brushed hers. Rosa cleared her throat. 'But I wouldn't want to put you out – the taxi's booked anyway.'

Talan gave a shrug and pulled a stool up next to hers. 'The offer's there if you change your mind.' As he sat down Rosa caught the delicious smell of lemony shower gel and clean skin. The flame of desire in her groin told her it might be just as well that she was short of time. If she stayed longer she might break the habit of a lifetime and throw herself at him.

Talan folded his arms across his chest, his right bicep flexing a leaping dolphin tattoo, his chest expanding in a deep sigh. Rosa suddenly found that she had to pay a lot of attention to the slate tiles on the kitchen floor.

'So I would like you to accept my most humble apology, Rosa. Am I forgiven?' He asked, her name on his lips in his quiet Cornish brogue creating a trail of goosebumps along her arms.

She lifted her eyes and found his regarding her over the rim of his coffee mug. 'Of course, I can quite understand how it all must have looked. You were only trying to protect your mum.'

He nodded and furrowed his thick dark brows. 'One thing that's been puzzling me. Why didn't you just ask me to arrange a meeting with you and Mum instead of asking if I knew a Daisy? It would have saved a lot of bad feeling.'

'Because at the time I didn't know Daisy was your mum. The spirit of your grandad said I should trust my feelings when trying to seek her out, but tell nobody about what he asked me to do. I trusted you, but I didn't know he was your grandad at that time. If I'd started coming out with the real reason I wanted to find Daisy, you would have thought I was a crazy person. And be fair, Talan, if I had asked you to set up a meeting with your mum you still would have thought I was after a story, wouldn't you?'

Talan pressed his lips together and ruffled his damp hair. 'I guess so. The whole story is pretty crazy to be honest ... so I'm not sure what you were supposed to have done. Glad you trusted me though and I'm sorry once again.'

His earnest expression and heartfelt smile made her want to smother him with kisses. Where were these feelings coming from? Come off it woman, you half-admitted to yourself in the wee-small hours that you could possibly be in love with him. It was looking more than likely to Rosa that Morganna and Jory were right. Then Kate's face came between them and she shook her head.

'That's enough apologising, Talan. I'm just glad we are friends again.'

He shot her a wry smile. 'There was a time when I'd hoped we could be more than that. Now I realise you just went out with me as a friend.'

Rosa considered another dodge but then instinct took over. This was a now or never moment. Kate's face was shoved under the table – all's fair in love and bloody war after all.

'Yes. I must admit I was hoping we could be more than friends too – even though a long-distance relationship would be difficult. Then of course everything went tits up – all finally and thankfully resolved now of course … But you have Kate.' She finished with a sad smile and little shrug.

Talan pushed both hands through his damp hair and scowled. 'What do you mean you wished we could have been more than friends? And Kate? I don't have Kate.'

The words *I don't have Kate* made Rosa's heart jump up in her ribcage and do a tap dance. Did that mean it had been just a fling? And the more than friends thing was *so* confusing her.

'More than friends, means more than friends, Talan. Didn't you learn about the birds and the bees in school? And for the record, I saw you and Kate snogging the face off each other outside the pub on the night of your mum's birthday. I dodged back the other way before you caught me.'

Talan raised his eyebrows at that and then shook his head. 'Oh, it was just a drunken fumble set up by bloody Aunt Clare and Kate between them. Clare told me that Kate was upset outside, said that she'd felt that she'd annoyed me somehow and would I go out and see her to put her mind at rest. I was pretty confused I can tell you, as we'd been getting on fine all evening. Still, I went out and she gave me a hug and then ...' his eyes grew round and he turned both his hands palm up in a gesture of incredulity, '... she just kind of pounced on me.'

Rosa nodded and narrowed her eyes. 'Well, from where I was standing you didn't seem too keen to fight her off.'

A blush crept up his neck and he slid off the stool and took his mug to the sink. 'Yeah, well I was pissed off after finding out about you and Willa I just needed to feel wanted. I know you didn't intend to hurt me ... but you did.' He turned to look at her. 'And now I have no bloody clue what to think since you just told me that you *did* want a relationship with me—'

Rosa jumped down from her stool and raised the flat of her hand towards him 'Whoa, there. Can we rewind just a second? What do you mean, me and Willa?'

Talan put his head on one side and raised a brow. 'She told Kate that you were her partner?'

The words were clear enough, the inference too, but Rosa could hardly believe what she was hearing. 'Willa told Kate that we were ... lesbians?'

'Yeah ... aren't you?'

'No! Well she is, but I'm...' Rosa put her hand over her mouth and shook her head bewildered. 'Fuck, just wait 'til I see her!' Furious beyond belief Rosa thumped the table rattling her coffee cup against a fruit bowl.

A huge smile spread slowly across Talan's face. 'So you were interested in me romantically, then?'

Rosa looked at him standing there so vulnerable yet so unfeasibly sexy and her breath caught in her throat. 'Oh God yes,' she whispered. Then as his eyes sent petrol blue flames of desire into hers she added, 'And I still am.'

Talan closed the gap between them in two strides and cupped her face in his large hands. 'You have no idea what that means to me.' Their eyes locked, connected. 'The times I have dreamt about you, lay awake at night fantasising about you.' The growl in his voice as he said those words left her in no doubt as to exactly what he meant.

Rosa traced her fingers gently over his lips and then brushed her lips against his. Talan's arms encircled her in a tight embrace and then she felt the heat of his mouth on hers, searching, opening her lips with his tongue, deepening the kiss so exquisitely that the flame of desire she'd just experienced now quickly became a fire.

He drew back and looked into her eyes, his own smouldering with pent-up desire. 'You have too many clothes on. Would you like to follow me into my bedroom and take them off?'

She could feel his excitement hard against her through his towel and the clingy material of her dress. The new brazen Rosa who had made an appearance the first time they'd met seemed to be in the driving seat again as she ran her hands over his firm buttocks and pressed her groin against his. 'No,' she panted, 'I'd like you to take them off for me.'

Talan took her hand and practically ran into his bedroom. He spun her round and with her back to him he pulled her hard against his chest. He lifted her hair and a shiver ran the length of her body as his eager mouth kissed her neck, while his strong hands travelled down her thighs. Rosa twisted her face up to his and he kissed her deeply, while his hands travelled back up along her tummy and cupped each breast, his fingers teasing her aching nipples.

'Now to get rid of those clothes,' he whispered into her ear and gently nipped her neck with his teeth.

Rosa kicked off her shoes as he walked round to face her and then he knelt before her, kissing her ankles, shins, knees, all the while pushing up the hem of her dress until his face was level with her crotch. He kissed the insides of her thighs briefly and Rosa gasped as she felt the heat of his mouth against her lacy knickers and the scratchy stubble of his face on her hot skin. Tantalisingly, his mouth continued up her body. He flicked her navel with his tongue, and then dropped hot kisses along her cleavage while deftly pulling her dress up and over her raised arms.

Getting to his feet Talan kissed her deeply again while he unhooked her bra, letting it slide down her arms to the floor. Then he hooked two of his fingers in the elastic of her knickers at each hip and sent them quickly to join the bra. Talan took a step back and cast his eyes over her full breasts and erect nipples, and then he slid his glance further down. Unbelievably, Rosa felt completely unabashed under his gaze and relished the look of admiration on his face.

'Will I do?'

'You are incredible, absolutely incredible,' Talan whispered stepping towards her.

Unsure where she found the confidence, she held up her hand and said, 'Wait. I think you need help with your towel.'

A slow sexy grin curled his lips and she stepped forward to kiss his neck, chest, and then on her knees, she traced her tongue down the line of dark hairs beneath his navel. The towel was coming loose under the pressure of his erection and one little tug of her fingers sent it to the carpet in a heap. Giving his body the same slow scrutiny as he'd given hers, she said huskily, 'You're incredible too, Talan.' Then she stroked her cool fingers up his thighs and guided him into her mouth. He gasped, twisted his hands in her thick curls and moaned as she slowly moved her tongue along the length of his shaft.

Moments later Rosa felt herself lifted into his arms and then placed on her back in the centre of his bed. As he opened her legs wider with his knee and then flicked his tongue over her most intimate spot Rosa grasped the metal bedstead and arched her back, her breath coming in short huffs. It occurred to her that the few men in the past that she'd slept with had never made her feel like this, never come close. Other men rapidly vanished from her thoughts as Talan's tongue worked its magic together with his long fingers. When she felt two slip inside her she cried out as her climax shuddered through her.

From somewhere up on the ceiling she felt Talan climb on top of her, tasted herself on his lips as he simultaneously thrust his hard length into her and kissed her deeply. She felt herself digging her fingernails into his back and matching his speed as she rocked her hips in time with his. Another mind blowing climax sent goosebumps up and down the length of her body, and then she felt him tense, swell inside her - his moan of ecstasy echoed her own.

Moments later after catching their breath Talan propped himself up on his pillow, looked at her and said, 'No doubt about it, that was *the* best sex I have ever had.'

Rosa laughed, 'For me too.' Then she felt her passion-fuelled raunchiness slipping away. 'To be honest, I have never been as ...' She struggled for the right words. '... As demonstrative as that. Never, um, took the lead in the way that I did.'

His eyes crinkled around the edges. 'Well, all I can say is thank goodness you did!' He kissed her on the tip of her nose and ran his fingers lightly down her cheek. Just that innocent gesture sent her libido into orbit again. What was happening to her? In the past she could either take or leave sex. It had seemed predictable, boring even, and she'd never been fulfilled. Her much prided, *I never sleep with men until I know them well* mantra had gone right out of the window too hadn't it? Sex with Talan seemed more than that. Yes it was mind-blowing physically – but there had been something else, something deeper. When he'd been inside her it felt as if he was connected to her spiritually. It felt right ... natural.

She closed her eyes and Talan brushed soft kisses on her lids and forehead. The emotion rising in her chest sent a prickle of tears behind her eyes. Thank goodness she had them closed. *Please don't let me cry.* She felt emotionally out of control, and that scared her. The jangle of her mobile phone snapped her eyes open and immediately a picture of a taxi appeared in her head.

'Oh nooo!' She leapt out of bed, grabbed her dress and ran to the kitchen.

'Rosa?' John's anxious voice asked.

'It's the taxi isn't it? God, so sorry I got ... caught up saying goodbye to a friend.'

'So what shall I do? He's outside waiting.' John's anxiety had switched to irritation and Rosa couldn't say she blamed him.

Talan appeared naked in the doorway. Rosa's attempt at wrapping her dress around her nudity hadn't quite worked; her left breast was exposed as was most of her backside. She was glad that this call wasn't a video link - that image made her giggle which didn't make John's temper any sweeter.

'Sorry Rosa, but I don't see what's funny. Do you want the man to wait or go? I think it would be only fair to pay him something if he's had a wasted journey.'

'Okay, hang on.' She pulled a face, covered the phone and explained what was happening to Talan.

'Ask John to slip him some cash and we'll see him right later. I'll take you anywhere you want to go.'

Rosa smiled. He had taken her to the most wonderful places already that morning. Places she'd never dreamed of.

CHAPTER 21

$\mathcal{R}$osa Fernley … was in his bed … *His* bed. Talan couldn't quite believe his luck and repeated the same sentence over and over as he made tea and placed two hot Cornish pasties on a plate. After they had made love a second time, she'd sat up, wrinkled her nose in that impish way that melted his heart and said, 'I would kill for a pasty. I haven't had one since I've been here.' So he'd got dressed and nipped across the road to the bakers.

Bob, the baker had commented that Talan looked like the cat that'd got the cream. Was it that obvious? He guessed a Cheshire cat grin and a twinkle in his eyes said, yes. Now as he took the tray through to the bedroom and saw her snuggled in his duvet, her glorious hair spread out across his pillow, a beautiful smile on her face, his heart flipped. He felt like a teenager with his first serious crush. But this wasn't a crush was it? No, this was…

'About time. I'm wasting away here,' Rosa giggled and sat up, the duvet slipping to her waist, her firm breasts bouncing as she got comfy. To his disappointment she tucked the duvet up under her arms and held her hands out for the tray. Just as well though, he thought, taking his shirt and jeans off and slipping in next to her, he doubted he'd have the energy to make love to her again just now.

The pasty tasted so good he nearly made a pig of himself. Must have expended a trillion calories during the morning. He looked across at Rosa who was devouring hers almost as fast and pointed to her cup. 'Not sure if you took sugar. I left it without.'

'No, I'm sweet enough, thanks.' She shot him that impish wrinkle, her jade green eyes bright with merriment.

'I won't argue with you there.' Returning to his pasty, a heavy weight suddenly descended across his shoulders. Soon she'd be gone. Of course she'd missed her train but there'd be another one, and life would return to normal. But then it never would, would it? It would never be normal again now Rosa had swept in and turned it upside down, turned him upside down. He could barely go a minute without his head filling with thoughts of her.

It was happening now as he popped the last bit of flaky pastry into his mouth. Thoughts of Rosa striding out along the cliff path last week, the wind in her hair, a pink glow in her cheeks. Rosa tackling a ham salad on a plate as big as a dustbin lid, her eyes round with surprise. Rosa half-naked on the phone. Rosa underneath him, her eyes aflame with need while he …

'You okay?' she broke into his thoughts. 'You look miles away.'

'Yeah, I couldn't be better.' Then he watched her sipping her tea until she frowned and opened her mouth to say something. Before she did, he jumped in. 'Actually, things *could* be better. I don't want you to go back to London. Isn't there some way you could extend your stay here? Just for a few days at least?'

Rosa's mouth broke into a melon-slice grin. 'I have been thinking exactly the same. I have the rest of the week technically, but I decided to go back early. I'll text Shelley and explain – well make an excuse. She'll be okay with it.'

'Fantastic! And you'll stay here with me?'

'No. I thought I'd ask if John had a spare room.' Then she burst out laughing at his crestfallen face. 'Of course I'll stay here. I can't think of anywhere I'd rather be.'

'You are so funny, not.' He wiped a crumb of pastry from her chin. 'Do you want a shower? I could do with one.'

'You saying I'm grubby?' Again the mischievous grin. Then she put her hand around his neck and pulled his mouth towards hers.

Before he kissed her he said, 'No, but I think I need to double check every inch of you to make sure.'

* * *

As it was such a lovely afternoon they decided to go for a walk. Talan had phoned in sick the rest of the day, much to his boss at Pendennis's chagrin. He didn't care though, nothing mattered apart from being with Rosa.

Rosa had been the one to suggest the walk and remained secretive about exactly where they were going. She seemed to be certain of where she wanted to go however and Talan had been content to follow her down the path towards the castle. He was glad, as they'd never had time to do more than talk about the place, so it would be nice for him to wax lyrical about points of interest – in short to show off a bit. What was he like? Perhaps he really was regressing back to his teenage years.

Talan was surprised however when Rosa pulled him left off the path towards the little bridge that ran across the stream and up through the bramble path towards the top of the hill. Panting along behind her he yelled, 'Slow down a bit. I'm guessing we're off to the church?'

'Yep. I adore that place. Come on, slow coach!'

Hand in hand they walked along the path through the graveyard, the grey slate headstones and Celtic crosses stirring up a mixture of emotion in his chest. It had been years since he'd come up here. The last time was for a Christmas concert when he'd been at school. Being here with Rosa made it feel special though – the old church had come alive somehow.

He watched her go to the arch doorway and place her hand on the keystone. The warm breeze lifted her curls and the scent of lilies drifted out of the open door. It was in that instant that his heart allowed him to see the depth of his feelings – the truth. It had been pressing of the corners of his mind all morning but he'd pushed it away. Even when he'd been furious, heartbroken at the way he thought she'd deceived him, his body had ached for hers, his arms had felt empty until she'd stepped into them at last.

He was in love with Rosa. Plain and simple.

That realisation rocked him on his feet and he turned his face towards the line of blue ocean visible through the fringe of meadow grass at the cliff edge. What to do about it? She would leave and … Talan silently admonished himself. There would be time enough to think about that later. Live for the moment. And, he added as he walked over to join her, try to think of ways to make that moment turn into forever.

'Put your hand on the stone and tell me what you feel,' she said with a smile.

He put his palm against the rough stone and felt the warmth of the sun in it and the ancient work of a chisel under it. 'Great craftsmanship.'

She frowned slightly. 'But can't you feel anything else?'

'Um, like what?'

'Well like,' she rolled her eyes up to the left, '… a sense of peace, and of those who have gone before, their hopes – dreams?'

'Not as you'd notice. I'm no psychic, sweetheart.' Talan sighed at her disappointed face. 'But I suppose I do feel peaceful up here though I thought it felt special when I walked up the path.' He waved his hand at the churchyard and then towards the sea 'I mean this is such a beautiful and peaceful spot isn't it?'

Rosa grinned. 'It sure is. Let's go and sit on that bench over there.'

Once seated, Rosa became quiet and shifted restlessly a few times. Then she seemed fixated with a bee on the clover. Clearing her throat, she said, 'Something told me to bring you here, I think it could be upsetting for you though.'

A finger of trepidation poked him in the chest. He didn't want to be upset today. He wanted to relax, take in this spectacular view and be close to Rosa 'Not sure I like the sound of that. Better show me and let's see.'

Rosa pointed to a craggy overhang to his left. 'You see that, Talan? That's where your grandfather fell. And this very bench we are sitting on – this is where Jory told me about his death and asked me to find Daisy.'

A wall of sadness rose up, closing the rolling sea and cliffs to his eyes. Growing up he'd seen a few pictures of his grandfather, but always by accident and his mother had quickly snatched them away. Her sadness had been too much to bear so he hadn't really found out much beyond the fact that Jory had taken his own life.

When he'd got older Daisy had mentioned that he'd done it because of a woman. Talan had so wished it could have been different, wished he could have met his grandfather. His paternal grandfather had died before he was born and when his friends had gone fishing, or to a cricket match or something with their grandads, Talan had felt like he was missing out. Then his dad left and his world fell apart.

'He looked so much like you, and like Daisy. You all have the same colour eyes.' Talan didn't trust his voice; he just stared out across the ocean. 'It was such a shame he couldn't have met you.' Rosa paused and nodded to herself. 'He's just told me that, and to tell you that you make him proud.'

A warm glow spread right up from his toes and into his heart. 'Did he? Can you see him?'

'He was here briefly. I didn't see him as I have before, he was just an impression. There was so much love for you, Talan,' she said quietly. When Talan looked into her eyes he saw an ocean of sympathy and caring. Something told him to go for it, tell her how he felt right there and then.

'Thank you so much for telling me, Rosa. You have no idea how much that means to me.' He drew her to him and she rested her head against his shoulder. 'In fact, you have no idea how much *you* mean to me. I know it might seem mad … but I think I'm already in love with you.'

Time seemed to stop. The rapid thud of his heartbeat in his ears and the call of a gull seemed magnified as he held his breath for her response.

Rosa lifted her head and looked at him, her eyes bright. 'Oh Talan,' she whispered and then kissed him, her salty tears warm on his lips. Then she drew back and cupped his face in her small hands. 'I feel exactly the same. I was thinking earlier about the reason why I had felt so close to you when we were in bed, why I enjoyed it so much compared to my past experiences. And I came to the conclusion it was because we weren't just having sex,' she dashed away a tear and gave him the melon-slice smile again, '... we were making love.'

Talan's heart was so full that there was no room for words. He just nodded and kissed her tenderly, aware only of the vanilla notes of Rosa's perfume, the sound of the waves below crashing on the shore, the sun on his skin and the taste of salt air mingling with her tears of joy.

Content to sit on the bench with Rosa snuggled under his arm, her head on his shoulder, lost in their own world of azure sky and cobalt ocean, he was a little disgruntled to find church bells breaking noisily into their silence. Rosa stood up, looking back to the church.

'Oh Talan, look it's a wedding!'

Talan twisted round on the bench and saw a beribboned vintage grey MG Midget parked at the church gates and a procession of cars filing down to the small car park nearby. From the car two men in top hat and tails emerged and waved to the growing crowd of people as they made their way toward the church entrance.

'Stylish car.'

'Car? What about the setting? Imagine how perfect it would be getting married here?' Rosa's face flushed and she gave a nervous laugh. 'Not that I'm proposing or anything.' Then her face grew serious. 'Did you know that your grandad wanted to marry my gran here?'

Talan didn't and the enormity of what Jory and Jocelyn had lost suddenly became very real to him. Now he'd found Rosa he could never imagine losing her. 'That is too hard to imagine. My poor grandad up here that night, remembering the time he'd spent with her, feeling so hopeless,' he said standing up and slipping his arm around Rosa's shoulders.

They watched for a few minutes as the photographer took a few photos and then everyone went inside. 'Look Talan, the bride's car!'

A black limousine glided to a halt and out of it stepped a grey-haired man in tails and then he held his hand out to the bride. She stepped into the afternoon sunshine, radiant in an Art Deco ivory design. The neckline swept elegantly from shoulder to shoulder, the silky gown clinging to her curves like cream on a spoon rippled down and swirled at her feet. Hair the colour of jet curled in a soft bob at her chin and on her head was another Art Deco-style silver filigree head band.

As she walked on her father's arm towards the photographer snapping away at the door of the church, Rosa heaved a sigh and said, 'She looks absolutely incredible. And if I ever get married, it would be in a dress like that.'

'And in this church?' Talan surprised himself by asking.

Rosa's head snapped up and she gave him a quizzical look. 'It would be a dream wouldn't it?'

'It would be amazing.' Then unable to read her expression and wondering if he'd come on too strong he said. 'Don't worry I'm not proposing either … well not yet anyway.' Talan looked back at the ocean unable to believe what he'd just said. It was like he had no control over his words. Perhaps Jory had a hand in it somewhere, he thought wryly. God knows what Rosa must be thinking.

Rosa slipped her arm through his and guided him towards the church. 'You never know what might happen in the future do you?' She looked up at him with that heart melting wrinkle of her nose.

Phew, thank goodness she'd not run away screaming. 'Nope. Well, I don't anyway. Morganna might though'

'Oh she does. She's already told me,' Rosa said with an enigmatic smile.

But no matter how hard he tried, Talan couldn't get her to say anything more about it.

* * *

Talan watched Rosa move around his kitchen as if she'd been doing it forever. She took out pans, cans, packets, found wooden spoons, herbs, and spices without once asking him where things were kept. And she moved with such grace and precision, as if she knew exactly what came next, focused, sure of herself - in control.

A low rumble growled in his stomach as the delicious aroma from the lasagne cooking in the oven filled his kitchen. 'So not only are you the most beautiful woman who ever lived, fantastic in bed, intelligent and funny – you can cook too. I think I could get used to this.'

Green eyes narrowed in mock chagrin. 'Don't think I'm cooking all the time, matey. Flattery won't get you everywhere.' Rosa pointed a garlic baguette thoughtfully at him. 'Do you think John was a bit grumpy this afternoon?'

Talan had noticed an edge to his voice when they'd popped in to collect Rosa's bags and pay him the money he'd given the taxi guy. 'A little … Perhaps he felt a bit put out, not surprising really when you left your bags in his hallway, said you'd be back in half an hour and then jumped into bed with me.'

Rosa threw back her head and laughed. 'But he didn't know that, did he? I would hate to think he'd been left with a bad impression of me.'

'You're hardly likely to stay there again are you?'

'No. But I might bump into him when I come up to this village often to see this Talan guy.' She grinned and wrapped foil around the bread. 'Do you know him? Tall, dark and handsome, sexy as hell and has this little arrowhead in his left eyebrow. Eyes as deep as the ocean, blue as the August sky and yet green too, like the sea-green depths under an anchored boat?'

'Wow!' Talan felt a rush of pride. 'Nobody has ever said that about my eyes. Poetic flattery *will* get you everywhere.'

'I can't claim it. It was Gran who described Jory's eyes in those words one evening, but in her dark little room I didn't quite get it. Then when I saw your eyes the description made perfect sense.'

'All I can say is your gran has a way with words.'

'And you shall meet her very soon…' Rosa put her head one side and for the first time that day he could tell she was unsure of him. She turned to the chopping board and began to slice a cucumber, the knife moving nearly as fast as her words. 'That's if you want to. I have to go up there on Friday evening, she's expecting me. But I quite understand if you don't want to meet her…with everything that happened in the past and—'

'Hey stop rambling, woman.' Talan walked over and placed his hands on her shoulders. 'I don't blame her for what happened. She did what she thought was best for everyone concerned at the time. The past is gone. I would love to meet the woman that my grandad fell in love with.'

Rosa put down her knife and turned into his arms. 'Thanks, Talan. I'm sure she will be over the moon to see you. I'll have to warn her how similar you look to Jory before you go in though, or we might lose her quicker than we thought.'

'Am I really so much like him?'

'In the eyes, yes.' Rosa traced a finger over his mouth. 'Your lips are fuller, your jaw is more square and your nose … perhaps a little longer. Once thing's for sure, you both had a similar effect on the women in my family.'

Talan tipped her face to his. 'You have a wonderful effect on me too. You make me feel truly alive and I can't believe how lucky I am to have found you, Rosa,' he said into her hair. And then he held her as if he'd never let her go.

Chapter 22

$\mathcal{H}$ow could one human being fulfil another so completely? From the bedroom door Rosa watched Talan as he slept, the morning light angling through a gap in the curtain illuminating a yellow sword across his taut belly. Rolling onto his side, the choppy waves of his hair tumbled over his closed eyes and his right arm flopped down over the side of the bed, the little dolphin leaping over his muscular bicep.

After supper last night they had talked, made love, talked again, each thoroughly at ease with the other, in sync with moods, views and aspirations. Rosa had been thrilled to find how similar their views on politics, music and religion had been, though her special sense had led her away from his common ground. It wasn't that he didn't like the extra dimension to her personality; he just didn't fully get it yet. And why would he? It was only last week that Rosa herself had embraced it completely. At least he wasn't a complete close-minded sceptic like her father.

A picture of the bride and her dad they'd seen yesterday sprang to mind. Would her father ever walk Rosa down the aisle? The way she felt at the moment she very much doubted it. Just thinking about her dad sent a rush of anger to her brain. Rosa picked up Talan's shirt from the carpet, slipped it on and tiptoed out of the bedroom.

Running water into the kettle, she thought about another

person who made her furious and had been on her mind as soon as she'd awakened that morning. Willa-sodding-Farquarson. Just what the fuck had she been playing at? If Talan hadn't had a compulsion to see Rosa and apologise, she would be back at her desk in London by now living the rest of her life without him. All because of Willa's lies.

So angry that she wouldn't have been surprised to see steam coming out of her ears if she'd looked in a mirror, a rational voice thankfully surfaced as she sipped her tea. She would have come back to visit Morganna and Daisy and probably have bumped into Talan at a later date, especially if Morganna's predictions of her future had been correct. Rosa blew a snort of exasperation down her nose. But that might have taken months, years even, and these lovely few days they'd spent together wouldn't have happened.
Before Rosa had time to change her mind she grabbed her mobile phone and pressed call. 'Willa?'

'Hey, you! You just caught me. I was almost in the car and off to work.' Willa's cheery voice grated more than Rosa imagined possible.

'I'm so glad about that, because I am *beyond* furious with you.'

'Oh.'

That *oh* spoke volumes to Rosa. 'What possessed you to tell such a huge fucking lie?'

'You mean about ... us being lovers?'

The knuckles of Rosa's hand stood white as she almost crushed the phone. 'Of course I mean that! Why, what other shit have you been spreading around Tintagel?'

'None.' Willa's voice wavered. 'I ... I'm so sorry, Rosa.'

'So am I! Can you please tell me why?' Rosa threw herself on the sofa and looked at a fly running across the ceiling. She imagined it was Willa and wanted to swat it.

'Because ... because I heard from Kate in the castle office that you'd been out with this Talan guy and just saw green.'

Rosa snorted. 'You mean red?'

'No, green. I was insanely jealous. You see ... I am in love with you, have been since you opened the door to me when I came round about the flat share.'

Rosa's jaw dropped opened and a lead weight settled in her chest. 'But ... but you tried to set me up with that Greg bloke you work with and –'

Willa heaved a heavy sigh. 'That was to make you feel secure about having me share the flat. I wanted to be near you and if you knew the truth it would make you uncomfortable and eventually you'd want me out.'

Rosa was at a loss. The whole conversation was surreal. 'But what if Greg and I had started dating?'

'I knew you wouldn't. I knew he'd irritate the hell out of you.' Willa gave a nervous laugh.

'Oh I'm sorry, but I *really* don't find any of this fucking funny.'

'No. No, I guess you don't, neither do I. In fact, I am awfully ashamed of myself. I wanted a chance at happiness for a change. My parents have a lot to answer for – guess I'm pretty messed up?'

Rosa felt a pang of sympathy, but even before all this her empathy for Willa had started to wear thin. 'Look, I know your parents are shits, but lots of other people have it far, far worse. At least you don't have to worry about where your next meal is coming from and how to pay your sodding bills!'

'Poor little rich girl, huh?'

'If the cap fits.'

'I agree with you Rosa, and you'll be pleased to know I have already started packing. What I did was wrong and I can't bear to be around you anymore knowing that we will ... never ...'

To Rosa's horror Willa began to cry. But she gritted her teeth and plunged on, there was no turning back now. 'It's for the best. Have you somewhere to go?'

'As you say there'll be no problem finding a place. I might just buy a wing of Buckingham palace.'

Rosa sighed and felt her anger fading. 'Well, perhaps two even.'

'Did you like the earrings?'

'Yes, but you shouldn't have—'

'Wear them and think of me from time to time.' Willa's voice almost broke into a sob. 'And will you see Talan again?'

'I will. Thanks to your antics we might never have got together, but luckily fate stepped in'

'Then I wish you every happiness. Goodbye, Rosa'

'Bye, Willa Take care.' Emotionally drained, Rosa ended the call and felt like a stiff brandy even though it was only eight in the morning.

Talan appeared at the door just in boxer shorts rubbing his eyes. He gave her a smile and yawned stretching his arms above his head. 'You okay? Thought I heard you shout at someone.'

Rosa didn't answer for a moment, so struck was she by the way the muscles in his arms and stomach became defined by this movement. A now familiar stirring told her breakfast in bed might be in order. 'Hmm?'

'You shouted?' Talan ran water into the kettle.

'Oh yes, I was on the phone to bloody Willa You'll never guess why she told Kate that we were lovers?'

He turned round and folded his arms across his chest. 'Because she was in love with you and was jealous of me.'

'Yes!' Rosa said surprised. 'So you are a psychic after all?'

'Nope. Just common sense. And thinking about the way she looked at you that night when you were both drunk – or shall I say you were - it was quite clear what was in her mind.'

The 'Elementary, my dear Watson' look on his face, hair stuck up on one side, eyebrows raised, made Rosa want to giggle. She kept her face straight however and said, 'Oh, so I'm short on common sense, eh?'

'Perhaps in this case, yes. Scrambled eggs, toast, bacon for you, my lady?'

'Cheeky aren't you?'

'Would you like me any other way?'

'Yes. After breakfast I'd like you naked in bed please.'

Talan winked. 'Your wish is my command.'

* * *

'I never imagined that when you said we'd walk down to Mawgan Porth another time that it would be after we had slept together.' Rosa twisted her hair into a clip to stop the wind lashing it into her eyes. 'In fact, at the time I didn't really think there'd be a next time, or that we had a future, even though I fancied you like mad.'

Talan stopped and look down at her, pushing his hair off his forehead 'Ah yes. That was the day that I accused you of being a dirty cheating newshound in league with the devil and all his works. I know how to end a date well.'

Rosa laughed and slipped her arm through his, walking him to the top of the steep incline leading down to Mawgan Porth beach 'I'm just glad it all came right in the end. No thanks to sodding Willa'

'Odd names her parents picked for her,' Talan said pulling a piece of meadow grass and chewing the end thoughtfully. 'No wonder she wants to use just Willa'

'Eh? She only has the one as far as I know.'

'Really? Well you always call her, sodding Willa, bloody Willa and even I think on one occasion, fucking Willa'

Rosa laughed and elbowed him 'Such a comedian Come on, let's get down to the beach'

The cliff path, already on a steep incline, became rocky in places and Rosa had to really be careful where she put her feet on the loose stones. On her right was the Atlantic, unusually grey and choppy for late May. The wind rode white horses over the waves and yanked the seagulls up and down across the sky as if they were kites on bits of string.

Even though Rosa loved the peace of the sea's calm blue days, when it was grumpy like this, it inspired her, made her feel alive and part of nature. Her face to the wind she walked from the path a few steps to the edge of the cliff, stopped, spread her arms wide, closed her eyes and inhaled. Releasing her breath she shouted to

Talan over her shoulder, 'You are so lucky to live in this part of the world!'

'Oh don't worry, I know it!' he yelled back. 'There's no way I'd ever live anywhere else!'

Rosa came back to the path and kissed his cheek feeling the cool of his skin and salt tang on her lips. Though she already knew that he'd never move (and she didn't blame him one little bit) it seemed to make the fact that they lived so far apart all too real. Her thoughts turned to Jocelyn as they crossed a little stream and up yet another incline. How must she have felt knowing not only did she have to leave this paradise and the man she loved, but she had to return to a loveless marriage with a violent man? Rosa at least only had to return to London.

A stunning landscaped lawn appeared unexpectedly on her left set with red cushioned seats, and beyond it a large structure of glass and chrome hugged the crest of the hill. 'Wow, what's that place, Talan?'

'That's a luxury hotel and spa – the Scarlet Hotel. It has an indoor pool, stunning sea views from the rooms and a menu to die for.' Talan shrugged and walked on down the path.

'Have you stayed there?'

'Ha! No. It's a bit too rich for my pocket. But you never know. One day there might be an occasion worth saving up for.'

Rosa smiled to herself as she hurried after him. She hoped that one day she might stay with him on such an occasion.

* * *

The Merrymoor Inn had one of the best views in the world Rosa decided as she looked at the beach from the window and sipped her Cornish cyder. The sun tried to pull back the corners of the thick blanket of grey cloud, while the ocean churned to the shore, sneering at a few brave surfers trying to hang on to a wave. The surfers had about as much success as the sun.

Talan came back from the bar windswept and glowing, a number seven on the end of a chrome stand in his hand which he placed in the table between them. 'Lunch will be about twenty minutes as the chef is still preparing the crab. Landed this morning, so can't get fresher than that.'

'Fantastic. Real Cornish crab with real Cornish cyder and a view of a real Cornish beach. And the best yet – a view of a real handsome Cornishman sitting opposite.'

The pride in Talan's voice was obvious as he remarked, 'We do our best to please those folk from up country.'

Rosa loved that expression. She'd heard it a lot since she'd been down here and at first didn't get the significance. Everything north of Cornwall was up country, Land's End proved it. 'You have certainly pleased me in a whole number of ways.' Rosa took his hand across the table, loving the way his long artistic fingers curled around her own.

'So what time would you like to set off to Skipton tomorrow?' Talan took a sip of his pint and licked the froth from his top lip. Once again Rosa's thoughts were less than pure.

'Um, well I think it will take at least six hours, so six o clock too early?'

'Fine by me.'

They had decided that they would drive up and then Rosa would get the train back to London on Sunday. 'I don't like to think of you driving back here all by yourself on Sunday afternoon.' She gave his hand a squeeze.

'I'll be fine. The train from here to there is a nightmare and has fifty trillion changes. And it takes longer than driving anyway. It will be less stressful in my car and we could stop off somewhere for a cooked breakfast.'

'A cooked breakfast again. Blimey I will be three stone heavier by the time I get to London, the amount of food I've consumed since I've been here.'

Talan squeezed her hand and winked. 'We have to keep your strength up don't we?'

That evening as she lay in Talan's arms listening to his rhythmic breathing and the steady sound of his heartbeat, she thought about the journey they'd take to see Jocelyn the next day. Rosa ached to see her and tell her about her summer in Tintagel in more detail, see her expression, hear her laugh. But another part of her – a kitten-shaped part - shrank from the realisation that it might be the last time she would see her wonderful gran alive.

Taking care not to wake him, Rosa rolled out from under Talan's arm, slipped out of bed and tiptoed out of the room and to the kitchen window. The corner view looked out over the sea and fields, and the half-moon sailed in a clear sky. It obviously had more experience than the sun at shifting clouds. Rosa wondered if Jocelyn was looking at the moon as she was wont to do and thinking of her granddaughter at this very moment. It was comforting to think that she might be.

Rosa put her hand to the cool windowpane, smiled at the moon and made a wish.

CHAPTER 23

'*D*id Kate believe you?' Rosa asked Talan as she handed him her suitcase.

'Not sure, but it's done now. I said I had family business to sort out and I do in a way. You're family.' He slammed the boot shut and ruffled her hair. 'I'll be back on Monday so she will just have to lump it.'

'My hero,' Rosa said, got into the passenger seat and then added as Talan started the engine, 'Talking about family, does Daisy know anything?'

'Mum knows lots of things. She's a very intelligent woman, don't you know?' He looked at her in mock surprise, the little arrowhead rocking in his raised eyebrow.

'You know what I mean, you mentalist.' Rosa poked him in the bicep. 'About us.'

'Oh yes of course. I phoned her yesterday morning when you were in the shower. To say that she was over the moon was an understatement.'

Relief and happiness filled Rosa's heart. It would be great to have a possible future mother-in-law who was as cool and as lovely as Daisy. The natural ease at which such a thought popped into her brain made her pull up with a start. Their relationship was perhaps a tad too young to even contemplate such things. Morganna had a lot to answer for. But then yesterday, Talan himself had hinted that the church would be a great place to get married in the future hadn't he?

'What's the secret smile for?' Talan asked as he pulled out of his driveway.

'No idea I was smiling, secret or otherwise.' Rosa said, feeling a tell-tale blush colour her neck. To distract his puzzled glances she said, 'And I wonder if Daisy will tell Clare and Kate about us?'

A wicked grin stretched his face. 'Oh no. I told Mum that I wanted that pleasure to be mine … all mine.'

At the traffic lights, Rosa craned her neck to try and see Morganna through the crystal bedecked window of *Heart's Desire*. 'Probably far too early for her to be in the shop.'

'We can park up there and pop in if you'd like? A few minutes won't make that much difference to the journey.'

'No it's fine. We'll see her another time.'

'Shame. I'm sure she'd love to know we're together. Also I could ask her about those mysterious predictions she made about us.'

Rosa treated him to a withering look. 'That's exactly why I don't want to go in there.'

They next three hours flew by as they whizzed up the M5 and were almost ready to join the M6 before their conversation about a multitude of subjects began to dry up. Talan suggested breakfast at a service station a few miles up the motorway as they didn't want to wander too far off course. It was hardly the nicest setting in the world but it hit the spot and forty-five minutes later they were back on the road again.

Making good time, Talan slowed the car into Skipton at just after twelve-forty and immediately suggested they find a nice little place for lunch.

'Is food all you ever think about?'

Talan raised an eyebrow. 'No, there *are* one or two other things,' he said looking her up and down suggestively.

'Eyes on the road, man!'

A few minutes later they were in the heart of the town. 'Wow!

'You never told me what a beautiful place this was. I pictured a cold and grim little northern settlement with a few sheep and a grumpy shepherd or two,' Talan said, gaping at the beautiful old stone buildings, the cobbled streets leading to quaint little shops and the rolling hills rising in the distance.

'There might be a grumpy shepherd or two, but I think you'll find my hometown is far from grim,' Rosa said and pointed to a sign for parking behind the High Street. This town has an historic market – which is on today by the way, is 'Gateway to the Dales', has a nine-hundred-year-old castle, and has been judged the best place to live in the UK by *The Sunday Times* no less.'

'I had no idea,' Talan said pulling into a parking space. 'So was it a farming town historically?'

'There has always been farming, but it was also known for the cotton trade.'

'Thought that was Lancashire?'

'Yes most people do, but Yorkshire had a thriving spinning industry too. The Leeds and Liverpool Canal runs through the town and was used to transport raw cotton in and manufactured goods out.'

'Right, and the market – just lots of lovely food?'

'No, all sorts. Why, are you really hungry?' Rosa couldn't believe it possible after he'd polished off a cooked breakfast complete with hash browns about three hours ago.

'Yep, could eat a horse.'

Rosa shook her head. 'They might have one for sale in the market.'

* * *

Rosa could almost forget why they were here as she led a tour of the town and did touristy things. Talan took photos of the huge but beautiful war memorial at the top of the High Street and the picturesque canal, explored the wares on offer on the market stalls and ate yet again – Talan, a homemade steak-pie and chips, Rosa a ham salad sandwich – and booked into a lovely B&B in the centre of town called The Woolly Sheep Inn for a two-night stay. Talan found it on the internet and said it had good reviews and ... great food.

In the distance, a church bell chimed three o' clock and Rosa realised that the carefree having-fun-on-holiday feel to the day must to come to an end. 'I told Gran we'd probably be at hers around now, Talan,' she said, guiding him away from a shop selling hand-made sweets.

He slipped his arm around her and kissed the top of her head. 'Don't be sad, love. I'm sure it won't be as bad as you think.'

'I'm just scared of walking in that bedroom to find her worse than before ... she already looked very frail and,' she struggled for the right words, 'it seemed like she was fading away before my eyes. Well, apart from when she was talking about Jory. Then she sparkled like a diamond.'

'Let's hope for the best. Didn't your mum give you a clue when you chatted last night?'

'She said she looked better to be honest. But Mum tends to sugar-coat things. She thinks I'm a kid still, can't cope with bad stuff.' Rosa admitted to herself that until she went to Tintagel she definitely couldn't.

'Perhaps it's true. Look on the bright side.' Talan squeezed her hand and added as they walked to the car. 'Did your mum wonder why you weren't staying at your gran's?'

'Yes. She was a bit put out that she wouldn't get these next few nights off as we'd planned, but I just said I didn't want to put her to any trouble changing the beds.' Rosa clicked her seatbelt in 'I think she thought I was worried at being in the house with Jocelyn in case she ... you know. Anyway, it's her own fault – she refuses to have carers come in to look after Gran.'

Talan nodded and kissed her hand. 'We could have stayed there. Jocelyn wouldn't have minded would she?'

'No. But I wouldn't have felt right sleeping with you under her roof ... daft I know.'

'Not daft – it's who you are and I love who you are.'

'I can't wait to see Mum's face when she sees you.' Rosa gave a little laugh as she texted her mum to tell her they would be at Jocelyn's in a few minutes so she could go. 'Gran is going to keep us a secret, and so it will be a big surprise when she gets here this evening! The whole story about who you are will wait until ... until she's no longer here. She doesn't want to rake over old coals in front of Mum.'

* * *

The old red brick Victorian house in the centre of a leafy gladed street brought a lump to Rosa's throat. Would Gran still be alive the next time she arrived here? Irritated that she was allowing dark clouds of maudlin and pessimistic thought to drift into her mind she clapped her hands and said, 'Right, here we are. Let's do this!'

Hand-in-hand the two of them walked along the drive and around the side of the house to the back garden. From the silver birch, the grey rope swing twirled idly in the breeze and the lavender now in full bloom scented the garden and childhood memories. 'See that rope, Talan? Gran used to swing on that with her skirt tucked in her knickers.'

'Did she? What a fantastic time you must have had with her as a kid.'

'We did – the best.' Through the tall bushes old wood peeped, the green paint upon it almost grey with age. 'And that shed there,' Rosa pointed, 'that was where we used to listen to her tell stories on rainy afternoons. We'd take a picnic in and pretend we were on a ship, up a mountain in a cabin, anywhere her imagination led us ... and it really doesn't seem so long ago that...' A knot in her throat blocked her words and she leaned into Talan's shoulder.

'My poor baby. Come on, there'll be time for sadness another day – let's go in.'

Turning the key in the back door she led Talan into the kitchen and then through into the sitting room. Thankfully the cleaner must have done a bit more whizzing since her last visit as no dust motes were disturbed as she opened the window, the frame gliding easily open. Talan made himself comfy on the sofa while Rosa put the kettle on and shouted up to Jocelyn that they'd arrived.

'Now, follow me up and wait on the landing with the tea tray until I come and get you, okay?'

'Yes, boss.'

Rosa grinned, heaved a big sigh and walked up the stairs, in her ears, her heart thumped louder than her footsteps on the thin stair carpet.

The door swung open and Rosa held her breath. Then she gasped as she realised that the wish she'd made the other night had come true. Jocelyn sat up in bed in a green cotton nightie, her chestnut hair tidy and with its old bounce, her cheeks no longer as pale as before and – it could have been Rosa's imagination – decidedly plumper. Her pale-green eyes sparkled and creased at the corners as a huge smile spread across her face.

'Rosa, little one!' Jocelyn threw her arms wide.

'Gran!' Rosa said as she hurried into her embrace. 'You look so well!'

'I got Polly to do my hair and freshen me up a bit as I was meeting Jory's grandson.'

'You told her?'

'No, just said I was fed up of looking like a dog's dinner.' Jocelyn gave a little laugh.

Rosa scrutinised her gran's face. 'It's more than a hair do and a freshen up, though. You do look healthier.'

'Well if I do, I'm pleased.' She stroked Rosa's cheek. 'I expect it's because you have been to help my Jory and fallen in love yourself.'

'Love? I never said I'd fall—'

'You didn't have to; it's written all over that lovely face.'

Rosa smiled. 'Do you want to see him before we have a good old catch up?'

'I thought you'd never ask.'

'Now I'll say again – he does look like Jory so prepare yourself, eh?' Rosa frowned and patted Jocelyn's hand.

'Don't worry, the shock of it won't do me in. I'm not ready to pop off just yet.'

'Talan, would you kindly bring in the tea?' Rosa called over her shoulder.

The door opened and a tea tray appeared followed by a smiling Talan. Rosa could tell he was nervous because of the way the cups rattled on the tray, but his voice was calm when he said, 'Great to meet you, Jocelyn.'

Rosa took the tray and set it on the side table, never taking her eyes from Jocelyn's face. This could prove too much for her after all these years. She needn't have worried however.

Jocelyn put her hand to her mouth her cheeks flushing a pretty shade of pink and said, 'My goodness. Rosa was right, you *do* have a look of your grandfather.' She patted her hair. 'It's the eyes. Your mouth and chin are different and ...' Jocelyn put her head on side. 'Something I can't quite put my finger on.'

'It's his nose, Gran.' Rosa said, pulling a chair up to the bed for Talan. 'Talan's nose is longer.'

'Yes, I think you're right!' Jocelyn folded her arms and stared at him. 'The hair colour is similar though and that expression he's pulling now.'

Rosa giggled when she noticed that Talan was beginning to look a little uncomfortable. 'Talan's taller too don't you think?'

'I *am* in the room you know,' Talan sighed and folded his arms.

'Who said that?' Rosa sat next to Jocelyn on the bed, her face deadpan.

After their tea and Jocelyn's many questions about Talan, his life and Tintagel, Talan left them to catch up properly. 'I'll go and have a wander around the garden and perhaps even shut my eyes for half-an-hour on that bench I noticed under the pergola. It was a long drive up.'

'Okay, sweetheart. You could do a spot of gardening while you're out there if you'd like to,' Rosa said and winked conspiratorially at Jocelyn Jocelyn chuckled and nodded.

'I can see you two are going to talk about me behind my back aren't you?'

'Of course,' Jocelyn said. 'You'd be disappointed if we didn't.'

Talan smiled, tipped his finger to his eyebrow and left the room

They listened to his footsteps on the stair and a door close downstairs and then Jocelyn grabbed Rosa's arm 'My goodness, he is absolutely charming – and drop-dead gorgeous as you young folk say nowadays! I am so happy you found each other.'

Rosa laughed. 'Me too. It seems Mr Right came along much quicker than I expected.'

'Well it was down to me and Jory sending you on the quest of course. We knew it would happen right from the off.'

Rosa's eyes grew round. 'Really?'

'No, of course not. I'm making it all up. We only have room for one psychic in the family.' Jocelyn twinkled, adjusted her pillows and made herself comfy. 'Right, now I'm all ears, tell me all about it.'

For the next hour Rosa gave her gran a blow-by-blow account of everything that had happened to her during her stay in Tintagel. There were many interruptions and questions on Jocelyn's part and some tears on both their parts when Jocelyn got emotional over Rosa's meetings with Jory.

'I am just overjoyed that you were able to help him go to his rest and for putting the record of the past straight for everyone. You can't imagine how guilty I have felt over the years thinking he'd taken his life because I didn't stay.'

'That must have been unbearable,' Rosa said handing a tissue to her gran while dabbing at her own eyes. There was a chance that she'd upset her further with her next question, but Rosa had to know. 'Do you think you made the right decision all those years ago?'

Jocelyn laid her head against the pillow and stared past Rosa's shoulder. 'I have asked myself that many times and I can honestly say I don't know. Even though the consequences were tragic, I know that your grandad wouldn't have allowed us to be together. I imagine he might have killed Jory, and perhaps even me, once he'd tracked us down.'

Rosa nodded. 'And if he hadn't killed you he would have ruined everything you had. If Jory hadn't slipped on the cliff that night, he would have been okay in the end ... he would have found someone else eventually.'

'Yes that's what I hoped would happen at the time. And you can't *keep* thinking about what if this or that happened, or you'd go mad. If I hadn't left, Jory wouldn't have got drunk and gone up to the church and fallen. But *if* I'd stayed, I know we wouldn't have made it anyway. The past is the past and the main thing to hold onto now is that everyone knows that Jory didn't take his own life. It must have been a great comfort to Daisy.'

'Oh it was. And she asked me to pass on her best to you too. She bears you no malice, not now she knows the truth.' Rosa did a potted history of Daisy and of Morganna too.

'Morganna sounds a real character,' Jocelyn said. 'Isn't it funny how you happened to go into her shop and meet her?'

'I think fate had a hand in it somewhere. Tintagel too. It is such a magical place, just as you said it would be.'

'It was magical for me all those years go, I wish I could have gone there one last time.' Jocelyn shrugged and gave a sad smile. 'It wasn't to be though.'

Rosa suddenly remembered the gifts in her suitcase. 'No you can't go there, but give me a minute and I'll see what I can do.'

Her suitcase was propped up against the sofa in the sitting room and she quickly pulled out two bags and hurried back to the door. As she did, she glanced through the sash and her heart flipped. Talan was in the garden, his shirt off, sun on his back, weeding the rockery. Bless his heart, he'd known they were joking about him doing the garden, but he obviously had forgone a nap because he wanted to help anyway. The garden was her dad's job, but it clearly hadn't been done for ages given the pile of weeds at Talan's feet.

Running back up the stairs she was grateful she'd found someone like Talan. 'They' said that girls look for someone like their dads as partners. How wrong 'they' were.

'Guess what, Talan's weeding the garden' Rosa laughed and perched on the end of Jocelyn's bed, the bags clutched to her chest.

'Oh, the poor boy. Surely he didn't think we meant it?' Jocelyn frowned.

'No, he's just a lovely man who wants to do the best he can for you.' Rosa took the smallest bag and handed it to her gran. 'Now this is from Morganna'

Jocelyn's hands shook a little as they took out a box wrapped in silver paper, a navy moon and stars patterned upon it. She looked at Rosa. 'Can you help me with the sticky-tape? My fingers aren't as strong as they once were.'

Just a simple statement, but it sent a pang of sadness into Rosa's heart and rammed home just how ill her gran was. Cancer reminded her that it was here in the room, just as it had always been. Perhaps more hidden than last time, further in the shadows maybe, behind cupboards - in crevices, but it was here. Waiting.

Rosa forced a cheery smile, unwrapped the box and handed it back. 'Now, Morganna impressed upon me to tell you that they are infused with positive energy. She did a spell or something – whatever white witches do apparently.'

Jocelyn lifted the lid and gasped. She gently lifted two oblong crystals from the box and held them to the light. Immediately they took on a pink hue around the edges and a shot of lilac through the centre. 'Oh they are so pretty!'

'Morganna said that when you feel like you need a boost, hold them in each hand and relax. Their energy will revive you.'

'She's so kind. I must write and thank her.' Rosa noticed her glance at her shaking fingers. 'Or perhaps I'll phone her. Would she mind that?'

'She would be over the moon' Rosa then put the larger bag on the bed. 'There are two things in here for you. I know you can't see Tingtagel again, so I brought a bit of it to you instead.' Bright though her smile was, it was beginning to feel a little stretched – a lock gate trying to hold back a tide of emotion.

The lock gate nearly burst as Jocelyn pulled out the painting of the church on the cliff top by a local artist. The older woman's eyes filled with tears and spilled over and down her cheeks like a silent river. It was a few moments before she could speak. 'Oh my little one, how different my life could have been if only I'd met Jory first. I will get this hung on the wall over there so it's the first thing I see when I wake.'

Rosa could only nod and then she said, 'There's one last thing if you can stand it.'

Jocelyn reached her hand back into the bag and pulled out an old olive jar full of sand from the castle beach. 'Sand?'

'Yes, I popped down and gathered it from the beach beneath Tintagel Island last night while Talan was in the bath. It hasn't had a spell cast on it, like the crystals, but whip the top off and have a sniff from time to time, I guarantee it will make you feel better.'

'I bet it will.' Jocelyn handed the jar to her granddaughter. 'Let's have a whiff now shall we? Then you'll have to leave the lid on loose for me and I'll always keep it right here by the bed.'

Kicking herself for being so stupid and thoughtless regarding the lid, Rosa opened it and handed it over. Jocelyn took a big sniff. 'Wow! If I close my eyes I can almost believe I'm right there, the wind in my hair the salt air on my lips.' Jocelyn grinned.

Rosa's smile could stand the strain no longer as the poignant image of her gran and Jory walking along that beach came to mind. Her face crumpled and a sob escaped. 'So sorry, Gran. You don't need me blubbing. This is such a happy day under the circumstances.'

She felt Jocelyn's cool fingers stroke her wrist. 'Don't be sorry. It is only natural ... all happy things have traces of sadness don't they? It's just the way life is.'

Rosa wiped her eyes and resurrected the smile. 'I promise that's the end of the waterworks today. Now do you want another cup of tea?'

'I would love one. I'd also like another look at that strapping Cornishman you've bagged yourself.' Jocelyn held up the painting again. 'Who knows one day you might get married here.' She winked at Rosa 'Now wouldn't that be something?'

Rosa shook her head and picked up the tea tray. 'As you were fond of telling us when we were little - let's not run before we can walk, eh?'

Just before the door closed behind her, Rosa heard her gran mutter, 'You've been walking for some time now.'

CHAPTER 24

$\mathcal{L}$ater that afternoon, Polly walked in on the three of them laughing fit to burst about something Talan had said, her face a mixture of surprise and puzzlement. 'Can anyone join in?' she said quietly and walked into her daughter's open arms.

'Mum! We didn't expect you until this evening,' Rosa said hugging her tightly and then holding her at arm's length to get a good look at her.

'I thought I'd like to spend a bit of time with my globe-trotting daughter while I have a chance.' Polly grinned and then nodded at Talan. 'And don't I get an introduction?'

'Yes, this is my boyfriend, Talan.' Rosa was ridiculously thrilled at the sound of those words out loud. 'We met while I was on a short break in Tintagel.'

'Pleased to meet you, Polly.' Talan stood and kissed her on both cheeks. 'And might I say I can see where Rosa gets her looks?'

Bright pink because of the kisses and compliments, Polly said, 'Pleased to meet you too. Though I'm sure you're just being charming.'

Rosa slipped her arm through Talan's and said, 'He is charming, but you do look lovely, Mum. Gran said last time how much I remind her of you when you were younger.'

Polly flapped her hand and sat down on the bed next to her Mother. 'When I was younger being the operative word.'

Rosa couldn't be bothered playing the 'fishing for compliments' game and sat back down. 'Don't you think that Gran looks well?'

'She does today that's for sure, must be because her favourite grandchild is back.'

'Now you know I don't have favourites,' Jocelyn said raising a brow.

'Hmm. We'll say no more on that one.' Polly said pulling a face.

'Talan's done the weeding, isn't he kind?' Rosa leaned into Talan and beamed up at him.

'Oh. That is kind, but your dad normally does that.'

'Not for a while he hasn't judging by the height of those weeds,' Rosa said.

Into the uncomfortable silence Talan said, 'We were just discussing a picnic on the lawn tomorrow if the weather keeps fine.'

Polly wrinkled her nose. 'A nice idea, but Mum might feel a bit left out.'

'No, I'd carry her down and she'd lay on the sofa which I'd put out there too.'

'It would almost be like old times. Not sure I'd manage the rope swing now, but I could tuck my skirt in my knickers at least.' Jocelyn gave a wheezy chuckle. 'Just to feel the sun on my face would be a dream come true.'

'But are you sure, Mum? We don't want you exhausted.'

'Stop fussing. If I get too tired Talan will carry me back up here again, won't you, my 'andsome?'

'Proper Cornish accent and all,' Talan laughed.

'Yes, I went there once years ago you know,' Jocelyn winked. Polly looked puzzled but said nothing.

Talan winked back. 'Of course I'll carry you. It would be my pleasure.'

Jocelyn squeezed his bicep. 'No, the pleasure will be all mine.'

'Mum, what's got into you?' Polly muttered from the side of her mouth, tipping an apologetic smile at Talan.

'Oh stop being so straight-laced. It was just a joke, you know.'

Polly shook her head in bewilderment and then assumed an

authoritative tone. 'Right, so if we're having a picnic we are doing it properly. I'll get the food from Waitrose and invite your brothers; short notice but hopefully they'll be free on a Saturday afternoon. Theo will come of course; perhaps we'll have a barbeque instead? Your dad always did a good barbie didn't he?'

Rosa's heart sank. Not only didn't she want a barbeque, she didn't want her dad ruining it all either. It would be very hard to be civil to him given what she now knew about his disgraceful behaviour concerning her special sense.

'The thing is, we wanted it to be like the old times when I was a kid here. We always had picnics on the lawn on the old blue gingham tablecloth. There was egg and cress and ham sandwiches, lemonade made by Gran and her cake … chocolate mostly?' Rosa looked at Jocelyn for confirmation.

'Yes, my signature bake.' Jocelyn nodded. 'We had homemade sausage rolls too once or twice.'

'Hmm.' Polly crossed her arms, clearly disgruntled that her ideas had been shunned. 'Well, Mum can't do the baking this time can she?'

'No, but you and Rosa can. I'll dictate the ingredients so you can get them at your fancy supermarket and the recipe too. Bob's your uncle.'

'Is he coming too?' Talan asked.

'Who?' Polly wondered.

'Uncle Bob,' Talan said with a chuckle.

Everyone laughed then, even Polly managed a grin.

* * *

Saturday morning dawned hot, sunny and still, the wind seemingly having forgotten how to blow or even pant. Talan reminded her that May had lost the battle with June by giving her a pinch on the bottom and a soft punch on the arm as they lay entwined in the rumpled sheets of the guest house bedroom, and her playful return had somehow ended up in lovemaking.

Rosa had lost count of the times that they had made love now. Like her special sense it felt as natural as breathing to her. From the bed as she watched Talan walk from the shower wrapped only in a towel, she wondered if she would experience something like cold turkey come Monday.

"Bout time you were up, lazy bones,' he said, unwrapping his towel and drying his upper body.

'I'll have you know that I stuck my head out the window and assessed the weather for us. I think the old gazebo will definitely be needed at Gran's.'

'No problem I'm looking forward to getting the garden looking its best.'

'Gran adores you, you know, and I think Mum is warming to you. She was thrown by your surprise appearance...' Rosa slid out of bed and slapped his backside. '... and the flattery!'

'Polly is a fine figure of a woman ... similar eyes and bossy nature to her youngest child too'

Rosa gave him a look, 'Me, bossy?' She'd never thought of herself as that.

'Well, only sometimes ... particularly when you want something urgently.' Talan grabbed her round the waist as she moved past him to the bathroom and ran his hands along her thighs and cupped her buttocks in both hands.

Twisting out of his grip she laughed and said 'No time for that now. It's eight-thirty, and I said we'd be at Gran's at ten You have to eat your own bodyweight in cooked breakfast, remember?'

Before she closed the bathroom door he called, 'You okay? You seem a bit flustered.' Rosa sighed and shrugged. 'Worried about seeing your dad aren't you?'

Once again he'd tuned into her apprehension - read her like a book. 'I just want everything to be perfect today. I want this day...' Rosa pushed away a swell of emotion '... perhaps our last full day together, to be filled with sunlight and hope rather than darkness and despair.'

'And it will be, my love. I'll do everything in my power to make it a day to remember.'

Rosa blew him a kiss and went to close the door again.

'Still worried about Theo though, I can tell.'

Pretending she didn't hear him Rosa reached into the shower and flicked it on. There was no way she wanted a confrontation with her dad on this last lovely day that she'd probably ever spend with Jocelyn, but she didn't see how could she avoid it.

With an effort she replaced these thoughts with those of lemonade and sandwiches, a blue gingham picnic cloth, homemade chocolate cake and Jocelyn's laughter.

* * *

Rosa looked at her mum's face as she poured the chocolate cake mixture into the tin. Her hair in a ponytail, a smear of mixture on her cheek and a half-smile on her lips. It was ages since they had spent any time together like this, in fact she couldn't remember when the last time had been.

When Rosa was growing up, Polly had worked full time in her bridal wear shop, Saturdays too. There had been precious little time to spare for Rosa, Ben and Simon, therefore, particularly during the teenage years as school work, exams, after-school clubs and the like had all seemed to take precedence. Polly would always try to make an effort but the years just seemed to get away from them. Now she'd sold the shop and had spare time, Rosa was away with her own job. Nevertheless, Rosa had always felt loved and wanted.

Dad on the other hand never seemed to even try to make time. He was always at school in important staff meetings, or in his study doing equally important things. Success and climbing the ladder was his priority. There was only two years left until he retired - God knows what he'd do then. There was the house in France of course, but Mum told her that he got restless after a few weeks there. He was never happier than when he had his 'head teacher's hat' on, pontificating in an assembly or giving talks in the local community. Rosa wondered if the 'dad's hat' actually fitted him anymore.

'Rosa?' Polly waved a hand in front of Rosa's eyes.

'Yep?'

'I asked if you could open the oven door, you're miles away.'

'Sorry, just thinking about how long it has been since we have done anything together.'

Polly put the cake in the oven and nodded. 'I know, the years just rush by don't they, my baby?'

Rosa took a damp cloth and wiped the cake mixture from her mum's face. 'They do. And we should make a big effort to slow them down a bit.'

Polly gave her a hug. 'We should. Your dad was only saying the other day how much he missed you.'

'Dad? Really? He always seems so preoccupied when I visit.'

Polly looked surprised. 'Well, yes, but that's Dad's way, isn't it? But he loves his children. He's lucky that the boys live close, but his 'little girl is always off to the four corners of the world' as he puts it.'

Before Rosa had time to think, she snapped, 'Pity he didn't think of that when he was blaming me for the death of Harry when I was little, isn't it?'

Polly's face went as white as the flour she was measuring out for the sausage rolls. The spoon shook in her hands and she sat down heavily at the table. 'So you remembered it all then?'

'With a little help from my friends, yes,' Rosa said sitting down too. 'How could you let him bully me like that, make me bury my psychic abilities?'

Polly couldn't meet her eyes and stared into the mixing bowl. There was no way Rosa was letting her off the hook and waited out the silence, watching the cake rise in the oven as the kitchen clock kept time with her heartbeat. Eventually Polly said, 'I ... I thought it was for the best. I was a bit frightened to be honest, Theo's mother was a medium and—'

'Yes I know all about that. My grandfather treated her appallingly. Poor woman couldn't help her sixth sense, just as I can't. And I for one don't want to. Don't you realise that there were so many people I could have helped over the years?'

Polly put her hand to her head. 'I don't know. Your dad said it was best left alone, that it was dangerous … I didn't understand it, love.' She looked into Rosa eyes. 'You must believe that I didn't want to hurt you, I wanted to protect you.'

It was obvious that her mum was telling the truth and Rosa felt her anger subside. 'Yes, I believe you, Mum. But it was still wrong and I'll tell Dad the same when he gets here.'

Polly made a face. 'Surely it can wait; we don't want to spoil our lovely day.'

Rosa sighed. 'I'll wait until the end of it but I must tell him. For one thing I need to get it off my chest and for another, I have a message from his father.'

* * *

Talan wiped the sweat off his brow, looked at Polly and Rosa and declared the picnic ready to commence. He'd mowed the lawn, put the gazebo up, brought out the old pasting table to put the drinks on, dragged the sofa outside complete with cushions, and spread the old gingham cloth on the lawn.

'My goodness, everything looks perfect!' Polly said patting him on the back. 'Thanks for all your hard work.'

'It's a pleasure. I'll go and grab Jocelyn now shall I?'

'Yep, and Mum and I will bring out the food. Dad and the boys should be here in fifteen minutes.'

Jocelyn heaved a sigh as Talan lowered her gently onto the sofa under the gazebo. 'Oh, it's a long time since I was in a man's arms, my boy. And I can't tell you how wonderful it is to be out in the fresh air!' She patted his hand and accepted a glass of lemonade from Rosa 'The truth is I never expected to leave that damned room again'

A car pulled into the drive and three men got out. Ben and Simon immediately raced over to them, followed more sedately by Theo Fernley. Rosa endured the compulsory hair ruffling and swinging around in the air ritual by her two brothers and then she introduced them to Talan.

Ben shook his hand and said, 'Grand to meet you, Talan' Then he pushed his floppy brown fringe out of his eyes and turned to Rosa. 'If I'd known we were bringing partners I'd have brought my fiancée Angelica'

'Yeah and I'd have asked Janine,' Simon a taller but almost identical version of his younger brother said, folding his arms and pretending to be put out.

'Oh stop it, you two. It was an impromptu thing – we'll do it again and send out gold embossed invites if you like,' Rosa said sticking her tongue out at them. The boys went over to see Gran and then Rosa's grin slipped away as her dad came across the lawn.

'Rosa, darling, give your old dad a hug!'

Rosa obliged, but took no comfort from the warmth of his embrace. In fact, her hand itched to slap his face. Before she was tempted to have a show-down right there and then, she grabbed Talan's hand. 'Dad, meet my boyfriend, Talan'

Theo pumped Talan's hand vigorously. 'Polly told me all about you. She's very impressed.' The smile was genuine, but Rosa thought she could detect a hint of jealousy in his words and eyes. At nearly six feet two himself, perhaps he didn't like being towered over by such a fine figure of a man. Dad had always 'joked' that he was still the tallest in his family even though the boys were grown men now.

Unwilling to enter into small talk with her father, she left him with Talan and nipped back into the kitchen to help her mum get the rest of the food.

The picnic went just as well as Rosa had hoped. Apart from the underlying feelings of bitterness towards her dad that she kept under lock and key, and the little glances of apprehension she received now and then from Polly, it was nigh on the perfect day to remember that Talan had promised her. They lounged on the grass, ate sandwiches, sausage-rolls, cake and drank lemonade and talked of old times and summers past. The boys even attempted a go on the rope-swing until it began to creak in an alarming manner.

'What a shame, lads,' Jocelyn laughed as they gave it up as a bad job. 'I was just about to have a go myself.'

* * *

Late afternoon shadows stretched along the lawn and the lavender rustled, its scent mixing with that of the freshly cut grass in the strengthening breeze. Rosa worried that Jocelyn, ill, and unused to fresh air would feel the chill after such a baking hot day. Though Rosa knew Gran had had a fantastic time, she could tell by the shadows under her eyes that she was getting very tired. Being Gran she didn't want to say so of course. She whispered to Talan that she was going to talk to her dad and then they'd think about making a move.

Rosa tapped her dad on the shoulder as he sat on the corner of the picnic cloth and inclined her head to the house. He frowned at her serious expression and then got up and followed her inside.

Indicating he should sit at the kitchen table, Rosa closed the door and sat opposite. 'Everything okay, sweetheart? You look a bit upset,' he said, his soft brown eyes full of concern.

'I am a bit as it goes. Before we start all that though, I have a message from your dad.'

Theo sat back, pushed his grey mop back from his forehead, incredulity removing all trace of concern from his eyes. 'My dad? What are you on about, he's been dead ten years?'

'Yep, but his spirit is alive and well and came to visit me as I drifted to sleep last night.'

Relief swamped his face. 'You'd have been dreaming, love. The mind plays funny tricks on us at that moment just before we fall into deep sleep, R.E.M.—'

'Cut the scientific crap for a moment and listen. Grandad Fernley wasn't a dream. He stood before my bed in his best suit, black mac over one arm—'

Theo shook his head clearly exasperated, 'Just like in the photo in the alcove that you will have seen countless times when you come round to ours—'

Rosa held up a finger, halting her dad mid-flow. 'He stood there and told me to tell you something that he said he'd never admit to when he was with the living. He said you were right.'

Theo scowled, 'Right? Right about what?'

'Before I tell you that, I have other stuff you might like to hear.' Then Rosa gave a little laugh. 'Actually you won't like to hear it but you *are* going to.'

She told him everything that had happened without mentioning Jory, Gran and why she'd actually gone to Tintagel in the first place. She had promised Jocelyn that would be saved for after she'd gone. Her dad listened, the look on his face running between pure amusement and barely concealed annoyance. His response after she'd finished was as she'd expected.

'So, you met a white witch who told you that you had psychic ability, which isn't unknown for these charlatans to do, especially in a place like Tintagel, geared for gullible tourists.' Rosa cringed when she remembered her words to Dan that first evening. 'Then you remembered all that nonsense from when you were little, and that poor boy's death and then you have the cheek to blame *me*,' he stabbed at his chest for emphasis 'for trying to correct such wild imaginings?'

Anger seared hot in her brain, but to her credit, Rosa kept her voice as calm and even as her stare. 'They were not wild imaginings. They were the truth and you were just scared shitless to admit it because of the disgusting way your father had treated your mother. You knew I had similar abilities, but because of your father drilling it into you that such things were embarrassing, dangerous, abhorrent and unscientific, you decided to do the same to me.'

Theo gripped the stem of a wooden spoon between his hands so hard Rosa thought he'd snap it in two, his mouth opening and closing a few times as if he was trying to swallow some angry words. 'My mother was delusional, an embarrassment and a weight around my dad's neck. I don't blame him for divorcing her. She wouldn't see sense and drop all that spiritual hoo-ha.'

'But you didn't always think that, did you?'

A shadow fell across Theo's eyes and she could tell he was trying to hide something. 'What do you mean?'

'Well, that's what your dad came to tell me.' Rosa sat back. 'He said that he threw your mother out a week before Christmas. On Christmas day just the two of you sat at the dinner table. You were twelve years old and crying because you missed your mum.'

Theo blanched and dropped the wooden spoon to the floor with a clatter. His breathing became rapid and for a minute Rosa thought he was going to cry, just like he had all those years ago. She pressed on. 'Do you remember what he said to you?'

Theo nodded and said in a small voice. 'Something about … I think, being successful.'

'Yes. He said your mother's ideas were medieval and had no place in the modern world. He said that success was the key to a happy life and he was damned sure you would follow in his footsteps. He also told you to stop crying and that you'd both be better off without her.'

Theo's eyes filled up with tears and he dashed them away with a shaking hand. Rosa almost gave him a hug but she had to finish what she started or she'd end up crying too. 'Do you remember what you said to him?'

'No.'

'You said you didn't care what her ideas were, she was your mum and you loved her. He slapped you across the head and said you'd never be successful with that attitude. Do you remember what you said next as you ran crying from the room?'

Her dad grew red in the face and pressed his lips together tightly but a sob escaped. 'I said success wasn't the most important thing in the world.'

Rosa realised tears were running down her cheeks too and grabbed her dad's hand across the table. 'You did. And last night Grandad said to tell you he was sorry and you were right.'

Theo, bewildered got shakily to his feet and said, 'I don't know what to say.'

Rosa thought he looked just like she imagined he would age twelve. A lost little boy missing his mother and bullied by his father. 'Then we'll say no more today. It will take your hugely scientific brain a while to process, reassess, and come to terms.'

Her dad sighed and drew his hands down his face. He looked like someone waking from a bad dream.

She moved round the table and hugged him. 'I feel so much better to have shared this. And really though I was furious at you to start with when I found out, it wasn't all your fault. We were both suppressed by our fathers; the difference is we have time to put it right.'

Theo looked down at her, a ghost of a smile playing at the corners of his mouth. 'You'll have to help me, love.' He drew her to him in a crushing bear hug, '…because right now, I don't know where to start.'

Rosa swallowed hard. 'I'll try my best,' she managed at last.

* * *

Talan waved as she came across the lawn arm-in-arm with her dad. His smile said it all and Rosa noticed a look of relief pass between him and her mum. From the sofa a pale Jocelyn shot her a grin too and held her arms open. 'Come and give your old gran a kiss.'

As Rosa bent to kiss her she whispered 'Glad to see you and your dad have mended a few bridges.'

'I hope so, Gran,' Rosa said sitting by her side. 'I think he's in shock at the moment but we'll get there. I told him something about his dad that convinced him I was telling the truth.'

'Oh that's wonderful, little one. And haven't we had a fabulous day? I couldn't have wished for better.'

'Me either. I have loved every minute of seeing you here – the great matriarch with all your family around you.' Rosa paused. 'I do think it's time that Talan carried you back up to your room though. You look done in.'

Jocelyn smiled. 'I think you're right. To tell you the truth I am exhausted. But I have those strong arms to look forward to, eh?'

Rosa laughed. 'I'm beginning to think I have competition here. I'll tell him he's wanted, and we'll stop by in the morning to say goodbye before we head off.'

Jocelyn's eyes moistened and she took Rosa's face in her hands. 'I do love you, my little one. And thank you for everything you have done today, the last few weeks and for bringing me summer in Tintagel to brighten my old room.'

'I love you too,' Rosa blinked rapidly and kissed her gran's soft cheeks. 'And I can say that it has been my very great pleasure.

CHAPTER 25

𝒯alan polished off the last of his cooked breakfast and patted his tummy. 'My goodness I'll miss all this good living, you know, when I'm all alone in my little flat with a bit of toast on Monday morning.'

Rosa sent him a mock scowl. 'If that's to make me feel sorry for you, I suggest you think again.'

Talan got up from the table. 'You're a cruel hard woman, Rosa Fernley. Come, on let's go check out and get going our separate ways. Bet you can't wait, seeing as I know you won't miss me one little bit.'

Rosa felt her heart sink and a real pang of sorrow settle somewhere under her ribcage. Though she knew he was just joking, the thought of going their separate ways was too awful to bear. 'You won't get rid of me that easily.' She said to his back as she followed him to reception. 'We've to say goodbye to Gran first.'

June was certainly busting out all over as they whizzed down the lanes of Skipton. The hills rolled green and pleasant, the wild flowers threaded purple yellow and white through hedgerows, and cows dotted the patchwork fields enclosed by a wealth of stone walling. 'This is just like Postman Pat country,' Talan said laughing. 'All we need is a black and white cat in a post van to hurtle past and it will be perfect.'

'It is lovely here.' Rosa twirled her hair around her finger and looked out of the car window at the scenery thoughtfully. 'But not as perfect as Tintagel. I miss the ocean and it's only been a few days.'

'Gord help you back in the big smoke then, shweedhart,' Talan said in an awful attempt at a London accent.

'And gord help you because you missed the turning to Gran's, you lemon. We're heading to the station.'

Talan buzzed the window down and his cheerful disposition blew out of it with his heavy sigh. He made a thin line of his lips and shook his head. 'I didn't take the wrong turn, Rosa.'

'You so did, look it says station parking right there!' Rosa threw her hands up but an uncomfortable feeling had begun in the pit of her stomach. Intuition, plus Talan's grim expression told her she wasn't going to like what was coming next.

'I know, that's where we are going.'

'But I don't understand. Are we not going to say goodbye to Gran?'

Talan swung into a parking space behind the station and turned off the engine. 'Come on, love. Let's get a drink in the cafe over there and I'll explain.'

Rosa's uncomfortable feeling had become an ache as she watched Talan bring a tray of coffee and cake over to her table. She watched his hands carefully set down two frothy cappuccinos and a huge slab of carrot cake while all the time her anxiety grew. Suddenly she could wait no longer.

'Talan, please sit down and tell me why we're here, nearly two hours early for my train and not at Gran's.'

He tapped a spoon on the table. 'Look, I'm sorry we're here early but not knowing the area I didn't really know where else to go and I—'

'Talan, stop tapping the spoon. It's normally me who babbles when I'm nervous, not you. Please get to the point.'

He put down the spoon and reached for her hand across the table. 'Okay, but please try not to get too upset. When I took Jocelyn back to her room yesterday she thanked me for everything and then asked me to keep you away today. She thought saying goodbye formally today would be too painful, and she'd said you'd both said all that needed to be said when you were outside on the sofa'

Rosa looked into his deep ocean blue eyes full of love for her, tried to pretend his words meant something else and bit the inside of her lip to stop herself screaming. 'No,' she said, after she'd managed to calm herself. 'No. I need to see her; it could be the last time–'

'Exactly. It would be too painful; you know it would. Jocelyn wants it like this. She told me to say she wanted no tears, just happy memories.'

Tears pushed at the back of her eyes now until she could barely make out Talan's features across the table. In her heart of hearts, she knew Gran was right. Perhaps she knew it was time to join Jory, perhaps she had only a few days, who knew?

Rosa did, if she was brutally honest.

But then an image of Jocelyn laughing with all her family gathered around sent sunlight into her heart, and Rosa laughed too, even as tears rolled down her cheeks.

* * *

'You should think yourself lucky that your journey will only be three hours or so,' Talan laughed, 'I have six hours ahead of me.'

Rosa looked at the open door to the train carriage behind his shoulder and nodded. His laugh was forced; fake, designed to make her think he wasn't as close to tears as she was. What was it about men and crying in public? Years of social conditioning that's what, she realised.

'I know. I just said that the journey will be a long one without you. I didn't mean the hours spent on the train so much as the days apart after we go back to our lives.'

Talan couldn't hold her gaze and looked away down the platform reaching out and pulling her close. 'Yes. It is going to be hard, but we aren't going back to our lives. We're going back to a small part of our lives ... You are the most important thing in mine now,' he said into her hair.

An involuntary sob escaped and she gave his chest a gentle thump. 'Don't say lovely things or I'll be a snotty heap on the floor in a minute.'

'Ugh, I think I might have just gone off you a bit.'

One eyebrow raised, Rosa looked up at him.

'Only joking. Even if you were swathed from head to toe in snot like a slug, I'd still love you.' Talan laughed at her disgusted expression.

'You say the nicest things.' Rosa snuggled closer to him feeling through the open-neck shirt, the warmth of him on her cheek, and inhaling the subtle tones of his cologne. Her heart was so full of love for him she felt a physical ache in her chest. Squeezing her eyes shut she tried to remember their 'big smile, no tears at the station' pact they'd made in the cafe.

Talan lifted her chin and kissed her softly on her lips. 'The train's about to go, the guard up there is slamming the doors.'

'I'd better get on, then.'

'So we'll talk every day and you'll be back in a couple of weeks, yes?' He murmured kissing every inch of her face.

'Try and keep me away.' The goose-egg-sized lump in Rosa's throat only allowed for short sentences. She wondered how her heart could survive the separation.

'One day soon you'll come back to stay for good,' Talan said, his voice wavering as he handed her suitcase up and closed the door behind her. 'Tintagel's in your blood.'

Through the open window she gave a bright smile and said, 'Do you know, I think you might be right.' The whistle blew and the train started to slowly pull away. 'You're in my blood too – I love you, Talan!' she called, annoyed that at the last moment she'd broken the pact.

'I love you more!' he shouted back. And though the train picked up speed and his features became unclear, if she wasn't mistaken, she thought he'd broken it too.

* * *

Talan wiped his eyes on the back of his hand as he walked back to the car. Once inside, he felt the heavy weight of parting lift slightly as he pulled his phone out of his bag. He smiled as he pressed call.

'She's on the train safe and I'm setting off back home in a little while.'

'Oh and I bet she was distraught, poor love.'

'Inside yes, we both were, but we managed to keep a brave face... well, almost. It's been an emotional visit all round. Still, I know it won't be long before she's back with me for good ... thanks to you.'

Morganna hooted. 'She'll go mad when she finds out you rang and grilled me yesterday.'

'She won't find out from me. And curiosity about what you'd seen in the cards, crystal ball, or whatever it is you do was eating me up.' Talan laughed, 'Besides you didn't need much persuading to spill all.'

'I wanted to make sure the course of true love ran smoothly. Plus, the fact I'm rubbish at keeping secrets!' Morganna laughed again.

'Well you'd better keep this one in case you speak to her in the near future. So, Morganna, exactly what was this ring like that you saw her wearing? I've seen some classy jeweller's shops here.'

A few minutes later he ended the call, and with a heart full of love and a spring in his step, Talan set off towards the High Street.

ABOUT THE AUTHOR

*A*manda James grew up in Sheffield but her dream was to eventually live in Cornwall. Having now realised that dream, the dramatic coastline around her home inspires her writing and she has sketched out many stories in her head while walking the cliff paths.

Known to many as Mandy, she spends far more time than is good for her on social media and has turned procrastination into a fine art. Amanda has written many short stories for anthologies and has four published novels. Two are about a time travelling history teacher, – *A Stitch in Time* and *Cross Stitch*, two are suspense – *Somewhere Beyond the Sea* and *Dancing in the Rain*.

Amanda left school with no real qualifications of note apart from an A* in how to be a nuisance in class. Nevertheless, she returned to education when her daughter was five and eventually became a history teacher, though she never travelled through time, apart from in her head. When Amanda is not writing she can be found playing on the beach with her family or walking next to the ocean plotting her next book.

Twitter – @akjames61

Facebook – mandy.james.33

Blog – http://mandykjameswrites.blogspot.co.uk/

SUMMER IN TINTAGEL

Urbane Publications is dedicated to
developing new author voices, and publishing
fiction and non-fiction that challenges, thrills and
fascinates. From page-turning novels to innovative
reference books, our goal is to publish what
YOU want to read.

Find out more at

urbanepublications.com